He didn't rel
right away...

"It's time to call it a day, Patrick. If you want to go, I can take care of locking up."

"No, I'm in no rush."

Melanie saw the shadow that crossed his face and realized that for Patrick going home meant going to Andy's place. She placed a hand over his arm and met his eyes. "Andy's home is your own. That's exactly the way it should be."

"I won't accept that while my dad's case remains unsolved." He watched her lock up the office, then walked her out to the car and checked it over.

As Melanie drove away, she caught sight of Patrick in her rearview mirror. He stood tall, his broad shoulders thrown back. A solitary figure in the gray shadows of night. He looked invincible. But his face, a pale mask in the moonlight's harsh glow, revealed another man, as well. Etched there was sadness and perhaps a trace of fear.

ABOUT THE AUTHOR

Aimée Thurlo is a talented writer with nineteen books to her credit, written under her own name, as well as the pseudonyms Aimée Duvall and Aimée Martel. For her first Intrigue, *Expiration Date*, Aimée has drawn on her own heritage as a native of Cuba to build the background for her heroine, Melanie Cardenas. When not battling deadlines at her word processor, Aimée enjoys riding her horses and practicing her marksmanship. She and her husband live in New Mexico.

Expiration Date

Aimée Thurlo

Harlequin Books

TORONTO • NEW YORK • LONDON
AMSTERDAM • PARIS • SYDNEY • HAMBURG
STOCKHOLM • ATHENS • TOKYO • MILAN

To the two people who made this book possible:
my husband, David Thurlo, and
my editor, Sue Stone

Acknowledgments

With special thanks to Officer Mike Sawyer and
Sergeant Mike Tarter of the Explosive Ordinance
Disposal Unit of the Albuquerque Police
Department.

Harlequin Intrigue edition published March 1989

ISBN 0-373-22109-6

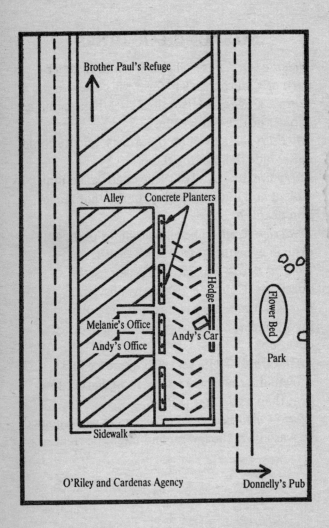

Brother Paul's Refuge

Alley   Concrete Planters

Melanie's Office

Andy's Office

Hedge

Andy's Car

Flower Bed

Park

Sidewalk

O'Riley and Cardenas Agency

Donnelly's Pub

CAST OF CHARACTERS

Melanie Cardenas—She'd sworn to find her partner's murderer, whatever the cost.

Patrick O'Riley—His father's death gave him a choice: justice or revenge.

Shy Eddy—He lived on the streets, and he could either hide there or die there.

Larry Clancy—Andy O'Riley had called him violent and unpredictable, but did that make him deadly?

Frederick Reed—The choices in his past could explain everything, except his death.

Conrad Reed—His father's past raised questions. Could he afford the answers?

Captain Mathers—He directed the police involvement, but was it to investigate or to cover up?

Mike Cooper—His years on the force had shown him that there was nothing harder to beat than a cop on the take.

Mario Cartolucci—An elusive man who claimed he was above the law . . . and might be right.

Chapter One

Melanie Cardenas knocked softly on her partner's open door and walked inside. "Are you almost ready to call it a day?" She stared in surprise as Andy reached into the bottom drawer of his desk and extracted a .38 caliber revolver. "What's going on? You haven't carried a weapon in years!" With effort, she managed to keep her voice even.

"It's just a little insurance. Nothing to get worried about," he replied, checking the cylinder to verify that the weapon was fully loaded. He glanced her way, but never quite caught her eye.

"Don't kid me, Andy. I know you too well." It wasn't like Andy to avoid looking directly at her. The observation made her uneasy. "If it wasn't necessary, you'd never carry a weapon." Her eyes stayed on the man before her.

Andy O'Riley was in his fifties, and had the tall, broad-shouldered build of an athlete who was always in condition. His body was trim and muscular, attesting to rigorous daily workouts. His thin red hair, streaked with white, gave him a distinguished appearance. "Right now, all I've got is a lot of suspicions based on circumstantial evidence, but I'll have more after tonight," he spoke hurriedly, his green eyes bright with energy as he finally met her gaze. "We'll talk tomorrow morning."

Andy placed the revolver on the desk before him, casually glanced out the window, then walked over to the closet to retrieve his shoulder holster and jacket.

She shook her head stubbornly. "If this agency is involved in something that requires you to start carrying a gun, I want to know about it as soon as possible." Melanie stepped over to the window, curious as to what he might be looking for. She saw nothing unusual. "If you're in a rush at the moment, how about meeting me at my place after you're finished with your appointment? We can send out for some dinner, or just have drinks, if you prefer. We can talk there, undisturbed." Andy was on the trail of something important, and it was unlike him to put her on the sidelines.

"I should have known that you wouldn't let it go." He pursed his lips pensively, then inhaled softly. "Okay. I've got a few things I want to check out first, then I can be at your apartment by eight-thirty. Is that convenient?" His mouth pulled into a mischievous grin. "I realize it's Friday night. I wouldn't want to be interrupting something."

She chuckled. "There's nothing to interrupt."

"Well, there should be," he admonished. "You're beautiful." He gazed at her large, expressive brown eyes and delicately sculpted features. Ebony hair fell softly over her shoulders, framing her face like the halo of a creature conceived in myth. At twenty-seven, Melanie Cardenas was a beautiful, desirable woman. "I've known you for the past six years," he commented thoughtfully. "Ever since we were both members of the San Francisco Police Department. I asked you to join me here when I started this agency four and half years ago. However, I still haven't been able to figure out how or why you've remained single."

Andy picked up his revolver, checking the chambers once more. After fitting the handgun securely in place in his shoulder holster, he slipped on his jacket.

"Stop trying to divert my attention. I'll expect you at my place at eight-thirty or so."

"No problem. I'll be there." He strolled out of the office whistling an old Irish tune.

Melanie cleared the computer material she'd been working with from her desk. Tired, she returned to her chair and sat down. The thick, leather chair sank comfortably beneath her weight. What was Andy up to, and why the gun? Gazing idly out her window, she watched him walk across the parking lot. Years of undercover work for the department had made Andy a cautious man. Nowadays their firm specialized in security background checks, scarcely what anyone would consider high risks. Their work was steady and profitable, but fairly routine.

Almost as if he'd sensed her looking, he stopped in front of his car, turned around and gave her a playful salute. She laughed and saw his face beam a bright smile back at her.

Andy searched his pockets for his keys, and walked around the car slowly, inspecting it carefully. It worried her because Andy O'Riley was much more than just her business partner. He opened the car door.

The concussion of the blast hit Melanie squarely in the chest, knocking the wind out of her. Shards of glass scattered everywhere. She struggled to catch her breath, as her mind vaguely registered that the window she'd been sitting in front of was no longer there.

Acting on instinct alone, she dived through the space the window had occupied and ran across the parking lot. The center of her world had just disintegrated before her eyes and become lost in a haze of smoke and fire. With the back of her hand she angrily wiped off the tiny, warm rivulets that were streaming down into her eyes. She knew it was blood, but undaunted, she pressed on.

Andy's car, and the one next to it, were consumed by tongues of orange flame. Billowing smoke obscured most of both vehicles. She tried to get near, but the heat was so intense that she could feel it searing her skin. She stepped back, gasping for air. Shielding her eyes with her arm, she tried to approach again.

Someone reached for her hand, pulling her back from the roaring inferno. She struggled to free herself, but the man wouldn't let go. Melanie could hear him speaking, but the words didn't make any sense.

Her ears were ringing. Her heart was breaking. She had to get to Andy. She screamed at the man, pushing him away, then turned toward the cars.

She was afraid she'd see Andy, and even more terrified that she wouldn't. As she drew near the blaze, acrid black smoke seemed to engulf her, burning her lungs, assaulting her face. She staggered backward.

Arms caught her and held her back. The enveloping smoke joined with the foggy darkness that was shrouding her senses.

An overwhelming sense of defeat seemed to be the only emotion that her numbed heart could register. Unable to fight anymore, she felt herself slipping into a black void, spinning out of control.

THE DARK GRAY CLOUD that had surrounded all her senses began to loosen its hold on her. She opened her eyes slowly.

She was in a strange room with pale green walls. She was lying in a narrow bed, her head resting on a small pillow. She felt awful, but worst of all, she couldn't remember how she'd got here. The smell of disinfectant stung her nostrils and her skin burned. She glanced down at her hands and noticed the loosely wrapped bandages that covered her forearms. She blinked several times, trying to make her eyes clear. They were wet, as if someone had just placed drops in them.

"You'll be all right, you're safe. You're at County Hospital now." A tall, thin brunette in a nurse's uniform moved closer to the bed. "You must have been in front of a window when the blast went off. You have quite a few cuts, and some minor burns, but everything will heal before you know it." She smoothed the light blanket that covered Melanie. "You were in shock when they brought you in."

Andy. The thought of him made her chest tighten. How could she have failed him? Her police training, her instinct, had amounted to absolutely nothing in the final analysis. Would Andy forgive her?

Her mind replayed the accident. No one could have survived that. But surely, he couldn't be gone. It wasn't possible. They'd come with news of him at anytime now. He was probably recuperating in a nearby room.

She started to speak, but then realized that it hurt to even try. The nurse held a glass of water and a straw up to her mouth. "Don't try to push yourself. You were very brave to try to reach that man."

She wanted to explain that it hadn't been a matter of bravery at all. Andy had been her partner, and her friend, the one person who meant more to her than anyone else in the world. She'd done what she had out of love and loyalty and it hadn't been enough. Her eyes began to brim over with tears, and she turned her face away. "Andy?" she managed to ask in a barely audible voice.

The nurse shook her head slowly. "I'm sorry, dear," she said kindly, "but you did all you could. I heard about the explosion from the paramedics. Your friend didn't suffer, be thankful for that. It was over before he knew it."

The words confirmed what she'd seen, and known in her heart all along. The senseless irrefutability of it all filled her with anger. She had to *do* something. It was a debt of love. She had to bring his murderer to justice. "Where are my clothes?" she asked in a raspy voice.

"They're in the closet," the nurse replied hesitantly, "but the doctors want you to stay overnight for observation."

She tried to pull herself together, but the pain inside her wouldn't let her think clearly. She had to find the person who'd killed Andy and lying around in bed wasn't going to help. She started to get up, but the pounding in her head got worse. She fell back onto the pillows.

"Let that be a lesson to you," the nurse said firmly. "For now, just rest. There'll be plenty of time tomorrow to take care of whatever needs to be done."

Melanie closed her eyes. She heard a quiet voice outside her door. "You'll have to question her some other time, Inspector. She's been given a sedative."

The voice seemed to get farther and farther away.

The next time she opened her eyes, sunlight was streaming through the window. Melanie lay still, trying to get her bearings. Her body ached all over, but her thinking was clearer. Gone was the jumbled confusion and disorientation that had plagued her. In her mind's eye she ran back the chaotic scene she'd witnessed the day before. An unbearable sadness gripped her and she found herself wishing the numbness would return.

A knock sounded at her door. "Come in," she said, her voice slightly stronger today.

"Hello, Melanie."

She recognized the tall inspector from the homicide division. He'd put on a few pounds over the years, but he still looked fit. "Hello, Mike."

"Melanie, I'm really sorry to bother you after what happened, but I've got to ask you a few questions." He pulled a chair closer to her bed, then took a notepad and pen from his coat pocket.

"Go ahead," she told him, determined to keep her voice steady. Her sorrow was too private a matter to share with anyone else.

The questioning took about twenty minutes, but going over the events leading to Andy's death left her feeling drained. "Mike, there's something I want you to understand. Andy was like family, and that means a great deal to me." She took a deep breath, and steadied herself. "I'll cooperate with the police and pass on any leads I turn up. However, I'd appreciate it if you'd also keep me informed on whatever progress you make."

"Fair enough." Mike Cooper stood slowly. "If you need anything, Melanie, or if you just want to talk to someone, you have my office and home number. Andy and I were buddies for years, and I'll miss him like hell, too."

She nodded, afraid that if she spoke, the tears would start flowing and there'd be nothing she could do to stop them. If only she'd kept Andy from going to his car. She should have forced him to tell her what he'd been working on before he left. Perhaps if she'd delayed him, or if they'd both gone out to the cars together, he'd still be alive. It was possible she might have spotted something amiss and prevented the tragedy.

Guilt and sorrow were relentless companions. Alone in the room once again, she pushed the covers aside and stood. She couldn't just lay there thinking of what had happened. It wasn't her way. A job needed to be done. After Andy's murderer was found, there'd be plenty of time for rest.

She dressed hurriedly; her smoke-damaged clothes reeked. Shutting out the memories the scent triggered, she walked over to the door.

As she stepped out into the hall, she collided with a stranger who'd appeared in her path. "Excuse me," she mumbled, distractedly.

"You must be Melanie," a masculine voice observed.

She glanced up, quickly scrutinizing the man. Melanie had never met him, but she recognized the person before her instantly. Patrick O'Riley was in his late thirties. He had his father's fair complexion and penetrating gaze. His hair was thick and wavy, but instead of Andy's bright red, it was a pale golden color. His Air Force officer's uniform gave him a commanding air. He stood erect, with the confidence of a born leader. It was to his azure eyes, however, that her attention returned. There was self-control and a quiet strength reflected in them that she found compelling.

"Patrick," she acknowledged softly.

"So, you know who I am," he replied quietly, with an approving nod. "Good. That'll save us introductions and explanations."

"I'm very sorry that we had to meet under these circumstances." She forced herself to remain perfectly calm under the intensity of his stare. "You look just like the photograph your father kept of you on his desk." Patrick had none of the warmth his father had always displayed, however. Then again, maybe this was his way of coping with grief. "You came quickly." Almost too quickly, she added silently, walking toward the desk at the nurses' station.

"The police called me. I took the first plane I could." He kept his voice low, but there was no mistaking the authority in his tone. "I want you to tell me everything you know. We can start by talking about what Dad was working on before he died."

It wasn't a request. She took a deep breath and tried to be patient. He was a man used to giving orders. Too bad she had no talent at all for taking them. "Patrick, I realize that you work for the Office of Special Investigations in the Air Force. Since you're a trained investigator, you'll undoubtedly want details. I warn you, though, I really don't know that much yet. Maybe by the time you're ready to go back to your base, after the funeral, I'll have learned more. I will keep you advised on the progress I make throughout my investigation." She forced herself to remain civil, but inwardly she bristled. Andy had been her partner and friend. She didn't have to answer to a son who'd come to see his father only after it was too late. "Rest assured, the person who killed your father won't get away with it."

"I intend to make certain of that," he assured her in a firm, but polite voice. "Between my thirty days bereavement leave, and the personal time I've accumulated over the years, I'll be able to stay in town for as long as I need. I won't be going anywhere until this matter is settled."

She pursed her lips tightly. She could see iron-willed determination to match her own mirrored in his face. "Patrick, take my advice and do yourself a favor. Don't try to interfere. You'll only slow things down," she admonished gently. "You have no contacts in this town, and you're too emotionally involved to think clearly."

His eyes locked with hers. "I'm a soldier. I can control my emotions, and keep my mind on the job no matter what the situation is."

"In an abstract sense perhaps, but can you remain objective when it's the death of your father you'll be looking into?" She'd kept her voice soft, trying to be kind in deference to his feelings. However, this was her investigation, not his. She'd shared Andy's life on a daily basis for the past six years. He'd been her partner and it was her right to find Andy's killer and bring him to justice.

Patrick, on the other hand, had been away for years. He hadn't shared a close relationship with his father at all. She recalled the times she'd seen Andy staring at Patrick's photograph. Andy had missed his son, of that she was certain. She'd tried to encourage him to call Patrick, but Andy had always refused, assuring her that it wouldn't do any good. She'd never pried, but she'd often wondered about the circumstances surrounding the breach between them. She knew that Patrick and Andy had barely spoken to each other for the past four or five years. What kind of son was he?

Patrick watched her walk off, heading toward the hospital's administrative section. He had no intention of leaving. She was his best lead, and there was no way he was going to let her off the hook that easily. He still couldn't believe his father was gone. He half expected him to appear from around the nearest corner, wearing his familiar grin. His dad would then offer to buy him a drink of the best Irish whiskey in town in exchange for the trouble caused by the false report of his death.

His face grew hot with anger. Someone would pay for what had been taken from him. Blood ties were unbreakable. And even if they'd always fought in the past, there was always the future, and that sense of possibility. One day they would have learned to be friends. Only now, someone had robbed them of that. He'd avenge his father. It was the one last thing he could do in the name of the ties that bound them.

He waited until she finished signing the hospital release papers.

Free to go at last, she looked around for a phone, hoping to call a cab. That's when she noticed Patrick walking toward her. "I didn't realize you were still here," she admitted, surprised.

"May I give you a ride home? I've rented a car," he offered.

She gazed at him speculatively. "Does that mean you'll be questioning me all the way there?"

"Yes," he conceded.

He was at once vulnerably honest, and arrogant. "All right, we'll do this your way," she paused and added, "this time."

He walked slowly, leading her to his car. Being with him was difficult for her. In some respects, he reminded her a great deal of Andy, especially his voice, but he lacked the amiability and compassionate insight that had made Andy so special to her.

Perhaps the comparison was unfair. She *had* only just met the man and he had just lost his father. Still there was an air of purpose about Patrick that obscured the human side of him. She wondered about the man behind the uniform. He was as handsome as the beautiful painting of the legendary Celtic knight, Cuchulain, Andy had given her last Christmas. She'd thought Andy had selected it because he'd known of her love for sword-and-sorcery novels. Now she wondered if the resemblance to his son had caught his eye and drawn Andy to that particular painting.

She cast a furtive glance over at Patrick, and then looked away again. This would get her nowhere. Patrick was nothing more than an added inconvenience. She'd have to persuade him to return to the military life he'd chosen and leave her to do her job. Still, if he insisted on staying, she'd have to learn more about him—from an adversarial point of view, if nothing else. Like Andy had taught her, it was the unknown factor in any investigation that posed the greatest danger.

She slipped inside Patrick's rental car, a rather ordinary looking four-door sedan, and leaned back into the firm bench seat. She remembered seeing Andy getting into his car, and the events that had followed replayed themselves vividly in her mind. She shut her eyes, willing the thoughts to stop.

"Where to?"

"Straight ahead. It's not far. I found a duplex that's only fifteen minutes from the office." She paused, then added, "Have you been by the agency?"

He nodded. "I went to look over the scene and to make sure the broken windows were boarded up. The building's maintenance people had already taken care of it." He glanced over at her. "I know so little about you," he added softly. "The only thing I remember was Dad telling me that you two worked together in the police department. Were you one of his inspectors?"

"Your dad and I became friends when we were both on the force." She hedged answering his question more out of habit than anything else. Experience had taught her that knowledge was power. Although obtaining information was the core of her job as an investigator, giving any out was seldom advisable. "I admired him a great deal. He was a hard taskmaster, but he didn't expect the impossible, only the improbable. What made him special was the fact that he usually managed to get it." She marveled at the control Patrick exerted over his emotions. Not once had he shown any outward signs of grief.

"Were you a police officer or a civilian working for the department?" he insisted.

So, Patrick had not been diverted by her evasion. Though he hadn't said anything, nor reacted in any way, he'd persisted with his inquiry without hesitation. That was the mark of a skilled investigator. She'd underestimated him.

"I was a cop, but not an inspector," she answered. "I was the liaison between the police and the press and media. Public relations really, though my title of Official Spokesperson was a bit fancier."

"What made you decide to go with Dad once he started the agency?"

Was he investigating her, or his father's death? She realized then that he was sizing her up just as she was sizing up him. "He asked, and I wanted to," she answered succinctly. She wasn't obligated to answer his questions, and she could see no reason why she should. Had he maintained closer ties with his father, he'd already know what he was asking her about now.

He glanced over at her. His hands tightened around the wheel then loosened their hold. As they stopped at a red light, he captured her gaze for a moment. "I know this is not easy for you, Melanie. It's difficult for me, too. But I have to learn all I can about my father's life prior to his murder in order to reconstruct what happened."

"I'll tell you what I told the police, which is really all I know so far." She paused and collected herself. "Andy was on the trail of something." She related their last conversation and the incident with the gun. "The problem is, he never did get to tell me what he suspected." Her voice cracked, but she cleared her throat and composed herself quickly. "I'll have to go over the files he kept in his office. You see, right now I don't even know which of his cases was the one giving him trouble. However, let's face it. His murder—" the words lodged in her throat, almost choking her "—may not be linked to any of the investigations he was conducting out of our offices. As an undercover cop, and then captain in charge of homicide, Andy made quite a few enemies before he ever started the agency."

He nodded, seemingly satisfied for now. "Tell me something about yourself. You most certainly know more about me than I do about you."

"I doubt it. Andy spoke of family matters from time to time, but never in any great detail. I know there was a breach between you two, but nothing more." She watched his reaction to her mention of that, but learned nothing from his stoic expression. "Andy never discussed the details behind it, and I respected him enough not to pry," she explained. "I will say this, there were times he missed you a great deal. I don't know if you know that or not, but it's true."

For several moments Patrick said nothing. He followed her directions automatically, but his mind seemed a million miles away. "I want to find the person who did this, and destroy his future like he did my dad's."

His words vibrated with a singleness of purpose that surprised her, yet his motives were unclear. If his love for Andy had run so deeply, then why had he stayed away for so long? It was one thing to move to another city, but quite another to sever all the ties that were natural between father and son. She knew that they hadn't even exchanged Christmas cards since he'd left town. Was it guilt or a personal vendetta of sorts? She could understand that sense of obligation that surpassed personal feelings. Her Spanish heritage was rich with tradition and unspoken codes that were passed from generation to generation.

Melanie glanced at Patrick furtively, trying to discern more about him. "I have no idea what condition I left my duplex in yesterday morning when I went to work. However, if general chaos doesn't bother you, I'd like you to come in. It won't take me long to shower and change. After that, I think you and I should have an honest discussion."

"That's a good idea," he answered simply. "What else did my father say about me?" he urged in a subdued tone.

Her heart went out to him. For the first time, she caught a glimpse of the pain behind the veiled eyes. She softened her voice again, and tried to recall details that would mean something special to him. By the time they arrived at her home, Patrick's mood was somber, though she couldn't say whether it was from regret or sadness. Perhaps it was a mixture of both.

She walked up the steps of an old Victorian house that had been converted into duplexes. To one side of the covered porch was a door that led to the upstairs apartment. She reached for a key that was buried beneath one of the bushes. "My other keys are still at the office where I left my purse," she explained. "It's not a problem, though. I hide another house key here, in case of emergencies." She started to unlock the catch when the door swung open. "What the . . ."

"Stay here," he ordered. "I'll go up and take a look."

Much to her surprise, he rushed past her. She collected her wits quickly and sprung forward. This was her home! She could handle herself in a crisis as well as he or anyone else could. She dashed up the stairs, and met him on the top step.

"I told you to stay put!" he whispered harshly.

"I don't take orders from you, Major," she countered in a low voice. As she tried to go through the doorway leading into her apartment, Patrick stepped forward. For a moment, they were both lodged in the opening.

Patrick moved aside, muttering an oath, and she shot ahead. Her apartment was in shambles. The contents of all the drawers had been tossed to the carpet. Paintings had been ripped from the walls and thrown onto the floor. Sofa cushions had been taken from the couch and were scattered around the room. Her potted plants had been uprooted and dumped on the floor along with the soil. Alert to danger, she crossed the living room and cautiously entered the kitchen. The door that led to the fire escape in the back was open. It creaked on its hinges as it swayed back and forth with the breeze. "Whoever was here is gone," she said in a weary voice.

"Sure looks that way," he conceded.

She walked to the bedroom and stared at the mess before her. The mattress lay on the floor. All her clothes had been ripped from the hangers and dumped in a pile. Patrick followed her in. "I gather this isn't what you meant when you warned me that your place might not be too neat." He gave her a thin smile.

She sighed. "Hardly. My home looks like it's been hit by a tornado."

He returned to the living room. "That's the least of your worries." Lost in thought, he ran a hand over her television set.

She took a deep breath and nodded. She'd seen her revolver lying on the floor next to her emptied nightstand. "They left all the valuables behind. This wasn't a robbery. They were looking for something."

"Which they obviously believe you have."

"That means Andy wasn't their only target. It's definitely something to do with the agency, and that puts me right in the thick of it."

Chapter Two

Careful to avoid disturbing the crime scene, Melanie stepped over to the wall. "They must have come today when my neighbors were at work." Rage and a sense of helplessness and futility washed over her. "My guess is that they hit the office, and maybe even Andy's place, too. I was probably last on their list. The good news is that if they came here, they probably haven't found whatever they were looking for."

Patrick's eyes turned dark and angry at the mention of his father. "I'm going over to Dad's right now and see what they've done to the house. Call the police and ask them to meet me there, all right?"

"Look, you can't just go charging into your father's home. You might be damaging evidence. Stay here, then after the police look over my apartment, we'll both go meet them at the office, then go to Andy's." She strode to the telephone and made the call.

Patrick paced restlessly. "I can't stand around here cooling my heels. I'm going over to Dad's now. I'll wait for the police before going inside."

"All right," she conceded, sensing it was useless to try to stop him. "Once they're through here, I'll head over to the office. I've got to see what condition they've left that in. After you're finished at Andy's, why don't you meet me there?" she suggested.

"No problem." He started toward her door.

"Patrick," she called out before he could leave. "I'm counting on you to give me a complete description of what you find at your father's house. Can I rely on you to give me an accurate report?" she asked bluntly. His interference was already creating problems for her. If he chose to omit details, he would end up jeopardizing her investigation.

"I'm a trained investigator."

"That doesn't answer my question," she insisted firmly.

"I'll give you an accurate report," he agreed, anxious to go. She was sharp, the kind who would make a great ally, and a bad adversary. The problem was that at the moment he really hadn't made up his mind which it would be. "I'll see you soon."

By the time he arrived at his father's home, the police were already there. With a station about a mile away, their trip had taken only a few minutes. A patrolman stood guard by the door. Mike Cooper, a police inspector his father had known since Patrick's high-school days, approached as Patrick entered the living room.

"Patrick, I came over as soon as I got Melanie's call."

Patrick shook his hand. "It's been a long time, Mike."

He escorted Patrick into the room. "It's a mess. They tossed everything. Did Melanie give you any idea of what they might have been looking for?"

"I don't think she knows, Mike." Patrick's glance took in the room before him. It was in shambles. He wandered around, sidestepping his father's possessions, which lay scattered all over the floor. There was a bitter taste at the back of his throat.

His gaze drifted gently over his father's favorite easy chair, memories flooding his mind. His father had always refused to part with it. Now it was tattered and overturned on the carpet. This house, which had been the center of his world and everything he loved for so many years, had been defiled. The knowledge felt like a sharp blade ripping at his insides.

The picture frame that held his mother's photograph lay in front of the mantelpiece, shattered. It had been on the shelf above the fireplace since her death during his junior year in high school. It was a place of honor, his father had said. The hearth, the symbolic heart of a family, was where the last photograph ever taken of her belonged. His father had seemed so lost without her. He'd never remarried. Now, at last, they'd be together.

"You okay?" Mike placed a hand on Patrick's shoulder.

"Sure," he snapped. It was as if someone were destroying all he'd valued from his past, all that had made him the man he was today. Patrick reached within himself for the discipline that had been ingrained into him as a military officer. He forced his thoughts back to the present. "It's literally been years since I've been here. If you and Dad stayed close, then you'll probably be better able to tell if anything's been taken."

"As far as I can tell, nothing big has. I've already checked. Right now, I've got the lab boys going over every inch of the place, but so far they haven't found any evidence we can use. It's my guess they won't. This was done by professionals."

"They certainly were thorough," Patrick commented.

"Our people will be here quite a while. On Melanie's suggestion, we dispatched another team to the agency's office. Someone's been there, too. We'll be dusting for prints at Melanie's apartment and the office today. What we'd like to do, in addition to that, is inspect all of Andy's office records. However, we can't do that without a court order. It would help a great deal if you'd speak to Melanie about it. She needs to give us permission. I wouldn't ask, Patrick, if I didn't feel it was important. Andy was acting strangely this past week, and I have a feeling he wasn't being as open with me as he normally was. His files would tell me exactly what he'd been up to, and that might turn out to be one of my best leads."

Patrick rubbed the back of his neck with one hand. "There's a matter of protecting clients' interests, Mike, you know that. Let me talk to Melanie, then I'll get back to you."

"Okay." Mike led Patrick back outside. "This is going to be rough on all of us, Pat. Would you like to come and stay with Cathy and me? Our home's always open to you."

"I appreciate the offer, but no. As soon as your people are gone, I'll go ahead and pick up Dad's place and stay here. I need some time alone. There's a lot I have to sort out in my mind." He met Mike's eyes in a direct gaze. "I'd like to ask you a favor, though. Will you keep me posted on the police investigation?"

Mike paused, and considered the request. "You're a professional. I don't see why we can't extend you that courtesy."

"How about letting me take a look at the photos of the murder scene?" His voice was steady, his body calm. He had to prove to Mike by his actions that he could remain professional. "I'm particularly interested in any physical evidence that was not part of the car itself."

Mike watched him for a few moments, then, satisfied that Patrick would be able to handle it, nodded. "Sure. Let's go over to the station now. You can follow me in your car."

Later, in Mike's office, he spread a series of photographs over the top of his desk.

Patrick went over each shot carefully, memorizing all the details. "There's a piece of wire here, still stuck to the door." His stomach tightened, grief threatening to erode his poise. "I suppose it was attached to the bomb."

Mike nodded. "The wire was fastened to the lower door panel with some instant glue. We believe the pull on that wire triggered the bomb. I can show you what we have in the evidence room, if you want."

"That might help." His heart wrenched in his chest, but he forced himself to keep his breathing steady.

Mike led him down the hall, then into a small room, where pieces of charred metal had been placed on a folding table. "The explosive was contained in a coffee can. Those are some of the fragments, the rest have been sent to the lab for special analysis. It'll take a few more days before any detailed reports come back, and we have more information."

Patrick concentrated on the metal fragments before him. Self-discipline and determination sustained him now.

"Patrick, if Melanie won't let me take a look at the files, then you're going to have to do it for me. See if there's anyone Andy was investigating who might have had the technical background necessary to build the bomb, as well as motive and opportunity."

Patrick nodded. "I'll take care of that right away, but it's been years since I had anything to do with Dad's work. I'm not sure how he's cataloged everything. Unless Melanie has a central file of some sort, I'm likely to have a hard time finding anything."

"Melanie is extremely organized. She looks like a porcelain doll, but believe me she's as tough and smart as they come."

"How long has she worked for Dad?"

"I don't think you understand." Mike gave him a puzzled look. "She did start by taking care of the administrative end of the business for him. However, once that was set up, she took on some of the background investigations. Pretty soon, she was taking on an equal number of cases. Then, about two years ago, Andy offered her a full partnership."

Patrick glanced up quickly. "What do you mean?"

"She isn't Andy's assistant, Patrick. She owns half the agency."

"What?" He stiffened, the news taking him completely by surprise.

Mike was about to elaborate when the door behind them was pushed open.

"What in the hell is going on?" A dark-haired, slightly overweight man in a gray suit strode into the room. His police ID badge proclaimed him to be Captain Mathers. "Cooper, what's this man doing in here?"

"Sir, this is Andy's son. He's an officer in the Air Force's Office of Special Investigations. I was affording him the courtesy of showing him..."

"I can see what you're doing, Inspector." He glowered at Patrick. Something odd and perhaps dangerous stirred in the back of his eyes. "Does the military claim official jurisdiction over this case?"

"No. This is of personal interest to me," Patrick replied. All emotion was gone from his voice, as if the pain of loss had draped him in a protective shell.

"Then I see no reason to have you in here, nor for the police department to extend you any special favors. I'm sure Inspector Cooper can show you the way out."

Mike led Patrick back out into the hall. As soon as they were out of earshot, he muttered an oath. "Sorry about that, Patrick. That jerk was one of Andy's enemies. Even someone as well liked as Andy had a few of those."

Patrick tried to will his anger to dissipate so that he could continue thinking clearly, but it took a lot of effort. "What was the problem between him and Dad?"

"Your father and Captain Mathers went up for the same promotion a couple of times. Andy always aced him out. The last time it happened, they were both up for captain. Your father tested out much higher, so he got the promotion. Then Andy retired early and started his own company just two years after he made captain. It took Mathers another three years to get to the position Andy had held. Only to him, it was a culmination of a lifetime ambition."

"And how did you feel about Dad going civilian and starting his own company?" Patrick asked, trying to put it all together.

"Andy was my friend, Pat, you know that. I wished him well when he left, and I was glad when the agency turned into such a profitable business. I think Andy did what was right for him. He was tired of all the internal politics in the department. I admired him for having the guts to leave and start over again."

"And what about you? You plan to stay a career man in the force?"

"It's what I do, Pat." Mike shrugged. "I'm a cop, first, last and always." He grinned slowly. "But I know how to bend the rules here and there. For starters, I'm about to give you a lead. I know you're going to get involved in this investigation no matter what anyone tells you, so you might as well pursue an avenue the department can't follow. There's a refuge for the homeless not too far from where your father's office is. It's useless for any cop to try to question street people. They know us in or out of uniform. To them, we're the bad guys, the ones who always make them move on, or bring them in."

"What do they have to do with this?"

"The alley beside the building that the agency's in is a shortcut to the refuge. Lots of vagrants use it. We've questioned the people in your building, and no one here saw anything unusual the day Andy was murdered. However, it's possible one of the street people might have."

They stopped at the side door of the station. "I'll see what I can do," Patrick said.

"It's going to be tough, Pat. They don't trust anyone. You could talk to Brother Paul, he runs the refuge and might be able to get some answers for you. He's very protective of the homeless that come to him, though, so tread carefully."

"Thanks, Mike, for all the help."

"If I learn anything that will be useful to you, I'll pass it along. But Patrick, I want you to keep me posted on your progress, too. We'll only set each other back if we start crossing paths."

"If I get anything, I'll let you know."

Patrick walked slowly to his car. The breeze coming from the bay was cold, but it had nothing to do with the chill he felt inside him. He remembered the tune his father had always whistled whenever he was under pressure. The little Irish melody echoed hauntingly in his mind.

He slipped inside his car. There was no time now to reminisce. His thoughts returned to Melanie. Had his father been in love with her? Not that he'd blame him if he had. She certainly had the looks to turn any man's head. There was also something else about her, a quality that was much harder to define. She possessed a delicate balance between fragility and strength that drew him despite his determination to remain unaffected. He wanted to wrap his arms around her and protect her from the hurt she was feeling. Yet he sensed that if he did, it would be her courage that would shield them both.

Had his father responded to her in the same way? Maybe she was really a shrewd little gold digger who had managed to con his father into giving away half of the agency. There was so much about her he didn't know.

He drove to the office quickly. It had been over two hours since he'd seen her last. A lot had happened since them.

MELANIE SIFTED through the papers that had been strewn all around the office. Their document files had been taken out of the cabinets and flung randomly about. A few folders were intact, but the contents of most had been scattered. The police had come and gone before she arrived. The building's superintendent had stayed with them until they'd dusted for fingerprints, and then left.

Between the chaos at her apartment, and now this, she felt a crushing heaviness settling over her. She wanted so much to escape from the grief, but felt guilty for even thinking that way.

Gathering herself, she walked over to the wall, crouched in the corner and removed a section of the wood paneling that was held in place by hidden catches. There was a box of computer disks encased in the hollow within the wall. Two sets of copies, hers and Andy's, had been left out in plain view and were now on the floor. However, the originals had remained protected and intact, nestled inside her secret hiding place. If anything had been taken from files or information had been altered, she'd eventually be able to find out. Then, perhaps, she'd have her first clue as to who was behind Andy's death.

Before starting that search process, however, she wanted to talk to some of the other occupants of the building. She put back the disks, closed the hiding place and spent the rest of the morning questioning the tenants whose offices faced the parking lot. Her investigation was fruitless. If anyone had seen anything significant that evening, the confusion that followed had obliterated it from their minds. Dejected, Melanie returned to her office just as repairmen were finishing replacing the windows. She slumped in her chair, and stared outside.

A fluttering movement caught her eye, and she leaned forward. Shy Eddy, one of the vagrants that frequented their area, was making his daily rounds, cutting through the alley beside their building. She could see him holding the apple he always carried but never ate. Andy and she had speculated on occasion if it was a real apple, or a wax replica. Shy Eddy would never let anyone close enough to him to end the mystery.

He sat down by one of the giant trash bins, and stared at the flower bed across the street. Her mind drifted back to the day of Andy's murder. She remembered seeing Shy Eddy that afternoon, sometime prior to the explosion. She'd been on the telephone and had noticed him walking by. Until now, the recollection had completely eluded her.

A knock at the door interrupted her musings. She turned around as Patrick walked in.

His eyes roamed over her in a quick, but thorough appraisal. Her white, long-sleeved blouse contrasted against her raven hair. Tan slacks accentuated her slim hips. She'd been pretty even this morning in tattered clothes, but now she looked beautiful. Yet there was an elusive quality about her. It seemed to wrap itself around him, beckoning and compelling him to delve past that air of reserve and mystery she projected. He stared speculatively at her.

"I see our intruders have been doing their interior decorating work with their usual flair." Melanie had already picked up the files from the floor, and stacked them in piles across the room, but drawer contents, paper clips, pencils, and other miscellaneous items were still strewn all over the carpet. "Have you been able to find out if they took anything?"

"Not yet, but I will." She started to tell him about the special hiding place she'd built for her computer disks, but then decided against it. This was her case, not his. He didn't really belong here in the agency. She still didn't know him well enough to be sure about him.

"I told you I'd give you an accurate report of what I found over at Dad's," he said, then proceeded in a taut voice to share his findings. "After that, Mike took me to the evidence room. However, before I could really study any of the items, Captain Mathers ran me out. He made it clear he wants to keep it strictly a police matter."

"Maybe he feels you're too close to the case," she suggested rather pointedly.

He gave her a wry smile. "Then he'll just have to adjust."

"I don't understand you," she said as she exhaled softly. "Why are you so determined to take over this investigation?" She shifted, her skin still sore in spots. At least the long sleeves covered up the bandages and most of the cuts.

He sat in the chair opposite her, and gave her a long, steady look. "He was my father," he answered succinctly.

"Yet you hardly had anything to do with him," she countered, perplexed.

He nodded slowly, his eyes trained on hers. "Yes, and that's precisely why I intend to find the person who murdered him."

"I'm more confused than ever," she admitted.

He paused for several moments. "Why is it necessary that you understand?"

She said nothing, trying to collect her thoughts. He was in her agency, trying to take over an investigation that was rightfully hers. "If you have to ask, then it's obvious you'd never understand my answer."

"Do you think that just because my father and I stayed apart, we didn't love or respect each other?" Patrick stood and jammed his hands into his pockets. He walked noiselessly around the office like a big jungle cat searching for prey. "Consider this, then. Maybe it was in deference to those feelings that I stayed away."

She felt her heart hammering against her sides. She remembered a conversation she'd had with her Cuban grandfather years back. He'd always insisted on the importance of family ties. Yet he'd also taught her that in order to do honor to that, she first had to be true to herself. Duty to family was best met by individuals who were satisfied with themselves and their lives.

That's when she'd made the decision to leave home, travel across the country and start a new life. She'd wanted and needed her independence, and autonomy. If her help was ever needed, she'd be back. In the meantime, she had an obligation to herself.

In some ways, perhaps, that was precisely what Patrick had done. She, of all people, had no right to judge him.

"What are your plans? Do you have any ideas on how to proceed from this point?" he asked, diverting the conversation.

She could tell he was uncomfortable talking about his feelings. "The first order of business is trying to figure out what cases Andy was working on. That's going to take some time. It wasn't unusual for each of us to be conducting five or six background investigations all at once."

"What if the person or persons responsible already have the information they wanted to retrieve? It's possible they've stolen a file or altered the information you keep here, then searched Dad's place and yours just as a ruse to cover their tracks."

"I know, but I have a system of checks and counterchecks. I'll be able to tell if anything has been taken or if any of our documents have been tampered with."

"I assume you keep extensive records stored in your computer diskettes in addition to whatever's in your file cabinets. Disks can also be altered, you know. Are you taking that into consideration?''

She rolled her eyes. ''Of course I am, Patrick. Let me handle that part of it? In the meantime, what line of investigation are you going to be pursuing?''

''Mike's waiting for the lab reports to come back. That's really the information I want. Still we can't afford to wait. You're in danger. Would you consider leaving town for a while, and letting me take over?''

It took all her willpower to remain calm. She answered, ''You just don't seem to be able to accept the fact that this is *my* investigation. You're the one who should withdraw, if anyone should.''

''I can't.'' He walked to the door of Andy's office, but did not go inside. He turned and faced her. ''As far as the line of investigation I'm going to pursue...'' He shrugged. ''I'm still not certain. Mike suggested that maybe the street people in the area saw something that day. That's a long shot though, at best. I think my time's better spent going through Dad's current files and compiling a list of those who might have had the knowledge to construct a bomb. Then, I'll have a buddy of mine check the names through the O.S.I. computer. We'll see what turns up.''

She nodded slowly. ''Okay. But whatever you learn has to stay confidential, unless you can find evidence or a motive that will link them to your father's murder.''

''I'm aware of that.'' His tone was somber. ''That's why I don't intend to turn over that list to the police, at least not right away. Having the computer run a check for me, though, will save lots of time. Technology is much more reliable than footwork.''

''I disagree completely. The best leads come from questioning people. One person seldom has all the answers, but clues can add up until you finally have enough to piece the puzzle together.''

''Maybe, but technology is faster and that's important to me at the moment. I'd like to have something to trade with Mike once he gets the lab reports back.''

"You don't need to do that with Mike, trust me on that. He was very close to Andy."

"I'd still like to have something for him in return," Patrick insisted. He gathered a bunch of files from the top of the cabinet. "I'll start with these."

"Fine." She stood up, a plan of action slowly forming in her mind. "I have a few things I'd like to do this afternoon, but I'll be back later."

"I'm sure the police have you under protective surveillance, Melanie, but if you prefer to have closer backup, I'll be glad to go along and keep an eye on things."

Was Patrick being chivalrous, or was he trying to find out what she was up to? She couldn't quite make up her mind. "I'll be fine by myself. I used to be a cop, and now I'm an investigator. I don't need someone to watch over me. That's why I declined police protection."

"That was a very foolish thing to do." He walked toward her, and stood close enough for her to feel the heat radiating from his body. "Are you really aware of the danger you're in? Whoever killed my father is playing for very high stakes. If he hasn't found what he wants, he'll come after you."

"I don't care for the position I've been put in, but I won't act like a frightened rabbit, either." Without as much as a backward glance, she walked out of the office and down the hall. The weight of the revolver in her shoulder bag felt strangely heavy after all those years without it.

She drove back to her apartment slowly. She didn't know what to make of Patrick. He was a dynamic mixture of courage and determination. He'd obviously charted a course for himself, and no amount of persuasion was going to dissuade him from it. His inner strength created an aura of power and impregnability. Yet there was also a vulnerable side to him. She'd glimpsed it before he could mask his feelings. The combination was appealing but the attraction dangerous.

She forced him from her mind, glanced at her watch and set a timetable for herself. By the end of this afternoon, if all went as planned, she might have some very definite leads. For now, there were preparations to make, and details to take care of.

PATRICK STARED PENSIVELY at Melanie's empty chair. Whatever else Melanie might be, one thing was for certain: she had a mind of her own and a fiery temper, although she did try to keep it under tight rein. He still believed she should leave town. Yet he couldn't help but admire her for staying, despite the risks.

He was glad she'd left the office this afternoon. The woman was too much of a distraction. Besides, he had an assignment he wanted to carry out and he certainly didn't want her involved. It was true Melanie had worked closely with his father, but the same blood that had coursed through Andy's veins flowed through his. This was a matter of family and honor.

He looked up the address of the refuge Mike had told him about, then found a secondhand store near the agency's office. That would be his first order of business. Compiling that list of suspects was important, but it would take time. He was hoping for an even more immediate break on the case.

With a bit of luck he'd have what he wanted by the end of the day.

MELANIE ARRIVED AT THE REFUGE shortly after four that same afternoon. She'd cut her red wig unevenly all the way around. Spiky bangs and ends protruded toward her face, accentuating splotches of dirt that covered her skin. A dark red scarf covered her head loosely, pushing her bangs against her cheeks and serving to obscure more of her face. She'd further enhanced her disguise by padding her clothes to make herself appear twenty pounds heavier than she was. She wore an army fatigue jacket a friend had once given her, and an old pair of overalls.

With patient determination, she forced herself to walk at the slow, shuffling gait the others around her used. Street people seldom spoke candidly to anyone who didn't share their life-style. Satisfied that she'd be able to carry it off, she started to look around for Shy Eddy.

She stood in one corner of the room, and studied the crowd before her. Her heart went out to them. Homeless and unwanted, their faces seemed to blend into a portrait of misery drawn by the harshness of their daily existence. She recognized Brother Paul, and a few of his assistants, but Shy Eddy was nowhere in sight. She started to walk toward the next room, when someone grasped her arm.

"First things first," one of the Brothers said gently. "I know you're eager to go into the dining area, but there's nothing set up in there yet. Your chore, helping us wash the pots and pans used to prepare tonight's meal, will speed us along." He grasped the arm of another man nearby. "You, Pete, can help us by sweeping the floors." He glanced back at Melanie. "We have plenty of food for everyone, and beds upstairs, but before we extend our hospitality, we insist that some work be done in exchange. There's no charity here, and no one has anything to be ashamed about."

Melanie walked through the dining room with Pete and the Brother, then entered the kitchen. When she saw the massive pots and pans that awaited her, she groaned inwardly.

After making sure they had everything needed to do their respective jobs, the Brother left them alone. Scrubbing the large vats was difficult work, but Melanie persisted.

"Where's Shy Eddy?" she asked her companion. "I haven't seen him tonight."

"Friend of yours?" Pete grumbled sourly.

She shook her head. "I just like him. He never says much, but he's always nice."

He pulled his worn baseball cap down so that the bill practically obscured his eyes, then started sweeping once more. "Eddy comes and goes, but it's hard to get to know him. He likes to keep to himself."

The next twenty minutes were interminable. She finished the large array of vats that had been set by the sink and walked out of the kitchen to join the others milling about in the hallway adjoining the dining area. She scanned faces looking for Shy Eddy, and saw him at the end of the line.

Cautiously she started toward him, not wanting to scare him off and give him reason to live up to his name.

She had almost reached his side when her gaze drifted over a tall man moving around restlessly. He'd talk to one person, then another, almost as if he were canvassing the room. He was dressed like the others, but he walked with an aggressiveness that didn't fit his appearance. As he turned around to speak to someone else, she gasped. With that dirty stocking cap on, she hadn't recognized him at first. How had Patrick learned about Shy Eddy, or more to the point, why hadn't he told her that he intended to track him down?

She stood to one side and watched him. Patrick was randomly striking up conversation. He didn't know about Shy Eddy, she concluded after a moment's observation.

She started toward Shy Eddy again. Patiently she worked her way across the room until she stood next to him in line. For several moments she said nothing. She was about to try to befriend him when Patrick approached. She slumped her shoulders and cast her face downward, staring at the floor. If he recognized her, he might inadvertently blow her cover.

"There was sure a heck of a lot of commotion a few days ago. I heard there was an explosion somewhere near here," Patrick commented.

She shrugged, but didn't look up. Shy Eddy didn't react.

"No use talking to Shy Eddy. He don't do much talking to strangers, mister," she mumbled.

"Well, maybe you can tell me about that day. I wasn't here, but I've been really curious."

She stifled the urge to curse. Turning away from him, she huddled against the wall, pulling her army jacket tightly against her. "Don't know nothin'. Go away."

Patrick edged closer, and in a conspiratorial voice added, "I think there's some money in it. I know a guy who's willing to pay for information, if it's good enough to help him catch the people who put the bomb in that car.''

"Go away,'' she nudged him on the shins with her shoe. She kept her face down so that he wouldn't get a close look at anything except her scarf and bits of the wig. Melanie started to move away from him, hoping that he'd take the hint and back off.

"Wait, you're losing your scarf,'' Patrick said, reaching for it.

Melanie felt him catch the hairs of her wig along with the scarf as he pulled at the loose end. The bobby pins that held the wig in place tugged at her scalp and came free. "Ow! Let go, you idiot.''

As he jerked his hand away, she felt the wig slip. Melanie reached up, but before she could catch it, the wig fell to the floor. It landed with a soft swoosh on Shy Eddy's foot.

"Melanie?'' Patrick narrowed his eyes, and looked closer. Her real hair was plastered to her skull like a hideous cap.

She ignored him completely and turned to Shy Eddy. "It's all right. Don't be afraid.''

Shy Eddy's hand went up to his own hair. He backed away from her, then turned and ran out the door of the refuge.

Melanie dashed after him, but by the time she reached the street corner, he'd disappeared.

Patrick joined her, and started to laugh. "Poor guy! He probably thought he was about to be scalped, too.''

"Nice going. You just loused up my investigation.''

"Me? I'd say it was the other way around.''

"Let's go back to the office, Patrick. It's time for us to have a long talk,'' she said flatly.

Chapter Three

Melanie paced in front of her desk. The anger within her was smoldering like the glowing coals of a furnace. "This just isn't going to work, Patrick. I was very close to a possible lead, then all of a sudden you loused up my chances. You have to leave this investigation to me. I worked with Andy for the past six years. If anyone can retrace his steps, I can." She tried to keep her voice smooth and appeal to his logic.

"Andrew O'Riley may have been your partner, but he was my father. That gives me all the right I need to take charge of this investigation. Had you told me what you were planning to do, this wouldn't have happened." His voice was too controlled to pass as natural. "I was willing to share the tip Mike gave me about the street people. However, I never agreed to be shut out so you could pursue it on your own."

She took a deep breath before answering. "You wait just one minute." There was no anger in her voice and that gave her words a peculiarly commanding effect. "If you recall, the lead Mike gave you was very broad. I was only interested in speaking to one man, Shy Eddy."

She could challenge him with an aplomb that he found surprising. He was used to cowering men three times her size with just a few crisply spoken words. "There's no sense in arguing about this anymore. The real question now is, can we find him again?"

"We'll have to wait." She stared at her reddened hands remembering all the pots and pans she'd scrubbed. "Right now—" The telephone rang, interrupting her. With a groan, she yanked the receiver off the cradle. "O'Riley and Cardenas," she snapped.

"Melanie, this is Mike Cooper."

"What's up?"

"Are you guys going to be there in another twenty minutes?"

"Sure, Mike," she answered, her voice softening. "Has the department come up with a lead?"

"I'll tell you all about it as soon as I get there," his voice echoed over the wire.

Melanie's eyes locked with Patrick's as she placed the receiver down. "Mike Cooper's coming over. It's a good thing we changed back into regular clothes again. His confidence in us would have gone down one hundred percent if he'd learned about this afternoon's fiasco." She faced him, hands on her hips. "You and I are going to have to come to some kind of agreement before he arrives. If you still refuse to drop out, then at least we have to set some ground rules."

"What do you suggest?"

"We share all the information we gather," she answered, "and coordinate our efforts better. I can't see you and I working as a team, but at least we can try not to trip over each other."

"I have no objections to that," he paused and deliberately added, "for now."

"You have a lousy attitude," she observed, forcing herself to remain civil. "Just remember, I'm in charge of this agency now."

Patrick's eyes darkened with fury. "Do you need to be reminded of how that came about?" The jab had been meant to shock her into awareness, and it had. "This is a family matter, Melanie. Don't try to get in my way."

"Get in *your* way?" She stared at the wall, struggling to maintain her composure. Her Spanish heritage had filled her with volatile emotions that existed precariously close to the surface. She refused to look back at him until she felt completely under control. To reveal one's thoughts to a stranger was a sign of weakness, and foolhardy.

Her grandparents had been largely responsible for that attitude. They'd lived in their native country at a time of political unrest. Their natural suspicions and distrust for anyone outside the family had been passed down in some form to her.

Her eyes focused on a photo of her and Andy standing beside the agency's new sign. Her heart constricted. Patrick was Andy's son. Out of respect for his father, Patrick deserved more from her than to be treated like a total stranger. She tugged at the sleeves of her silver gray blouse, then reached down to smooth her ankle-length teal skirt. "Patrick, I understand why you can't withdraw from this investigation. I also know I've been partly at fault for our inability to work together. Can you meet me halfway on this and admit that you haven't been quite fair, either?"

Patrick exhaled quietly, and his gaze softened. "I suppose you're right." He extended his hand. "Truce?"

She placed her hand in his, and shook it. "Until the next battle," she baited with a rueful smile.

He laughed. "Okay, I'll accept that."

For an instant, she saw Andy mirrored in the sparkling blue eyes that held hers. The seriousness of the situation they faced was brought crashing back to her. "Will you also accept the fact that I know more about what's been going on in this agency than you do? You should be clearing your plans with me."

"Don't push it," he warned, his features hardening once more.

Melanie shrugged. "It was worth a try." She was about to say more when a knock sounded at the door. She turned around. "Hi, Mike. Come in."

Mike looked from one to the other, a curious expression on his face. "And how are you two getting along?"

She couldn't tell if he'd heard part of the exchange between Patrick and her, or whether he'd simply sensed the tension between them. She smiled and hedged his question. "I'm glad you're here. You really got my curiosity up on the phone."

Mike recognized the tactic. "Once a cop, always a cop," he said and held up a thin folder. "We got the lab report back. I figured you two might like a copy. It contains some very interesting information."

Melanie diplomatically placed it on the center of her desktop, and laid it open between Patrick and her.

"What's this about Composition C plastique?" Melanie asked, eyebrows furrowed. "Is the lab saying that the explosive used dates back to World War II?"

"I thought that would get your attention," Mike replied, taking a seat. "According to what I was told, Composition C is known for its long-term stability, but of course, it's no longer available. Today, C-4 plastic explosive, an improvement on Composition C, is used."

"So the question is, how did someone get this stuff?" Patrick observed.

"And that's not all. The formulation of this particular explosive was one used exclusively by *German* combat engineers during the war years. Each country had their own 'recipe' or chemical formula for the equivalent of C-2, I'm told, and no two were exactly the same."

"Then if we can figure out how someone managed to obtain a quantity of obsolete foreign explosives, we'll have a link to the killer." Melanie gave Mike a questioning look. "So what has the department done in their search so far?"

"We can't track it through the usual sources. Since it's no longer manufactured anywhere, it's not something that's easily traced. Dynamite, for instance, has lot numbers, and other explosives have some identifying characteristic that helps us follow a trail to a particular source, or at least to the manufacturer. Of course, once we find the killer, if he still has the slightest trace of the explosive around, it'll be damning evidence. But I doubt if it'll help us much before that." He stood. "Maybe it will be more use to you."

"Thanks, Mike, I appreciate your sharing this information with us." She walked Mike to the door, then rejoined Patrick. "I realize you were only in the evidence room a short while, but I need to know everything you can remember about the bomb." She paused. "I hate to ask this of you. But some detail might give us a lead," she explained, "if we can tie it into the information we already have."

Their eyes met and an unspoken understanding passed between them. They both had their own private hells to contend with. Andy's death had left a gap in their lives that no one would ever be able to fill.

Melanie steadied herself, knowing instinctively that she'd be useless as an investigator if she didn't manage to put some distance between her feelings and her job.

Patrick told her about the coffee can filled with shrapnel and the pull wire that had triggered it. "I've come up with an idea that might help us," he continued slowly. "The police cordoned off the parking lot and searched it, but that blast would have sent fragments flying quite a distance. Something could still be out there that we *can* trace."

"You're right, Patrick. The explosion really rocked the building. There's no telling how far debris could have been scattered. We could take a look in the city park across the street."

"All right. Let's go rent a couple of metal detectors and take a look. I'll get my jacket." He went back into his father's office.

Patrick stepped over to the wooden coatrack in the corner, and lifted his tan sports jacket off the brass hook. Melanie silently noted a pistol in a shoulder holster with two extra ammo clips attached to it, hanging on the same hook. Patrick expertly slipped on the shoulder rig and adjusted the holster so it rested beneath his left arm. Without any wasted motions, he put on his jacket. Patrick noticed Melanie standing in the doorway.

"Part of my regular O.S.I. gear," he said. "Just in case." He checked the magazine on the nine-millimeter Beretta, then placed the self-loading pistol firmly back in its holster.

"Probably a good idea," she commented, again feeling the unfamiliar weight of her own .38 caliber revolver in her handbag. Carrying a hand gun reminded Melanie of her rookie days on the force, when she'd been taught to think of herself as a potential target. She knew she was a target again, and the knowledge was chilling.

They were both at the door when the telephone rang. "I'm closer," Patrick said. "I'll answer it."

"O'Riley and Cardenas," he said into the receiver. His face grew somber.

Melanie couldn't really hear the voice at the other end.

"There won't be a funeral, Mr. Kelly. My father detested any kind of ceremony. In fact, I've already made arrangements with the mortuary to have Dad's remains cremated and entombed in the crypt next to my mother's. He would have preferred each of us to say goodbye to him in our own private way." He listened for a few minutes more, then added. "I'll be at your office then, and I'll pass the message along to Melanie. Thank you for calling." He didn't look up right away.

"Patrick?" she called gently.

"When my father's murderer is found, then I'll say goodbye to him. But not before," he said, his voice husky with emotion. Taking a deep breath, he forced himself to meet her gaze. "There won't be a funeral."

She nodded. "You're right. I remember Andy talking about that." A ghost of a smile touched her lips. "He made me promise once that if I ever wanted to do something to honor his memory, I should go out, buy a bottle of Old Bushmills Irish Whiskey and toast to him. That's exactly what I intend to do—when this is over."

Patrick nodded. "That sounds just like him." He cleared his throat, then added, "By the way, the lawyer wants us both there tomorrow morning for a reading of Dad's will. Is that going to be a problem?"

"I'll be there," she said flatly.

An hour later they were outside, working the far perimeters of the parking lot and extending outward. Each of them was equipped with a metal detector. It was six-thirty in the evening, and with most of the cars gone, their search was easier. They moved cautiously, all too aware that while they were preoccupied, Andy's murderer might be watching them. During the next forty minutes they found enough change and bottle caps to fill a small trash can. The detectors were constantly giving off signals.

Patrick was checking the edges of the park that faced their building's parking area, while Melanie went over the flower bed. When the audio tone in her headset sounded once more, alerting her that something metallic lay imbedded in the soft earth, she bent to brush aside the loose earth with her fingertips and uncovered a small brass tube. The metal at one end had been peeled back like a banana, and was scorched almost black. Inside the casing was a steel spring.

Melanie studied it for a moment in the fading light. She was about to call Patrick, when she heard him approach.

"It's time to call it quits, Melanie. Scouring the area with metal detectors was a good idea. It's a shame it didn't pan out."

She showed him the tube. "Don't be too sure. It's not much, but I think this either came from the car or the bomb itself. Look at the way the surface is scorched and split."

"Let's take it to a mechanic and see if it belongs to the car. If it could have been part of the bomb we can have the residue on it checked, and see if we can learn anything new." Patrick placed their discovery in one of the small plastic bags he had brought along, and squeezed the self-sealing ends closed.

"I know just the garage we can take this to. The man who runs it has been my mechanic for years. He also knows cars. If this came from an automobile, he'll know."

"Fine." Patrick checked his watch. "But it's after seven, so I guess we'll have to wait until tomorrow."

Melanie shook her head. "Santiago is usually in the garage until dinnertime—Cuban dinnertime that is—around eight-thirty or so. Come on."

When Melanie pulled her compact up into the driveway of the two-stall auto repair shop in the Mission District, both garage doors were closed.

Melanie led Patrick down a narrow walkway toward the back of the old brick building where a door was open. Sounds of Spanish music filtered out from inside. "Santiago, are you here?" She entered the large garage area and looked around.

"We're closed," came the brisk reply.

"It's me, Melanie Cardenas. *¿Tienes un momentico?*"

A man crawled out from beneath one of the cars. "For you, *siempre.*"

Ignoring the grease on his clothes, she walked up and gave him a hug. "How have you been doing?"

"I'm fine, but Teresa and I heard about what happened to your partner. We were worried about you. If you need anything, you know that all you have to do is call."

As Patrick stepped up, Santiago's eyes fastened on him.

Melanie introduced them. "Santiago Gomez, this is Patrick O'Riley. Andy's son."

"I thought as much. The resemblance is there. I'm sorry to hear about your father." He wiped his hand on a rag, then held it out. Patrick took it in a firm handshake. That settled, Santiago's gaze returned to Melanie. "What can I do to help you? I know you've come here at this hour for a reason."

She handed him the bag with the brass tube. "Santiago, I need to know if this came from a car, and if so, what kind? Anything you can tell me will help."

He studied it for several minutes. "This isn't from a car. It wasn't from a truck or a bus, either." He studied the scorched surface. "But it's been stressed. Look how it's burned and indented on one side, and split at the end. I have no idea what it came from originally, but it was exposed to very intense heat and pressure."

She nodded slowly. "Okay. That's what I needed to know."

"Now I need something from you," Santiago replied.

"Name it." Her answer was quick and came without hesitation.

He nodded in approval. "These people who killed your partner, will they come for you?"

"It's possible, but I can take care of myself. Don't worry." Privately she wondered if all their precautions would be enough if the murderer wanted her dead. After all, Andy had been the finest police officer she'd ever known.

"Let me install a tamper alarm on your car," Santiago insisted. "Just to be safe. It'll take a half hour, maybe forty-five minutes to put in."

"I don't know, Santiago. I appreciate your concern, but chances are, if they try to get me, it'll be in a different way." The idea of using Andy's death as a lesson in how to better protect herself seemed too cold and calculated—profiting from what happened, abhorrent.

"Dad didn't have one, and it could have made a difference," Patrick coaxed softly, as if sensing her feelings. "It's foolish to take chances when you don't have to. Dad would have been the first to tell you that."

"All right," Melanie acquiesced, eager to put an end to their discussion.

Patrick nodded at Santiago in approval. "When could you do it for her?"

Santiago turned to Melanie, his jaw set firm. "First thing tomorrow, at your apartment. I know an all-night electronics shop with everything I need."

"Santiago, I'd like Patrick's sedan rigged up, too. Can you do that for me?" She glanced at Patrick and added, "We're in this together now, it looks like, so we'll be sharing the risk."

"It's a good idea, but my car's a rental," Patrick countered. "We can't do anything to it."

"No problem," Santiago joined in quickly. "I'll fix it so you can remove it yourself later. It won't hurt the car in any way. How about it?"

"Give me the bill when you're done, Mr. Gomez. It's a great idea," Patrick replied.

"Just for the parts. I'm doing this for Melanie. I'll need your address, Mr. O'Riley, and phone number. I'll call before I come over."

"Thanks, Santiago." Melanie gave the man another hug.

"Be careful, Melanie." He shook his head. "I wish you'd have picked another occupation for yourself. Being a detective is no place for a woman."

"It's the place for me," she answered gently, urging Patrick casually toward the door.

"Sorry about rushing you out back there," she apologized as they walked to the car. "But I just didn't have the heart to deal with that argument today." She merged with traffic and headed back to the office.

Patrick studied the small brass tube in the plastic bag. His fist closed tightly around it. He remained silent as she weaved through traffic.

"It's a strange feeling to hold part of the bomb that killed my dad," he commented at last.

"Why don't you put it inside my purse, Patrick?" she suggested, suppressing the shiver that ran up her spine. Melanie pulled the car into her parking space near the side entrance. "We can keep the component in the office until it can be analyzed. Agreed?"

He nodded, then followed her inside. "I'll send it over to the lab that evaluates evidence for the O.S.I. tomorrow. We'll see what they have to say."

"O.S.I.? No way, Patrick. This is a police matter. We should go through the proper channels. We want the police to cooperate with us, and the only way that's going to happen is if we do the same in return. We should take this over to Mike in the morning." She pulled a chair away from her desk, and positioned it beneath a light fixture. "However, since the police lab does take forever, I have no objection if you want to try to talk him into letting you send it to the O.S.I. lab. In fact—" she stood on the chair "—I'll even help you."

"What are you doing?" he asked. "The light bulb's just fine."

She glanced down and saw his gaze traveling upward from her legs, then straying provocatively over her breasts. The intimacy of the gesture made her body tingle. "I'm hiding the brass tube here in the light fixture. If they decide to search this place again, which I doubt, they'll never find it here."

She slipped the tube onto the dish that covered the bulbs and had started to step down from the chair when she realized that Patrick had moved directly into her path.

"Let me help you down," he said, his voice deep and resonant in the silence of the office. He grasped her by the waist, then lifted her down to the carpeted floor.

Although his strength had been evident in the effortless way he'd supported her body, his touch was surprisingly gentle. He didn't release her right away, and the warmth of his hands against her sides seared through the thin fabric of her blouse. Her mouth went completely dry, her heart hammering.

She hesitated briefly, then forced herself to move away. "It's time to call it a day, Patrick." She needed to put things into perspective. Her attraction to Patrick was real and very disconcerting. Yet with both their lives in the balance, she couldn't think of a less appropriate time to give in to those feelings. "If you want to go, I can take care of locking up."

"No, I'm in no rush."

She saw the shadow that crossed his face and realized that for him going home meant going to Andy's house. She placed a hand over his arm, and met his eyes, allowing him a glimpse into her own pain. "Andy's home is now your own. And that's exactly the way it should be. It's your place and your time. Do you understand what I'm trying to say?"

He shook his head. "I won't accept that while my dad's case remains unsolved." He watched her lock up the office, then walked her out to the car and checked it over carefully.

She slipped behind the driver's seat and switched on the ignition. "What time does the attorney expect us for the reading of the will?"

"Ten."

She took a deep breath then let it out slowly. "Try to get some rest. We have a long day ahead of us tomorrow."

As she drove away, she caught sight of Patrick in her rearview mirror. He stood tall, his broad shoulders thrown back. A solitary figure in the gray shadows of night. He looked invincible. His face, a pale mask in the moonlight's harsh glow, revealed another man as well. Etched there was sadness, and perhaps a trace of fear.

THEY MET at the police department the next day. Patrick, attired in a gray pin-striped suit, was waiting at the front entrance when she arrived. He looked as if he hadn't slept much the night before.

"You okay?" she asked as she reached the top step where he stood.

"I'm fine," he assured, following her inside the building.

"I hope you don't mind my calling you so early this morning. I wanted you to meet me here instead of at the office. I thought it would save you a trip," Melanie ventured. "I tried to get hold of you until late last night, but I never managed to reach you."

"I went back to the office for a while," Patrick answered. "I couldn't sleep, so I decided to get to work on that list of possible suspects. I'll tell you about that later. Right now we better concentrate on our meeting with Mike."

Melanie led the way. Mike greeted them at the door to his office. "Now what's this new information you wanted to share with me?"

"Mike, are you sure you want to talk here? I understand Captain Mathers doesn't exactly want Patrick, nor I imagine me, looking into this."

"You know the captain, Melanie. He doesn't like private investigators, and Andy's always been a touchy subject with him."

"So, do we go someplace else?"

"Captain Mathers is out of town for the day." Mike gave her a smile. "If only we could get him to take more out-of-town trips . . ." he added wistfully.

Chuckling, she extracted the plastic bag containing the brass tube from her purse. "We did a search of the area near the parking lot with metal detectors yesterday. We found this just beneath the ground in the flower bed across the street. We've already checked, and it's not a car part."

Mike studied the metal tube, and then glanced back at her. "It looks like it might have been part of the bomb."

"That's what we thought, too," Patrick said. "How long do you think it'll take the police lab to run some tests on it?"

"Ten days, at least." He picked up a memo from his desk and showed it to Patrick. "That came in yesterday. There's a backlog at the lab so unless it's categorized as a class A priority, which is nothing less than an emergency situation, we've been warned to give everything a few extra days. We may even have to send it to L.A. or San Diego."

"Mike, if you let me send it in to the O.S.I. lab," Patrick offered, "I can have results back here in a week at the very latest. Plus, with some of the equipment the Air Force has at its disposal, I can almost guarantee you'll see a much more detailed report than what the city lab will be able to provide."

"I wouldn't have any objections," Mike replied, "but the captain's out of town. If I give you the go-ahead, he's likely to bust me back down to patrolman."

"Maybe not," Melanie interjected quickly. "If I know Mathers, he'll say that the police have already gathered enough evidence from the site. They know about the bomb and the explosive used, and that's all they could have hoped for. At best, he's going to view this as a rehash of what they've already learned—at worst, as a drain on the lab's valuable time. Once he finds out it came from us, I'll be surprised if he doesn't cancel the lab request on it completely."

Mike grinned slowly. "You've got a point there."

She smiled back. "I doubt sincerely that he'll mind if you send it to the O.S.I. lab for analysis. Or if he does, he'd never tell you so. To do that, he'd have to also admit that the evidence was important. Besides, you can always point out that you were trying to save the police lab the extra work. That interdepartmental memo you received made it clear they were swamped."

"Very clever," Mike chuckled softly. "Patrick, can you guarantee that the department will get a full report?"

"I sure can. And if the information turns out to be valuable, the department will be able to act on it that much sooner. I'll have a copy sent directly to you, and another to our office."

"For the sake of diplomacy, Mike," Melanie added, "why don't you have Patrick send it in on behalf of the captain? If it pans out, Mathers'll get the credit. If not, then you can point out how much time he saved the police lab, and he'll still come out ahead."

"Good idea. Nothing like covering your back, I always say."

Patrick glanced at his watch. "I'll send it to the lab by express today."

Minutes later, Patrick stepped outside the building and reached for his sunglasses. "It was really handy to have you along with me today," he commented. "Mike was about to turn me down, but thanks to your powers of persuasion, we'll be able to send this to the O.S.I. lab like we wanted."

"*Have* me along?" her voice rose slightly. "I think you're forgetting I was the one who found that tube," she lowered her voice, her tone taut. "I'm not here with your permission. I'm here to do a job."

"Oh, come on! Don't be so touchy. If the cops hadn't been cooperative—which they were only because Mathers wasn't there—you'd have needed the O.S.I. And face it, you couldn't get them without me."

"Maybe you'd like to see how far *you'd* actually get on this investigation without my contacts or help," she replied in a frosty tone, jamming her hands into her suit jacket pockets.

"It wouldn't take long to find my way around the office, Melanie," he said calmly. "I know my father's methods. I'll find my father's killer with or without your help."

"No one is going to stop me from trying to find my partner's murderer, Patrick. And I think that in future we should pursue this investigation from angles that will require only minimal cooperation between us."

"Fine with me. We can work that out at the office later." He started toward his car then stopped. He scribbled an address on the back of a card, then handed it to her. "Dad's will is going to be read in another forty minutes. That's Mr. Kelly's address. I'll see you there."

Melanie stopped by the doughnut shop and treated herself to the first cup of coffee she'd had all morning, and two doughnuts. Sitting at a corner table, she watched the room, ever vigilant for trouble. If only Patrick would go back to the military. Unfortunately he had inherited Andy's stubbornness.

She stared at her coffee for several long moments. Yet there was no way she could fault him for wanting to stay. Although he was driving her crazy with his constant interference, she had to admire him for having the courage to see the matter through. A man who exhibited that type of family loyalty was someone who deserved her respect.

Then again, perhaps that was the whole problem. On a personal level, there was much to like about Patrick. She found him compelling and undeniably appealing. However, that also made him a distraction, and that was the last thing she needed. This case could prove to be her last. Danger dogged her footsteps like a second shadow. And professionally, Patrick was an incredible hindrance. She owed Andy. She had to find his killer, despite the obstacle his well-meaning son posed.

By the time she arrived at John Kelly's office, Patrick was already there. She'd tried to brace herself for the task that lay ahead. It was heartbreaking to witness the cool, dispassionate distribution of all the possessions Andy had loved and valued throughout his life.

The lawyer's voice seemed to drone on endlessly. Finally he glanced up. ''There's a lot of legal jargon here, so let me summarize it for you.'' He met Melanie's eyes. ''A few of Andy's personal possessions, like the chess set you admired so much, and Andy's collection of Irish Folklore books, are yours, Melanie.'' He shifted his gaze to Patrick. ''The rest of his belongings are left to you.'' He cleared his throat. ''That includes the agency. You now own fifty percent of O'Riley and Cardenas Investigations, Patrick, but in order to retain this equal partnership, you must resign your commission in the Air Force within sixty days. Otherwise your half will revert to Melanie.''

Melanie gripped the sides of her chair with both hands. The terms of the will had come as a total shock. She'd always assumed that when Andy was no longer an active partner, she'd get the opportunity to buy out his share of the agency. She'd believed that to be Andy's intention, too. The knowledge that Andy had obviously wanted Patrick and her to become partners stunned her. Andy's last wish had been for Patrick and her to work together. She gave Patrick a bewildered look.

His eyes met hers. ''It looks as though you didn't know about this, either. Well, partner, this time Dad took us both by complete surprise.''

Chapter Four

Hours later, Patrick stood inside his father's office. His gaze traveled slowly around the room. The desk, the chair, the small leather sofa, the paintings on the wall, the oak bookcase lined with books on criminology, all held his father's stamp. Andrew Sean O'Riley was gone, but the room was still his. "He wanted us to be partners, like you and he had been. Those were his last wishes," Patrick said softly.

Melanie leaned against the wall, and stared pensively at an indeterminate spot across the room. This office had been Andy's domain, the one outside, hers. Each had intruded on the other's with the easy grace of visiting monarchs from allied kingdoms. She fought the spidery touch of sorrow that drained her spirit. "Are you going to stay at the agency for good?"

"I don't know. I'll have to think about it." He rubbed the back of his neck with one hand. "In the meantime, we both have some decisions to make. Dad expected us to work together. I think we should try to honor that, despite our personal feelings."

On one hand, her duty to Andy seemed clear. She had to find his murderer, to see justice done. Yet, now, to work alone toward that goal was to ignore Andy's last wishes. She exhaled slowly. "Agreed."

Patrick walked around the desk. He reached for a file he'd placed inside the metal tray on the corner of the desk, and gestured toward the sofa. "Have a seat, and I'll tell you what I worked on last night."

He brought out several sheets of paper. "From the evidence we've uncovered so far, I believe the person who placed the bomb in Dad's car was either a World War II veteran, a collector of military weapons or both. That makes sense when you figure that the type of explosive that was used must have been obtained between 1943 and 1945, or shortly thereafter. With that in mind, I began making a list of suspects. I compiled the names of all the people Dad was making background checks on. Then I mailed the list to a contact of mine in Alcohol, Tobacco and Firearms. They regulate permits for gun dealers and collectors so they have an extensive file on related criminal activities. My contact will check to see if any of those people or their relatives turn up in his files."

"Good thought." She paused for a moment. It was time to confide in him completely, as Andy had wanted. "I didn't say anything before, but I have a special hiding place where I store the agency's original computer disks. The two sets I keep out in the office are only copies. This was my way of making sure we'd be protected in case of a break-in." She gestured for him to follow her into the next room. Crouching down, she removed what appeared to be a heating vent at the bottom of the wall. Inside were several boxes filled with diskettes. "What I'd like to do now is check your list against the data I've kept in here. Let's see how it matches up."

"Excellent hiding place," he observed with admiration. "A phony vent. No one would ever think of looking there."

She smiled, noting his tone. "Nothing like the obvious to throw people off the track," she explained. "I've also maintained a computerized data file that serves as an instant reference to everyone we're currently working on. It gives me names, addresses and telephone numbers, as well as the position they're being considered for." She placed the original disk inside the computer and brought it up on screen. As she read each name that had been assigned to Andy, Patrick checked it against his own list.

"I don't have a record for two of the people you mentioned," Patrick said after she finished. "Larry Clancy and Steve Waite. I checked through all of Dad's files, so if I didn't include them, it's because they weren't there."

"Let's recheck." Melanie walked over to Andy's file cabinet and with Patrick went through each individual folder. "You're right. They're not here. It looks like some of our files have been stolen. We'll have to check all our records and see if any of the inactive folders are missing also. That can probably be a low priority. Right now, let's start with the current cases whose records are missing. Do you agree?"

He nodded. "At the same time, we should take a closer look at the other four people Dad was in the process of investigating." He stood braced, feet apart and hands in his pockets, regarding her for a moment. "That's a total of six. We can cover more ground if we split the load, but it's okay with me if you want to stick together."

"Andy wanted us to be partners—" she smiled, a twinge of sadness etching her face "—not Siamese twins."

He chuckled softly. "Okay. How about if you take the top three names and I'll take the rest?"

"Fine."

He glanced inside his father's old office. "I've got to make more room for myself in there," he muttered almost to himself. "I'll telephone my three and make the appointments from Dad's desk." He started toward his father's office, then stopped. "By the way. I've had a cellular telephone placed in my car. I'm using Dad's old exchange, so keep in touch. If you run into any trouble, don't try to handle it alone. Remember that, at the moment, you're more of a target. They may not even know about me yet, or may think I'm only here for a few days."

"Will do." Melanie scheduled her stops one after the other, allowing for travel time. Since most of their clients were currently unemployed, and awaiting the results of their background investigations, getting cooperation was an easy matter.

Ready to leave, she entered Andy's former office and saw Patrick still busy on the telephone. Melanie scribbled a quick note telling him when she'd be back, then with a casual wave, left the office.

Her first appointment went by quickly. The man was a stroke victim who had only recovered partial use of his arms. It was highly unlikely he'd be able to put together the intricate mechanism a bomb would require. He'd also recently accepted a job as a bookkeeper with another corporation, making any background check they would do completely unnecessary.

Melanie proceeded to the second person on her list. No one had answered the phone when she'd called earlier, so she didn't really have an appointment. But the man's residence was near her first contact, so she was hoping that he'd be home by the time she drove by.

Conrad Reed was a civil engineer, and as such, would probably have some knowledge of explosives. Also, people in his profession worked around construction sites all the time. Reed would have easy access to the explosives routinely used there, which could conceivably include unused stock as old as those they were looking for.

She parked in front of a large, two-story frame house. A swing had been hung from the large oak tree in the front yard, and swayed gently back and forth in the breeze. A late model station wagon was in the driveway.

She was in luck. A thin, rather tall man about her age answered the door. He wore wire-rimmed glasses and had the pale, untoned physique of a man used to working indoors with ideas, rather than outside with his body. A little girl with straw blond hair, about three years old, clung to his hand. Melanie introduced herself, then followed him into the living room, where Reed offered her a chair.

"How can I help you, Ms. Cardenas?" He turned and picked up his daughter, sitting her beside him on the sofa.

"My partner was killed, Mr. Reed, as you may have read in the papers, and I'm trying to complete some of the background surveys he was working on. I know that Mr. O'Riley questioned you before, so all I really need to do is verify some of the information in your file. Then we'll consider the case closed."

"Fine," he replied, crossing his arms in front of his chest.

Melanie smiled when his daughter mimicked her father's gesture. "Let's see, you applied for an engineering job with the Bendrix Corporation, and were formerly employed at Western Tech for the past eight years. Is that correct?"

"Yes, but that's old news." He started to say more, but Melanie interrupted him.

"Please bear with me, sir. I assure you we'll be finished shortly. My partner already gathered most of the personal information we need on you, and we have your signed release granting the agency permission to make inquiries about your family background. Now all we have to do is verify your father's employment history, and we'll be through. Every time someone applies for a position with a defense contractor, we have to check the family's history at least one generation back. Your father's last employer?"

"My dad retired a few years ago, but he had been a professor at Golden Gate University. Ms. Cardenas," he said irately, "this hardly seems applicable now." He shifted again on the sofa crossing his legs.

She glanced up. What in the world was he being so nervous about? "I'll be through in a moment, sir. A little bit of your time now will help us complete our background check. You'll be considered for the job with Bendrix that much sooner."

"I've withdrawn my application," he stated flatly.

Melanie blinked. "I beg your pardon?"

"I'm no longer an applicant for that job. I've withdrawn—for personal reasons."

"Are you currently employed then?"

He was silent for a few seconds, then in a voice that held a raw edge, he continued. "No," he answered. "You see, my father recently died, Ms. Cardenas, in an accident. We were very close, and it's been a difficult time." Reed put his arm around his daughter, and pulled her close to his side. "For the past two weeks I've been home taking care of Cindy while my wife's at work. But my reputation as a civil engineer is solid. There'll be plenty of time for me to find another job, and I'm financially secure right now. At the moment, I have personal matters to take care of."

"I'm sorry," she said with genuine sympathy. "I had no idea." She noticed a photograph of Reed, his wife and an older man placed prominently on the fireplace mantel. Conrad Reed favored the man in the photo, obviously his late father.

"I did phone and inform your former partner, Mr. O'Riley. Under the circumstances, though, I understand how the information never reached you. Don't give it another thought."

Feeling guilty about intruding on his grief, she excused herself and returned quickly to her car. The part of the report Andy had finished on Reed showed him to be clean, not even a traffic violation. With a record like his, Conrad Reed would have had no motive to kill Andy. His father's death was easy to verify, and not the type of thing anyone would lie about. She would make the necessary call later that day to check it out and then close the file.

The drive through traffic to the southern end of the city seemed interminable. She couldn't help but wonder how Patrick was faring. Why had Andy placed her in such a difficult position? Patrick understood so little about her relationship with his father! No wonder he felt it was his right, as Andy's son, to be solely in charge of the investigation. Patrick thought that Andy and she were only casual friends and working partners. Yet it had been so much more. She'd loved Andy as if he'd been her own father. He'd filled the void her own dad's death had left in her life eight years ago. And to Andy, she'd been the daughter he'd never had. Her claim to investigate his murder was as valid, if not greater, than Patrick's.

The last person on her list, Larry Clancy, lived in a shabby section of south San Francisco. Children played in the streets, while a street gang clustered around the outside of a small bar, seated on top of someone's parked car. Melanie drove around the corner. Iron railings contrasted against the worn brick exteriors of several apartment buildings.

She stepped inside the small foyer of Clancy's building and checked the mailboxes, verifying his apartment number. As she climbed the stairs, she was pleasantly surprised to see that the inside of the building was meticulously clean. It wasn't as run-down as the outside had appeared to be.

Melanie knocked on the door and was met by a tall man wearing tan slacks and a white T-shirt. His bulging muscles strained against his clothes and his hair was cropped short, military style.

"I have an appointment to see Mr. Lawrence Clancy."

"Are you the lady who called this morning?" he countered briskly.

Melanie nodded. "I'm Melanie Cardenas. Are you Mr. Clancy?" If he was, he was in excellent physical shape for a man their data listed as in his early sixties.

"Yeah." He stood aside and waited for her to enter.

Her instincts were working overtime. There was something hostile about the man's attitude. Her skin prickled as it usually did when her sixth sense warned of danger. She faced him, keeping the purse, which concealed her weapon, securely by her side. Quickly she surveyed his apartment. Everything was in place; Clancy was obviously an orderly man. He wasn't married, according to what Andy had already written. Military books and survivalist magazines filled several bookshelves, and a table lamp made from an artillery shell stood next to a large reclining chair. A weight bench with a massive set of barbells occupied the far corner.

"Are you here to apologize? If so, don't bother, it's too late now. Your partner did a hell of a number on me."

"Apologize?" She turned as he did. Melanie regretted at once that he now stood between her and the door.

"Blackstone Laboratories called and said that my application was no longer being considered. Since that other guy from your agency was here just a few days before, asking questions, I think it's safe to say the two were connected. Don't you agree?"

"I doubt it," she answered smoothly. "Your background check was not completed." However, Andy had been known to give clients preliminary oral reports. She decided not to mention that particular fact. Melanie moved casually around him, angling toward the exit. As she did, she caught a glimpse of the next room. Rifles, mostly military issue, hung in racks on the wall. A glass case with two pistols she recognized as Lugers, old German issue weapons, stood in the hall.

"I'm not buying any excuses, lady. You guys had something to do with me not getting that job, I feel it. Your agency did a hatchet job on me. A man with my war record shouldn't have to put up with people questioning his integrity. I fought for my country during World War II, and I'm damned proud of it." He gestured toward the hallway. "I brought back a few mementos with me, I saw you looking. Do you want a closer look?"

"No, thank you." She made her way discreetly toward the front door. "Maybe some other time. I've got another appointment."

"If you're not here to apologize, then why are you here?" He blocked her way, and smiled slowly.

Melanie swallowed. Her throat was infernally dry. The feeling of danger was overwhelming. She forced herself to meet his gaze. "My partner was murdered, Mr. Clancy," she explained in a steady voice. "I'm trying to close up all the cases he was working on."

"Murdered?" He shrugged. "How careless of him," Clancy uttered sarcastically. "Then again, I don't suppose you make too many friends in a business where you can destroy a career before it even gets started."

His inhuman attitude sent a chill through her. She forced her body to remain very still, sensing he'd feed on any outward signs of fear.

"I certainly hope you don't think *I* had anything to do with his death," he baited.

Gathering her courage, Melanie faced him boldly. "Well, since you brought it up, exactly where were you last Friday between noon and 6:00 p.m.?"

He pretended to mull the question over in his head for about twenty seconds. "Watching television here in my apartment," he said, then added with mock sadness, "all alone. You see, I don't have a job now." He took a step toward her, then laughed when she automatically moved to one side. "Am I making you nervous?"

"Not at all," she lied, determined not to give him the satisfaction.

"That's good," he added, mocking her tone. "Maybe you should stay and question me more thoroughly. I'll try to cooperate," he told her smoothly. "Of course, it depends on how nice you are to me. I'm not so agreeable when I'm upset."

That was it. He was not the type of suspect anyone should question solo. She tried to move around him, and walk to the door. He blocked her way again, crossing his arms in front of his chest.

"Step aside, mister," she ordered in a hard, uncompromising tone. "I'm not pleasant to be around, either, when I'm angry. I make a lousy victim, so don't push me." She transfixed him with an unblinking stare. Her fingers imperceptibly began to push open the folds of her shoulder purse.

Clancy laughed and then with a bow, gestured toward the door. "Well, if the lady's changed her mind about wanting my company..." he deliberately let the sentence hang. "But I think I'll look you up from time to time, Melanie. If you were interested enough once to come and see me, then there's no telling what the future could hold for us. I'll just have to make sure I make myself available to you." His laughter was soft and menacing.

Melanie walked past him, then quickly strode down the hall, ever alert for movement behind her. Out on the sidewalk moments later, she took a deep breath and tried to quiet her frazzled nerves. There was a quality of evil about Larry Clancy.

She returned to her car, and leaned back against the seat, adrenaline still surging through her. She felt charged and eager for action. Nonetheless she realized the need for caution.

Switching on the ignition, she drove out of sight of Clancy's apartment, then parked on what seemed like a safe side street. She stared in her rearview mirror as she considered what to do next. There was no real evidence against Clancy yet, but he had suddenly zoomed to the top of her list of suspects. The next step would be talking to his neighbors and some of his former employers. Remembering his gun collection and the mention of a military record, her thoughts switched to Patrick, and what he'd said. That's when her car phone began to ring.

"Melanie? This is Patrick. I wanted to check in with you and see how you were doing." His voice was distant but clear.

"Patrick, I think maybe I've found our man. I don't have any solid evidence against him, but let me tell you what I've learned so far." She told him about her visit. "I'm going to talk to his neighbors now, and see what other information I can get."

"Where are you?"

Melanie gave him Clancy's address, then added, "I decided to drive down two blocks north and park at the corner. I didn't want to leave my car where he could see it while I was talking to some of the others in his building. I'm sure he doesn't know I'm still here. He didn't follow me, I've been watching in my rearview mirror."

"Good thinking. Now stay put, I'm on my way to meet you right now. Don't try to go anywhere near his building alone. You'll need a backup on this one, Melanie. His file was one of those missing. If he thinks Dad found out something that was worth killing him for, he might start thinking that you're also a threat and know too much. Besides, from what you said, it looks like he's blaming the agency for his current unemployment. That doesn't put you in a good position. You were lucky to get out of his apartment when you did. Don't push your luck."

"What about your leads, particularly Steve Waite, the other man whose file was taken?"

"He's already employed, and in fact was at work the day Dad was killed. The other two turned out to be dead ends also. The way I figure it, Steve Waite's file must have been taken to purposely mislead us, or by mistake."

"Patrick, you don't have to come over here. I can take care of this. What you should do is check with your sources and get Clancy's military record. See what branch he served in, and anything else that might be useful."

"I'm going to do both. Now stay put. I'll be there within half an hour."

Melanie tapped her fingers against the wheel. He was starting to encroach on her part of the investigation again. Patrick simply wasn't the type of person who could work with someone else without trying to horn in on absolutely everything. Although the military encouraged teamwork, Patrick's field and rank guaranteed him quite a bit of autonomy.

She left the car, and locked the door. Of course, there really wasn't any reason for her to have to put up with this. She wasn't in the military.

By the time Patrick arrived, Melanie had already completed two interviews with apartment residents in Larry Clancy's building. She was back in the lobby writing down the names of more prospects, when Patrick came rushing toward her. "What the hell are you doing here? You were supposed to wait for me in the car."

"I didn't want to waste time. I went ahead and interviewed a few of the tenants, instead of just sitting outside in the heat. Now calm down. From what I've learned already, people are afraid of Larry Clancy. He drinks. He's hassled almost everyone here at least once. One woman thinks that the only reason he hasn't been evicted is because the landlord is afraid of him.''

"All right. Let's get out of here for now," he said, quickly leading her back out of the building. "A friend of mine from the Naval Air Station is going to check Clancy's military record for us. We should have something in a few hours. All he has to do is wait for a chance to log on to one of the computer terminals.''

She fell into step beside him. "Patrick, I admit that if I was going to question Clancy again, I'd like to have you there. However interviewing a few of his neighbors is something I can do on my own. The way you rushed right over when my lead panned out makes me wonder. What's more important to you, catching the murderer, or making sure that *you're* the one who brings him in?''

Patrick stopped and faced her. "What do you think?'' he challenged.

"I'm asking you.''

He held her eyes for a few moments then looked away. "Melanie, even if you don't agree with this, catching the murderer and bringing him to justice is my responsibility. When this goes down, I want to be there.''

"Andy may not have been my father, but I couldn't have loved him more if he had been, Patrick. I think you should know that,'' she said firmly.

"Dad thought a great deal of you, Melanie. The terms of the will make that obvious.'' He ran a hand through his hair, then shook his head. "Let's not get into this. We're not going to convince each other. Let's just do the best we can together, and take things moment by moment.'' He fished his keys out of his pocket. "I'll meet you back at the office.''

"I'm going to stop at the department and talk to Mike. I want to check Andy's arrest records for a few years prior to his leaving. In particular, I want to know if he made any long-term enemies, and if anyone he sent to jail's been released lately.''

"You know where I'll be," he said briskly, then turned toward his own car.

PATRICK WALKED SLOWLY down the corridor leading to the agency's office. So much was happening, and his attraction to Melanie was only making things more complicated. He couldn't really define what was drawing him to her. Was it lust, or perhaps something more complicated? Maybe it was the feeling they'd shared for his father, and their need to bring his killer to justice.

Yet no matter how he rationalized it, instinct told him he was only seeing part of the picture. Melanie was a very special woman. He liked her fighting spirit. She took a back seat to no one, and was not afraid to stand on her own. Although it certainly made her harder to deal with, those were qualities he admired. Undeniably there was also a powerful dose of sensuality in every move she made. Under ordinary circumstances, Melanie was the kind of woman he'd have fought to keep by his side. But these weren't ordinary circumstances.

The telephone was already ringing when he stepped inside the office. Switching off the answering machine, he picked up the receiver. "Patrick O'Riley."

"Hey, Sherlock, how's it going?"

Navy Captain Michael Murphy had been his friend since high school. "How ya doing, Mick. Did you get what I needed?"

"Sure, I did. In fact, I thought I'd come across the bay to hand deliver it to you. It's a doozie, if I say so myself."

Patrick sat on the corner of the desk, his muscles tense with anticipation. "How long before you can get here?"

"About thirty minutes if the traffic's going my way."

"Then come over. I'll wait for you."

When Michael Murphy walked into the office a while later, the tall redheaded man in Navy khakis grinned as he saw Patrick's conservative gray suit and maroon tie. "Hoo boy! Look at this! Civilian life is subverting you already!"

"You're just jealous, you old bag of wind. You're married to that uniform and grouchy because you're finding out it's a lousy companion on a cold night."

Murphy grinned. "So what's going on, that all of a sudden the Air Force's most confirmed bachelor should start brooding about cold, lonely nights?" he teased.

"I'm not brooding and I never claimed to be a confirmed bachelor. That was your department."

"Disclaimers now." He rubbed his chin. "If this is what a stint of civilian life does to a perfectly normal career officer, remind me to avoid it."

Patrick laughed. Mick gloried in his words. "Mick, I never said I wanted to stay single for the rest of my life. I'll get married someday if I find a woman I'd like to spend the rest of my life with." He grinned slowly. "The problem is that first I have to find a woman who's as good a catch as I am. That takes some looking."

Mick laughed loudly. "Same old Pat."

"Now where's my report, you idiot," he growled.

He opened his briefcase and handed Patrick several printed pages bound with a paper clip. "Pat, this has been rough for you, I know," Mick said seriously. "If there's anything I can do, just ask." Mick stood and jammed his hands into his pockets. "I'll tell you something, though. I wanted to hand deliver that report. I think once you have a chance to look through it, you'll see why."

As they stepped into the outer office, Melanie walked in. She smiled politely at Mick, then glanced at Patrick. "Hello."

Patrick introduced them, then focused his attention on Mick. He could see the mischievous gleam in Mick's eyes and was afraid of what he might blurt out.

Mick's eyes locked with Patrick's. "You just try to stay warm, Pat. I'll have all the men out looking for your uniform." Murphy opened the door, stepping halfway out, then turned and grinned widely.

Patrick slowly shook his head. "Goodbye, Mick." As Murphy left, Patrick started toward the office again.

"What was he talking about?" Melanie ventured.

He cleared his throat. "Mick? Don't listen to anything that man says. Mick gives new meaning to the expression blarney."

"Was he just visiting?"

"No. He brought me a copy of Larry Clancy's service record. Why don't you join me on the sofa and we'll both take a look at it. It's in Dad's..." he stopped, then continued, "it's in my office." It was time to accept the present, and stop looking to what had been. His father would have approved.

Melanie nodded, understanding. "How complete is it?"

"It's several pages long. Let's take a look." Patrick glanced at the first sheet, then handed it to her. He repeated the process until they'd gone through the entire seven-page report. "So, Clancy received demolition training. That means he's got the expertise to make a bomb."

"It fits with the World War II connection," Melanie observed.

"Did you read the last page yet? After all those charges of black marketeering were finally dropped, he was dishonorably discharged for striking an officer."

Melanie pursed her lips thoughtfully. "He blames Andy for the fact that he wasn't hired, so that gives him a motive. And being unemployed gives him the opportunity," Melanie added.

"What we don't have is any direct evidence linking him to the crime."

"But now that we know where to look, it shouldn't be too difficult to find it. Let's call Mike Cooper. I think we should bring him in on this."

Patrick nodded. "We might be coming to the end of the line," he said in a quiet voice.

Melanie walked back to her desk, needing to confirm the number of Inspector Cooper's private line. Pulling the Rolodex card out, she picked up the receiver. She'd just started to dial when she heard footsteps behind her.

Before she could turn, someone reached around her, pinning her arms to her sides. She was jerked backward hard, a vicelike grip immobilizing her completely. Melanie felt the tip of a knife pressing against her back, almost cutting into her skin.

"Melanie, what's that noise..." Patrick came into the room.

Her captor spun around to face Patrick, towing her along roughly. "Don't move, O'Riley, or I'll carve up your pretty little lady friend."

Chapter Five

"Put your gun on the floor and slide it away from you," Clancy ordered.

Patrick took his pistol out of the holster and slid it to the side of the room opposite Clancy.

"You two just couldn't leave it alone, could you?" Larry murmured. "O'Riley, go lock the door, and if you try anything, it'll be the lady who pays for it."

"Take it easy," Patrick answered, moving slowly around Clancy and toward the door. "Just tell us what you want."

Clancy's laughter was low. "I'm here to teach you a little lesson, O'Riley. You can't go around messing up people's lives and expect to get away with it."

Patrick reached over and turned the door latch. "I haven't done anything to you, Clancy. Neither did my father. He was hired to do a background check, that's all. You knew when you applied for that job that your past would be investigated. What's the problem?"

"You guys go around digging up every piece of dirt in a guy's life, and you can't figure out why some people would get sore?" He chuckled softly. "You're not too bright, are you?"

Melanie forced her body to relax. Clancy had shifted his hold on her slightly and now held the knife point at her side. If she was careful, she'd be able to use that to her advantage.

"If you believe my father's report wasn't fair, why don't you tell us your side of it? We can go to the company who hired us to do the check on you, and correct any errors we might have made."

"It's too late for that." Clancy's eyes stayed on him. As Patrick started to put his hands into his pockets, Clancy tightened his hold on Melanie. "Keep your hands where I can see them?"

"Then why are you here?" Patrick dropped his hands to his sides.

Melanie felt Clancy relax once more, his hold easing ever so slightly. She willed herself to remain patient and bide her time.

"You're starting to nose around in my business again. I've had enough trouble with you people. I'm warning you now—stay out of my life!" He rubbed his cheek against Melanie's, and she could smell the liquor on his breath. "This pretty little thing said that the guy who came to see me before went and got himself killed. I assume that was your old man." He grinned slowly. "Maybe you should learn from his mistakes—that is unless you want to end up the same way."

Patrick's eyes hardened. "Are you telling me that you're responsible for my father's death?"

Clancy stood rigid, his smile taunting, lethal. "Don't look at me to make your job easier. You have nothing on me, do you? You can't prove a thing." He stared hard at Patrick. "But you still don't get it, do you? Trust me, O'Riley," he mocked. "You don't want to give me a reason to hate you." He waved the knife at Patrick to emphasize his point. "There's no telling what can happen then, is there?"

Melanie seized the chance. Stepping down hard on his instep, she bent her arm at the elbow, and brought the back of her fist up, slamming it against his face. Taken by surprise, Clancy staggered back, the knife dropping out of his hand.

Melanie spun free, and the next instant the heel of Patrick's foot smashed against Clancy's midsection, sending him crashing against the wall.

Melanie dived for her purse and pulled out her gun. As she whirled around, Clancy, tall and powerfully built, scrambled to his feet. In a rage, he lunged at Patrick.

Patrick sidestepped, catching Clancy with a hard punch that sent him slamming against the wall. Clancy quickly rolled to one side. Swinging a foot around, he caught Patrick behind his knees. Patrick fell to the floor, but was up again instantly. As Clancy threw a right jab at his chin, Patrick spun around, evading the blow and chopped his hand across Clancy's kidneys. Clancy doubled over with a gasp, landing face down on the carpet.

"That's enough!" Melanie ordered sharply, pointing the gun directly at Clancy. "Stay exactly where you are. Patrick, before we call the police, there's a pair of handcuffs in my desk drawer. Cuff him."

Patrick approached Clancy slowly. "There's nothing I'd like more than to take you apart with my bare hands, so if you feel like trying something, go right ahead. You can take your best shot," he said in an ominously calm voice. "Then, I'll take mine."

"Easy, Patrick," Melanie warned.

Clancy remained passive as Patrick placed the handcuffs on him.

"Too bad," Patrick commented, then roughly forced Clancy into a chair. Retrieving his gun from the corner of the room, he pointed it at Clancy. "I'll cover him, Melanie. Phone the police."

Melanie finished the call, then cast a glance at Patrick and Clancy. Both men were silent, but the animosity between them made the room vibrate with tension. In preparation for the arrival of the police, she unlocked the door, opened it and came face-to-face with half a dozen of the other tenants.

"We thought we heard a fight, but then everything went quiet," one of the women, a real estate agent, said. Her eyes were wide and her voice shaky. "We called the police, just in case, though."

"I appreciate your concern . . ." Melanie started.

The man in front interrupted her. "Listen, we're not just worried about you. We want to keep an eye on your offices for our sakes, too. If I had my way, you'd be out of the building. It's too dangerous to have an agency of your sort around here."

Melanie started to reply angrily, but then took a deep breath. She really couldn't blame them. They were scared. Fear was an emotion she knew well, and respected. "You have no more reason to worry. Everything's under control now. The police will be here shortly," she assured them, "and as soon as this matter is cleared up, we can all go back to the way things used to be. Peaceful." She smiled gently. "Believe me, no one wants that more than I do."

There were a few grumbles but for the most part, her reply satisfied the crowd. As they began to move away, she saw two uniformed police officers approaching. Just behind them were Mike Cooper and Captain Mathers.

Mike came forward in a hurry, making sure he reached Melanie first. "Are you all right?"

"We're both fine, Mike. Patrick's inside." She began to recount the events of the past thirty minutes as she led both Mike and the captain inside their office.

As Clancy was taken away, yelling and cursing, Melanie continued the story, and Patrick filled in details.

Mathers paced back and forth, pointing his cigar at them as he spoke. "That's the problem with private investigators. You two should have called us in on this immediately, instead of keeping it to yourselves. The last thing the department needs now is to have you two souring the case by going off on some fool vendetta."

Patrick forced his voice to remain even. His gaze was as glacial as a polar ice cap. "There is no vendetta involved, Captain. What we have done is deliver a suspect and our evidence against him to you." He stood by the door. "We'll be in to sign a statement later, Captain. As I'm sure you realize, both my partner and I have had a trying day."

"Some partnership," Mathers muttered as he turned to go. "More like the blind leading the blind."

Mike tarried, and as soon as the captain was out of sight, gave Melanie a thumbs-up sign. "Good work. I'll get back to you as soon as we find out anything concrete." Mike glanced at Patrick and exchanged a level look. "You handled Mathers well, Pat. Andy would have been proud."

Patrick watched Mike leave. He stood rock still, and said nothing for a few moments. "So, it looks like we have our man. I should feel relief, or satisfaction, yet all I feel is empty."

Melanie nodded. "It's not over yet, Patrick. Not by a long shot. I'm sure you've testified in enough military proceedings to know how long it takes for the wheels of justice to turn. I hope that the police will be able to build a good enough case against him."

That's when Melanie learned the difference between silence and utter silence. Patrick stared at some indeterminate spot across the room for what seemed like an eternity. "I intend to make sure they do just that. I'm staying in town until I'm certain that the police have an air-tight case. I owe my dad that. I'll keep in close contact with Mike and help him in any way I can."

"Patrick, Mike's a cop. He knows how to get the evidence he needs. Besides, you forget, I'm in on this, too."

He met her eyes in an unyielding stare.

"Why do I even try to reason with you?" she sighed, and walked to her desk.

"Well, for the time being, the case is in the hands of the department," Patrick observed. "I can't just sit around while they're conducting their investigation. I'll take over Dad's caseload, and let you get back to yours."

She nodded, realizing there was no way she could dissuade him from doing that anyway. "I do need to start attending to the agency's regular business. Financially this firm can't afford to put things on hold indefinitely."

Patrick entered his father's office and sat behind the desk. Sorting through the stack of office reports his father had failed to complete required a lot more space than the desktop alone could provide. Reaching to his right, Patrick extended the slide-out work surface. As he did, he discovered a manila file folder taped to it. "What's this?"

Melanie poked her head in. "What's what?"

Using a letter opener, he carefully removed the tape that held it in place. "This file. It was taped to the extension by the corners, sealed shut. If I hadn't needed the slide-out surface, it might have taken me days to spot it."

Melanie furrowed her eyebrows, puzzled. "That doesn't sound like Andy. If he was trying to hide it, he'd have chosen a better place." She stepped closer to get a better look. "What is it?"

Patrick began to leaf through it. "Interesting." He rubbed his chin, lost in thought. "Someone Dad wanted to keep anonymous hired him to investigate a local crime figure by the name of Mario Cartolucci. He's suspected of operating illegal betting establishments, running numbers and other related offenses."

"I can't believe this was there," she said, bewildered by the information. "I've heard the rumors about Cartolucci, of course. He's been on the news and in the papers, but this is not the type of case our agency handles." She scanned the pages as Patrick handed them to her. "If I hadn't seen this myself, I'd have never believed it."

Patrick let out a slow whistle. "According to this, Dad was trying to prove that Cartolucci has been bribing several law enforcement officers. Those payoffs are the reason the prosecutor's office hasn't been able to gather enough evidence on Cartolucci to get an indictment. This claims Cartolucci's people had been tipped several times prior to police raids, giving them time to cover their tracks. Also, that evidence had been purposely lost, or destroyed, right before the arraignment."

Melanie seated herself on a chair that she had pulled away from the wall, and scanned the pages before her. "Andy never told me any of this."

Patrick pulled out several small sheets of paper that had been clipped to the back of the folder.

"What are those?" Melanie asked, sitting up and leaning forward.

"Notes Dad typed to himself." He read through the first two, then turned them over to her. "What do you think about this?" He met her eyes in a penetrating gaze.

Melanie saw the suspicion mirrored there, and felt a shiver run up her spine. She read the notes, her mouth agape. "I don't understand," she admitted. "These seem to be a record of the times and dates Andy received threatening telephone calls at home, warning him to stop investigating Cartolucci. There're quite a few here, Patrick." She stood and began to pace before the desk. "But it doesn't make any sense. There's no way Andy would have kept this from me. Also, it wasn't like him to type notes to himself like this. Andy had a little pocket spiral notebook he carried around or else he used whatever was handy. He might have scribbled notes of this kind on the back of a matchbook, or a take-out food menu, but this—" she held up the neatly typed papers "—isn't like him at all."

"I'll tell you one thing, this is exactly the type of investigation that could have led to my dad's murder," Patrick commented pensively.

"There's a note here on the last page that says no other copies of this file exist." She furrowed her eyebrows and stared absently across the room. "Now *that* doesn't make any sense. Andy kept duplicates of absolutely everything. I wish his notebook hadn't been destroyed in the..." She took a deep breath, trying to get her bearings. "I'm going to check the computer and see if anything is logged in there."

"He may have made a more cryptic type of backup. Nothing extensive, just enough to jog his memory if something was needed. Maybe it's hidden within another folder. I'll take a look."

Melanie walked back to her office. She'd seen the distrust in Patrick's eyes.

Melanie diligently searched through all the computer disk files pertaining to Andy's active cases. At the end of an hour, she admitted defeat. As she entered Patrick's office once more, she saw him searching through Andy's file cabinets. "I didn't find any mention of Cartolucci anywhere. How about you?"

He shook his head. "So as it stands, there's no official record of that case in his files, the computer disks or through your personal knowledge. Is that right?"

Melanie nodded. "I know what you're thinking, Patrick, but you're wrong. Andy and I worked as partners and we trusted each other implicitly. Besides, like the Irish, Spanish people hold the family sacred, and to me, Andy was like family. I knew I could count on him, just as he knew he could count on me. Think what you want, but that's the way it was."

Patrick said nothing for a few moments. Was it possible Melanie knew about that file, but out of loyalty to her old police associates was keeping quiet? If she believed it didn't pertain to his dad's murder, it was possible she might do just that. To her, he was the outsider, not the police. "Melanie, relax. There're too many variables and options here for me to jump to any conclusions."

"Yes, you're trying to keep an open mind, and look at it from all angles," she conceded. "However, you're not willing to reject the possibility that your father might have been conducting an investigation that he deliberately kept secret from me."

"I trust my instincts, Melanie. You never would have harmed my father. Your loyalty to him is evident in the way you started to work with me, even though you didn't want to, in deference to his wishes. But, you're right to assume that I'm not willing to discount the information we've found in this file. Perhaps Dad had other reasons to keep you out of it. Once we look into it more, we might find answers we never even considered."

"So now what? I think that we have an obligation to turn this over to the police. This file brings up the possibility of mob involvement in Andy's death. Let's face it, you and I alone wouldn't last long investigating those people, not unless we had the police working on the case, too. And it's not as if we're duty bound to protect a client in this case. That client was Andy's, if he ever existed, and he's remained anonymous." She brushed a few stray locks away from her forehead. "I also really believe that if there's corruption within the department we should let someone we trust know about it."

"All right, Melanie. We'll go over to the department and talk to Mike. Only I'm warning you ahead of time, they're not exactly going to welcome this type of information."

"That's not our problem."

"It might be," Patrick muttered under his breath, as they got ready to leave the office.

The drive didn't take long, but it seemed an eternity to Melanie. Silence hung heavy between them. An uneasiness rooted in distrust seemed to charge the air. They walked directly to Mike's office.

"I'll save you some time," Mike said as soon as they were seated. "Clancy's turning out to be a tough nut to crack. We haven't been able to get anything out of him yet. We're working on him in shifts, so he'll start to talk sooner or later."

"We've got some new information." Melanie's heart went out to him. Mike looked as if he needed a good eight hours sleep. "I'm not sure how this ties to Clancy, yet, but maybe together we'll be able to figure it out." She gave him a photocopy of the file, and explained how they'd found it. For the next ten minutes Melanie reviewed their findings.

Mike listened patiently, then quietly muttered an oath. "I'm going to have to bring the captain in on this, you two." He stood reluctantly. "You both had better brace yourselves. This isn't going to go over well."

MATHERS GLARED at Patrick and Melanie, pointing a stubby, unlit cigar at each in turn. "You two are bad news. First you try to do the police department's job. Then, when we force you to accept that we're the ones handling this case, you try to discredit us. I should have you two thrown in jail for interfering with a police investigation."

"Captain, you could never make that stick," Melanie answered quietly, but firmly. "We've bent over backward to cooperate with the department."

"All I know is that you're making our job more difficult. And as far as making it stick . . ." He shrugged. "It really doesn't matter. You might be out by tomorrow morning, but you'd sure as heck spend one miserable night in jail."

"How does a false arrest and harassment lawsuit, made very public, sound to *you*, Captain?" Patrick countered in a low monotone.

Mathers glared at him for several moments. Finally he walked over to the window and stared outside, jamming his hands into his baggy pants pockets. The stogie was clenched between his teeth like a licorice stick. "O'Riley, I don't like the cloud this places on the department. This means that someone felt it necessary to hire an outsider to investigate us. We don't need the type of press this generates. On the other hand, this information may be the lead we need to crack this case wide open." Mathers turned and hitched up his pants, trying to cover his ample midsection. "Cartolucci will undoubtedly have an ironclad alibi for the day of the murder, but with enough time and patience we'll find the hit man. Of course," he added quickly, "we may already have him. Clancy could turn out to be exactly the person we need to shut down Cartolucci and his operation."

It took another twenty-five minutes before the police finished questioning Patrick and Melanie. In silence, they returned to the car and drove back to their office.

Melanie slumped down in her chair, and took a deep breath. "It's ten o'clock. I'm absolutely beat. I think I'm going to call it a day."

Patrick leaned against the file cabinet and regarded her thoughtfully. "Do you think Clancy is Cartolucci's hit man?"

Melanie began to clear her desk. "No, not really," she answered. "Clancy isn't the type to take orders, and he's completely unreliable, if we're to believe anyone who knows him. Those aren't qualities the mob would accept in a hit man. The biggest argument against that theory, though, is that it would be highly unlikely that any of Cartolucci's people would hire a hit man who was already being investigated by our firm. It makes far more sense to believe they'd find a professional killer neither Andy nor I would know. Unless Clancy was set up," she speculated idly.

She made sure the files were all securely locked, then walked slowly toward the door. "I'll see you tomorrow." For a moment she stood by the door, her eyes meeting his. He no longer saw her as his father's trusted partner. She could feel it. Even though he hadn't said anything, it hurt to see the uncertainty mirrored on his face.

"Be careful, Melanie," he said quietly. "Clancy is under arrest, but I don't believe that all the players have been accounted for." He locked the office, and walked her to her car, despite her protests. Patrick watched as she checked the door alarm and the tamper light, unlocked the car and reached inside to enter a code number on a small device attached to the steering column. The time delay on the anti-tamper alarm for the door allowed her ten seconds to deactivate a loud siren. Certain the alarm wouldn't sound now, she looked up at Patrick once more.

"I'll watch it. You do the same." She started the engine, letting it idle. "Will you be going home now?"

He shook his head. "I'm going to sit at my desk for a while. I need time to sort out my thoughts. We'll try to come up with a game plan tomorrow."

As Melanie drove away, Patrick walked back to the office. Melanie was difficult to know. She always kept her guard up, and never allowed him to see what lay beyond those inscrutable eyes of hers. Still he was slowly learning

more about the woman his father had worked with for so
many years. Melanie was honest and lived by a code that
valued tradition and honor highly. Her loyalty to his father
was without question, but what about her relationship to the
department?

She hadn't broken those ties completely. Had his father,
in order to spare her feelings, kept her out of the Cartolucci
investigation? Or had he feared that Melanie's loyalty to the
force might cloud her objectivity? Patrick wasn't at all sure
how Melanie would react if someone she knew, a friend, was
on the take.

Melanie was starting to pose other more difficult problems for him, too. His feelings for her were changing. He felt
a growing desire for her presence, for her touch, and more.
Elemental thoughts that made his blood turn to fire had
come unbidden and lingered in his mind throughout the day
until a steady pressure pounded through him.

The confines of the office seemed stifling all of a sudden. Taking his jacket from the rack, he started toward the
door. Tomorrow, he'd force her from his thoughts.

But tonight, she'd haunt his dreams.

PATRICK AWOKE EARLY. He'd managed to beat the alarm
clock by an hour and a half. Listening to the ticking of the
grandfather clock in the hall, the one his dad had built by
hand, acutely reminded him of his father's absence. All the
years he'd lived at home, the house had never seemed so
quiet, or so empty.

He got up slowly, and fixed himself a cup of coffee. Odd
how the grief he felt could be made tolerable by the sense of
purpose the investigation gave him.

His thoughts drifted to Melanie as he mentally reviewed
their latest findings. Slowly a plan began to form in his
mind. There really wasn't any choice. There was only one
way to handle the investigation from this point. He'd have
to work the Cartolucci lead on his own, and follow it wherever it led.

PATRICK ARRIVED AT THE OFFICE eager to get to work. The implications made by the Cartolucci file were too important to ignore.

Melanie glanced at Patrick, who was clad in a conservative blue jacket and slacks, as he came in the door. She'd been aware of him from the moment he'd pulled into the parking lot. After Clancy's unannounced arrival the previous day, she was keeping an eye out for unwelcome visitors as well as for any signs of trouble. Up to now, she really hadn't expected anyone to try to create problems for them inside the building during normal business hours. The incident with Clancy had caught her completely by surprise. But not again. By mutual agreement, Patrick and she had decided to keep the door latched during office hours for the time being. Also, according to her instructions, the superintendent had installed a peephole that rested in the middle of one of their suite numbers, making it almost invisible.

"Good morning," Patrick commented.

"I'm glad you're here," Melanie began. "There's something I wanted to talk to you about. I've been giving this Cartolucci thing a lot of thought, and I think the police department will have to be the ones who handle that investigation. I trust Mike to make sure things are run as they should. Besides, the department has the manpower and the pull to be able to do that job. What we can and should do is keep looking through the agency files and see what else we can turn up. A cursory check on the cases Andy was handling has given us two suspects already. We might also extend our search to include investigations he completed this last quarter. Maybe there are several suspects hidden there we haven't even considered yet. For instance, there might be others who, like Clancy, hold a grudge or consider Andy responsible for their not getting a particular job."

"Are you starting to doubt Clancy's guilt?" Patrick asked, his attention now focused sharply on her words.

"No, to be honest with you, I believe he did it. Only I don't think it was connected to Cartolucci. I think he acted out of revenge." She returned to her desk. "However, in the interest of being thorough, we should check out everything else. Who knows what we might uncover?''

"I think you're right." He nodded slowly. "I'll help you follow that up." He watched her as she walked to a storage box and extracted several computer diskettes, then gathered a stack of written files from a file cabinet.

It was clear to him that Melanie was very reluctant to pursue the Cartolucci lead. Perhaps she was afraid to find out who in the department was taking bribes. What if his father had discovered that someone they both knew, maybe Mike Cooper, was involved with Cartolucci? The possibility was an intriguing one. His thoughts centered around Mike, the policeman his father had known for the longest period of time.

Patrick had met Mike when he was a boy, but times and people changed. Had Mike gone sour? If Mike had discovered Andy on his trail, how would he have reacted? Prison was a very unhealthy place for a former cop.

The telephone rang, interrupting his musings. He picked up the receiver. "O'Riley and Cardenas," he clipped out.

"O'Riley, recognize my voice?" The man spoke in a barely audible tone, but there was no mistaking the identity of the caller.

Chapter Six

"I won't forget that you got me arrested," Clancy's voice rose in volume. "You're turning out to be as big a pain in the neck as your old man was. The same goes for the pretty little lady you work with. I'm out, your charges didn't stick. And I have no intention of letting bygones be bygones."

"Clancy?" Patrick's fist clenched into a tight ball. "Let me give you a piece of advice. I make a very bad enemy, and threatening me or my partner is the best way I can think of finding my bad side."

Melanie glanced up quickly. Her eyes focused on Patrick. She waited until he hung up the telephone, then quickly asked. "What was that all about?"

"Clancy gave us a friendly call. Apparently he's out on bail," Patrick said lightly.

The news took her by surprise. "Tell me what he said," she insisted. The thought of that knife near her ribs made her heart beat faster. She couldn't resist the impulse to look outside, to see if he might be lurking nearby, waiting.

Noting her anxiety, he complied. "You know," he added at length, "I'd almost welcome him coming back here. This time, I'd do enough damage to make him think about it for a while."

"That never works with people like Clancy," she answered, wondering if her voice really sounded higher pitched than usual. "It only escalates the problem." She paused, collecting her thoughts. "What we need to do is find out why he was released, and see what we can do to get him back in jail where he obviously belongs.''

Patrick heard the strain in Melanie's voice. Was she reacting to the stress she'd been through? He thought about Mike and the allegations made in the Cartolucci file concerning the police department. Was Mike part of a web of corruption, and had any of that played a part in Clancy's release? It would be useless to discuss the possibility with Melanie until he had some proof.

"I'm going to give Mike a call," Melanie said, "and meet him someplace. I want to know what happened with Clancy. Mike'll be able to talk more freely at a coffee shop than at the station, or over the telephone."

"Good idea." Patrick hoped that Melanie was not going to be given the standard police line, or worse, allow Mike Cooper to misdirect their investigations. "While you're doing that, I'll go through Dad's back cases thoroughly. Then, once I'm finished, I'll check the work load he'd scheduled for the next month."

"It's a lot of work, but it needs to be done," Melanie agreed and picked up the telephone and dialed.

Patrick walked into his office. It was true he intended to study his father's case records extensively, but that was not all he planned to do this afternoon. There was no way he could just sit back and wait to see if the police could link Cartolucci to his father's murderer.

Melanie came in a few minutes later. "I'm on my way to meet Mike."

"Fine. Did he tell you anything on the telephone?"

"No, but I didn't ask," she replied. "Cops never open up on the phone. I'll be at the Coach House, about two miles north of here, if you need me."

"Melanie, just remember that Clancy's out. Don't take any chances. If you think something's not right, trust your instincts. Call me, or the cops immediately."

She nodded, having just checked the revolver in her purse. "I'll be careful. And don't worry, I know how to take care of myself."

He smiled. "I don't doubt that for a moment."

Patrick waited inside long enough to insure Melanie was really gone. He checked his watch, switched on the answering machine, then locked up the office. The drive to the newspaper office didn't take long. He strode through the front doors and went directly to the city editor's desk. "Harvey, how ya been?"

"Patrick." He shook his head. "I'm really sorry about your dad. He was a good friend, and I miss him a great deal."

"So do I," Patrick admitted somberly.

"Now tell me what I can do to help you, Pat. I figured you'd be investigating this on your own when I heard you were back in town to stay for a while."

"Who told you that?"

"I ran into Mike Cooper about a week ago."

How close was Harvey to Mike? It was difficult to know whom to trust. "Harvey, I need a favor. I know the newspaper keeps a clipping file downstairs, but it's not really open to the public."

Harvey held up his hand. "Say no more. I'll take you down there myself." He led the way to the elevator. "What are you looking for, if you don't mind me asking?"

Patrick didn't really want to volunteer information, but this was something Harvey could easily have checked. "I thought I'd find out all I could about Cartolucci and his local ties."

Harvey nodded. "Yeah, I heard that the police were investigating a possible connection between him and your father's murder." As the elevator door slid open, he led the way out. "We should have a truckload of information on Cartolucci that you can study. He's been in the news almost every week lately."

Harvey introduced Patrick to the librarian, then started back toward the door. "You're free to use our resources anytime, Pat, and I'm also privy to a lot of information we don't print because for one reason or another we can't verify it. If I hear anything about your father's case, I'll pass it on."

"I'd really appreciate that," Patrick said candidly.

Patrick made himself comfortable at one end of a long table while the librarian brought him the files he'd requested. He opened his briefcase and placed his copy of the Cartolucci file on his right, as a reference. He began to sort through the myriad of information the newspaper had collected when the librarian returned again.

"I thought you might also like to see this file." The young, heavyset man placed another smaller folder before him. "I don't know if this will have the type of information you need, but you're welcome to look through it."

Patrick glanced up. "Anything at all you have on Cartolucci will help, even related articles."

"In that case, you'll want to study both files. The smaller one contains mostly biographical data. The larger file pertains to his rumored connection to organized crime operations."

Patrick read each article carefully. Cartolucci had been in the public eye for a very short time. Nonetheless, he'd made quite a reputation for himself. He was considered ruthless. Several members of rival factions who had reputedly challenged his meteoric rise to power had turned up dead. Though Cartolucci was suspected to be behind the murders, no one had been able to prove anything against him.

As he sifted through the articles, Patrick began to see a pattern. The information in the newspapers closely matched the data in his father's file. Of course if the stories were accurate, and his father's findings correct, similarities were to be expected, but this was too much for coincidence. In one instance, the phrase used to describe Cartolucci's temper precisely matched the one his father had made in his notes.

Patrick's attention was then caught by a story detailing Cartolucci's early years. That's when he spotted an inconsistency that made the hairs at the back of his neck stand on end.

He compared the newspaper account to the information his father had supposedly gathered. The article in the clipping file indicated that Cartolucci's home state was Iowa, however, this information had been crossed out in ink and corrected to read Ohio. A small erratum had appeared in the next day's paper.

What he found so disturbing was that his father's report had also listed the wrong place of birth. It was obvious the information had been gleaned from the same, inaccurate newspaper story.

After a few hours work, Patrick returned to the office. Melanie was already there when he arrived. "I was wondering where you'd gone off to," she said, sounding cheerful.

"You're not the only one who likes to eat occasionally, you know," he hedged.

She followed him to his office and stood in the doorway leaning against the frame. "I've got some good news. Clancy isn't out at all. It seems that he must have made that call from jail. He gets to make one phone call a day, so he apparently decided to harass us."

Patrick turned around. "He's still in jail?"

"Mike said that there's no way they'd ever release Clancy. They know he's hiding something and they're trying to get some evidence to tie him to Andy's murder."

Patrick rubbed the back of his neck with one hand. When he'd thought that they'd only held Clancy overnight, he'd been almost certain that there was corruption at the police department. Now he was willing to concede that perhaps he'd been too hasty in his conclusions. By the same token, he still wasn't ready to completely discount the possibility of police involvement in his father's death. Yet Mike's actions had reaffirmed some of the trust he'd once had in him. He was pleased. Suspecting a man he'd known to be one of his father's dearest friends had left a bitter taste in his mouth.

Patrick set his briefcase down by the edge of the desk. Out of the corner of his eye, he saw Melanie focus on it. His excuse about going out for a bite wasn't going to hold up after all. "I meant to ask you something about Dad's methods of investigation. How did he usually gather background information on people? What type of sources did he like to use?"

"Andy made extensive use of police and employment files, but most of all, he relied heavily on personal interviews." She smiled, remembering. "He'd do it so casually that people would never even notice how much information they were giving out."

Patrick nodded. His father had been very good with people. He possessed an easy charm that allowed him to weave past an individual's defenses. It had been quite a gift. "Do you know if he ever relied on newspaper articles as sources?"

"Usually only as a last resort," Melanie replied. "He avoided secondhand sources. You see, he was a stickler for accuracy. I grant you that his daily logs and record keeping may have appeared at first glance to be haphazard. However, I can assure you he always verified and double-checked every single detail contained in his reports.

Patrick opened his briefcase and removed the copy of the Cartolucci file from it.

Melanie recognized it immediately. She waited for an explanation, but then realized none was forthcoming. "I see you had a working lunch. Anything I should know about?" She kept her tone light.

"I went to the newspaper's clipping file library to get some more background and general information on Cartolucci. I took our file with me so I could refer to it if I needed." He placed the file back into the cabinet casually. "Did you see yesterday's article in the paper alluding to a connection between Dad's murder and Cartolucci? Someone apparently leaked it to the press," he commented, hoping to divert her attention. "It wasn't you or me, so that leaves..."

"The police," she finished. "That explains something else," she observed. "I noticed when I was coming back from my meeting with Mike that none of the street people seem to be hanging around like they normally do. I've been hoping to spot Shy Eddy, so I've been keeping my eyes open." Her shoulders slumped. "If the newspaper ran a story connecting Andy's murder with Cartolucci, word is probably out everywhere for people to keep their mouths shut." Melanie forced herself to shake the heaviness that had settled over her. "Now tell me more about your visit to the newspaper's library."

"Like I said, I was trying to familiarize myself with Cartolucci's activities in this city."

Melanie stared at him for a moment, waiting for the rest. Faced with his silence, she knew he had no intention of telling her anything more.

Patrick met her eyes and saw that icy wall of indifference she could instantly erect as a barrier between them. By not freely divulging the information he'd gathered, he'd managed to further alienate Melanie. His gut twisted with frustration.

"Keep me posted." She turned abruptly and left.

Patrick seated himself as she stormed out of his office. Grim lines of tension settled around his mouth. He didn't like having to exclude her, but he still didn't feel comfortable involving Melanie in the Cartolucci investigation. He intended to stick by his decision and work on that alone.

Melanie had just confirmed his suspicions. He'd found it difficult to believe his father had relied on newspapers as a source. So what did all this say about the file itself? Cartolucci was bad news. According to what he'd learned about the man, if his father had indeed been investigating him, Cartolucci could have made a lethal adversary. The fact that some of the information in the file was not the sort his father would have gathered, did not necessarily mean the file was bogus. There was another possibility....

MELANIE PACED in front of her desk. She couldn't remember ever being so angry. Patrick was deliberately withholding information from her. Again!

Taking several deep breaths, she forced herself to view the situation dispassionately. Patrick had obviously found the

Cartolucci file interesting and worthy of closer study. Perhaps it was time she also inspected it carefully. If Patrick had learned something important from it, she had to find out for herself what that was.

Melanie walked inside his office and pulled the original folder from the cabinet. "I need to borrow this," she stated flatly. Before he could say anything, she was out of the room.

She hadn't gone more than a few steps when the telephone rang. The timing couldn't be better. She smiled. "Patrick, it's your turn to take the call." She really wasn't sure whose turn it was, but taking turns answering the phone had been Patrick's idea and now it would divert his attention.

She went through the papers carefully, but it wasn't until she reviewed them a second time that she realized what else was wrong with the report.

Melanie stared at Andy's signature on the last page of their agency's preliminary data form. She then pulled another sample of Andy's writing from the file cabinet and set them side by side. Even taking into account normal variations in writing, the signatures contained definite differences in style. Admittedly they were close but unless she missed her guess, Andy hadn't signed his name to the Cartolucci report at all. It had been forged. This could turn out to be the evidence she needed to prove to Patrick that the file had been planted.

Yet she had to be sure. She wasn't a handwriting expert. Taking her purse and the file, she poked her head inside Patrick's office. He was still on the telephone. This would give her the perfect opportunity to duck out without having to offer any explanations.

Scribbling a note, and sticking the self-adhesive paper on his door, she informed him she'd be back in ninety minutes.

BY THE TIME SHE RETURNED, Patrick was pacing back and forth between their offices. "You're back, finally."

"Has something happened?"

"No, but I've been very curious as to what you're up to. First you storm out of my office, then you sneak back in, take a file I've been using and leave. Care to tell me what's going on?"

She met his hostile gaze with a cool one of her own. "I'm going to tell you what I've found out, but I expect the same from you. You're withholding things from me, Patrick, and that's no way for us to make any headway on this case."

He threw his hands up in the air, at the end of his patience. "All my life I've heard that Spanish women respected a man's authority, and were happiest when they could stay in the background and support his efforts. But you're like an Irish woman. No one can tell you anything!"

"Thank you for the latter part, I consider it a compliment. However, your view of Spanish women needs some updating. You're a generation or two behind." Her eyes narrowed, but she kept any anger from showing in her voice. "And don't try to sidetrack me from the real issue, Patrick. It won't work."

He smiled slowly, a playful gleam appearing in his eyes.

"Now, I'm going to tell you what I found out," she continued, undaunted. "Then it'll be your turn."

He gave her a snappy salute. "Yes, ma'am."

Flinching at the memory of Andy's last moments the salute evoked, Melanie continued.

"There was something about the Cartolucci file itself, beside the facts that I had mentioned to you before, that nagged at the back of my mind. I felt there was something I should have been seeing, but wasn't. Then when I realized you'd been studying it, and using the file as a legitimate lead, I knew I had to take a closer look, too."

"And what did you find out?"

"Andy's signature didn't look quite right. So I pulled a sample of Andy's writing I knew to be genuine, and then took it and the Cartolucci file to a friend of mine at the state police. He's the West Coast's leading forgery expect. I knew he would help me, unofficially, if I asked. I purposely

avoided using the department's people, for your benefit.''
She sat behind the desk and rested her arms on the sides of
her chair.

"That wasn't Andy's signature on that report. There's a
certain unevenness in the script at the end of each letter. It's
almost as if the forger is out of practice.'' She continued
slowly, enunciating each syllable. "That file is not legitimate, Patrick, and this should prove it to you.'' She leaned
back against her chair and waited for his reaction.

Patrick seated himself across from her desk. "I already
knew that the file wasn't a product of Dad's work,'' he admitted, exhaling softly.

"What?'' She straightened abruptly. "How?''

He told her about the data that had been gleaned from the
erroneous newspaper article. "I really found it difficult to
believe that Dad would have compiled a report using only
newspaper accounts as a source. Later you verified that for
me.''

"Why didn't you tell me?'' Her voice rose slightly. Realizing that her anger would get the best of her if she didn't
calm down right away, she took a deep breath and slowly
counted to ten. "You realize that we've duplicated each
other's efforts again, don't you?'' Her voice was void of
inflection and perfectly controlled. "We're never going to
get anywhere at this rate, Patrick.'' She leaned forward,
clasping her hands in front of her. "I understand that mutual trust takes time to develop, but unless we learn to confide in each other, it may end up costing us our lives. And
Andy's murderer may get away scot-free .''

"You're right,'' he admitted. He stood and placed both
hands flat on her desk. "All right, we've identified the
problem. Now we have to deal with it,'' he said briskly.

She saw the determination in his face, and for a moment
she truly sympathized with him. He didn't want to work
with her, yet in deference to his father, he would. She was in
exactly the same position. *Oh, Andy, what did you do to us!*

"First, let me start by sharing a few thoughts with you,''
Patrick added. "Although we both agree that the informa-

tion in the Cartolucci file has been planted, we differ in one major point. You're ready to discard the entire thing. I'm not." He paced the front of her desk.

"How can you say that? We tackled this from two different angles and proved that the file was a phony."

"The information inside it wasn't collected by Dad, that's true. However, consider this. What if whoever broke in replaced the real information in that file with data anyone could have gathered from the newspapers?" He pulled a chair out from the wall and straddled it, facing her directly. "The person might have figured you knew about the investigation, and to remove the file altogether would be dangerous. Instead he decided to make a cover file using Dad's own typewriter and he kept only the sections of Dad's report that were already public knowledge. The rest of the mess that he made when he broke in was to cover up what he'd really done. Maybe the other break-ins were also part of the scheme."

He cleared his throat and continued. "Of course, I can see Dad not wanting to have a computerized backup to that file, particularly if he was trying to keep you from getting involved. I think if we search thoroughly, though, we might be lucky enough to find a second copy of Dad's real report somewhere. Dad might have purposely said there was no other copy just to throw someone off the track."

"That *does* sound like Andy," she admitted. "But there's a flaw with that theory." She stood and began to pace back and forth between the door and her desk. "Andy would have never accepted a case that could have placed me in danger, if only through association, and kept me in the dark about it."

"I understand what you're saying, Melanie, and I've considered that angle, too. The problem is, we can't be sure what Dad's reasons might have been at that time. He did let you know he'd started carrying a gun again. Maybe that was his way of warning you there could be danger ahead. Until we manage to find evidence that proves or disproves the

Cartolucci connection, we just can't afford to eliminate him as a suspect.''

Melanie nodded slowly. The truth is, she wasn't so sure anymore. Was it pride that kept her from admitting the possibility that Andy might not have confided in her? Or was it really her own personal knowledge of her former partner and friend? "You have a point," she admitted reluctantly.

She rubbed her temples, a headache beginning to pound inside her head. Hearing a knock at their door, she went to answer it. A package express deliveryman was standing in the hallway just outside. "May I help you?"

"I have a package for Major Patrick O'Riley," he informed her.

"I'll sign for it," she offered. She'd been used to accepting packages ever since the office had opened. She reached for the clipboard with the shipping paper, but the deliveryman drew it back. "I'll need to see some identification before I can release this. It's to be accepted by Major O'Riley only."

"Here I am." Patrick retrieved his wallet from his back pocket and showed his military identification card. "I'll take that now," he said, reaching for the overnight packet.

Melanie suppressed the embarrassment she felt. Ever since Patrick had stepped into her life, it seemed that she was losing more and more control over her environment. Not being able to accept a package at her own agency made her feel inadequate somehow. Piqued, she walked to her desk.

Patrick waited until they were alone. "Sorry about that," he said, sensing her mood, "but it's military procedure."

"Military?" she asked, somewhat mollified. It was uncanny. For years, she'd prided herself on being able to hide what she was thinking. Yet Patrick seemed to have a special knack for being able to read her true feelings, breaking through the cool exterior she always tried to project.

He ripped open the padded envelope and extracted a lengthy letter. A few moments later, he glanced up. He handed the contents to her. "It's the O.S.I. report. Apparently the computer came through just as I thought it would. It was able to compare the information from the police reports with what was learned about the component we sent in. The scorch pattern on the brass tube, the telltale marks that indicated how the spring was attached, and the physical evidence collected by the police have all been correlated with historical records. They've concluded the bomb was similar in design to a German S-mine." He paused, sorting his thoughts. "Larry Clancy is getting to look more and more like the murderer. He's got the know-how, and he collects weapons and paraphernalia dating back to World War II."

"I'll stand by my original opinion, though, that he acted on his own. He might have furthered Cartolucci's objectives, but he certainly isn't affiliated with organized crime in this city. No way."

"This O.S.I. report will help the police know what to look for when they search Clancy's apartment. Between what they have on him now, and this, I believe they'll be able to find enough solid evidence to convict him." He clenched his fist into a tight ball. "I hope they send him away for the rest of his life. And when he gets up every morning, he'll have a chance to think about what he took from—" he paused for a moment "—from both of us," he continued, "as he looks out from between those steel bars."

Melanie was about to answer when once again a knock sounded, interrupting them. She peered through the viewer and saw Inspector Mike Cooper standing in the hall. She opened the door and invited him inside. "Hello, Mike. What brings you here? Is it the copy of the O.S.I. report? We just got ours."

"I received mine about an hour ago," he answered. He waited for Melanie to sit down, then made himself comfortable on one of the leather chairs in front of her desk. "You guys aren't going to like what I have to say one bit."

Patrick sat on the edge of the desk, his legs spread in a slight V. "What's going on, Mike?" His tone was filled with a wariness he made no attempt to disguise.

"We've had to release Clancy from jail. I thought you should know right away. I've got a gut feeling he's going to come after you two."

Chapter Seven

Patrick's eyes blazed. "The police department released Clancy, even after they saw the O.S.I. report? Whose side are you guys on?"

Mike's expression grew hard. "Patrick, I'm going to let that pass because I know how hard this has been on you."

Melanie saw the fierce determination on both men's faces, and instantly stepped forward. "Mike, Clancy probably killed Andy. He also sneaked into this office, assaulted Patrick and me with a knife and then made a threatening phone call from jail, no less. It's a safe bet he's coming after us. After all that's happened, how could the department have just let him go?"

"A very expensive private attorney, John Hutchins, showed up. He forced the issue, and without some very definite and solid evidence to link Clancy to the murder, we had to let him out on bail," he explained. "Let's face it. We don't have any physical evidence linking Clancy to Andy's murder and we're not even close to establishing a connection between Clancy and Cartolucci. All we have is that assault charge against you two. We did manage to get the bail set high, but he still made it."

"Where did Clancy get the money for the attorney or to make bail, for that matter?" Melanie asked, her mind racing. "I thought he was unemployed?"

"We're not sure. We're checking on that now. If we find anything fishy, we're pulling him right back in. But the fact that Clancy has no witnesses to corroborate his where-abouts on the day Andy was killed isn't enough to keep him in jail and the rest of what we have is circumstantial. You both know it." He gave Patrick a long, hard look. "The law is the law. You should realize that, Pat."

"That's not the way I see it, Mike." Patrick jammed both hands into his pockets, shoving his sports jacket aside. "We've cooperated with the police, but you guys don't seem to be getting anywhere. We hand you the perfect suspect, and right away he's back out again. I think the department is stalling because they don't want to take a real close look at their own people."

Mike stood and faced Patrick. "The department I work for isn't like that. Your father was a cop, and a damn good one. I expected more from his son."

"And I expected more from my father's friend," Patrick replied pointedly.

"I'm doing what I can," Mike growled.

Whether or not Patrick would see it, Melanie knew they needed the department's help. To alienate Mike was only going to make matters worse. "Look, Patrick, the depart-ment has an internal affairs division that comes on like the Soviet secret police. Believe me, cops have no rights when they're being investigated. Civilians, on the other hand, have a lot more legal protection. If an attorney comes in and demands the release of his client, the department has no choice but to set terms. Their hands are tied unless they can produce strong evidence to hold him. What we have to do is work together with Mike and see if we can come up with some solid evidence."

Patrick said nothing for several moments. "Once a cop, always a cop," he said slowly. "Is that the way it is, Mela-nie?"

She felt her own temper begin to get the best of her. "You better be real careful what you say right now, Patrick. You're angry and you want to lash out at someone, but there's no one here who deserves that," she answered coldly.

"Mike came over here because he was concerned. You don't treat your friends this way."

Patrick's eyes hinted at the turmoil going on inside him. He strode to the recently replaced window and stared outside. "Thanks for the warning, Mike," he said at length.

Mike gave Melanie an exasperated look, but she held up her hand, shook her head and walked him to the door.

Patrick strode back into his own office.

Melanie lingered with Mike at the doorway. "Don't judge him too harshly. I'm learning more about Patrick as each day goes by. He's just reacting to his frustration with this case. It feels as if we keep losing more ground than we gain. Of course, the pressure to stay alert all the time also takes its toll."

Mike nodded and gave her shoulder a squeeze. "Don't allow yourself to get complacent, Melanie. Clancy's bad news. I'll have the cops who normally patrol this area keep a special lookout on your office. If you sense trouble, or spot anything that makes you uneasy, just give us a call. We'll be here like that." He snapped his fingers. "You have a lot of friends in the department. We'll do everything we can do make sure nothing happens to you."

"Thanks, Mike, I mean that," she answered candidly.

MELANIE RETURNED to her desk slowly. She couldn't quite erase Patrick's crack about "once a cop always a cop" from her mind. Did he honestly think she'd side with the police department and consciously aid a cover-up? Now that Mike had left, it was time to bring some things out into the open.

She walked directly into Patrick's office without knocking, and took a chair. "Patrick, you owe me an apology. I may have been a cop once, but that doesn't make me the enemy here."

"Melanie, I sympathize with what you're going through. You love the department and defend it like you were still on the force. But right now your priority should be the objectives of this agency. When our goals are undermined by what the police are doing, you shouldn't side with them. I think your loyalties are confused at the moment.''

She stared agape at him. ''Are you implying that I'm not fit to investigate Andy's murder?'' This time there was no controlling it. Her anger spewed to the surface. ''For me, nothing takes precedence over finding Andy's killer—not the department, not even you, Patrick. I let my partner down once, but I won't fail again.'' Her words were taut, held together by bitter regret and sorrow. ''Maybe if I had gone out to the car with Andy, I'd have spotted the bomb and he'd still be alive.'' Her voice cracked, but she forced the raw emotions from it. ''I can't change that now, but I sure as hell intend to find the person who murdered him.''

Stunned, he couldn't find the words to reply. Before he could react, Melanie picked up her purse and strode out of the office. Patrick went after her a moment later, but by the time he reached the parking lot, she was pulling away in her car. Melanie blamed herself for his father's murder? But that was crazy! She couldn't have made his dad any safer by dogging his footsteps. Chances were if his father hadn't spotted anything amiss, she wouldn't have, either. If she'd been with him at the time, she'd probably have been killed, as well.

He returned inside. She had given him a glimpse of her soul, and what he'd seen had taken him completely by surprise. He felt an overwhelming desire to hold her against him and comfort her. Despite the tough exterior, she was vulnerable and in pain. If only he'd handled things differently!

Over an hour passed before Melanie returned to the office. Patrick left his chair and met her by her desk. ''Where did you go?''

''Out. I had to cool off,'' she answered succinctly.

He'd wanted to say so much to her, to tell her that he wasn't the cold-blooded bastard she believed him to be, but now the words wouldn't come. They seemed to be lodged in his throat. ''Melanie...''

She picked up a file from her desk, and glanced up at him with those frosty, impassive eyes. "I have to finish a background report. After that, I'm going to hand deliver it to the client. It's overdue, and I don't want to keep him waiting any longer."

"With Clancy on the loose we should try to stick together as much as we can," he warned in a gentle voice. "It's dangerous taking off abruptly like you did earlier, without telling me where you're going or when you're coming back. Fatal mistakes are made that way."

"You're right," she conceded. "It won't happen again," she added briskly. Mentally she kicked herself for having allowed her emotions to get the best of her. The last thing she needed was for Patrick to lose confidence in her as a professional. Her spirits plummeted as she considered the possibility that what she feared had already happened.

Then, slowly, another more startling realization began to form at the edges of her mind. She truly did care what he thought and how he personally felt about her. It mattered to her a great deal. Her own feelings toward him had been changing in a most subtle and pervasive manner.

"Why don't we go together when you're ready to deliver that report?" he suggested.

"Sure. If you'd like, it's okay with me." Disguising her turmoil, she kept her tone noncommittal.

Again Patrick tried to tell her what he felt. "I wanted to explain..." He saw the enigmatic look in her eyes and concluded that his timing wasn't right. "Never mind. It'll keep." He returned to his desk.

An hour later, the report ready, Patrick accompanied Melanie to his car. Frequent glances over their shoulders, the rigid posture of their bodies, all attested to the strain they both felt so acutely. Yet deeply ingrained survival instincts prevented them from dropping their guard.

Patrick pulled his car out into the street.

Melanie, lost in her own thoughts, did not interrupt the silence between them for several minutes. Then, when she realized that Patrick had turned in the wrong direction, she started to warn him.

His expression jolted her. His jaw was set grimly, and his lips were pursed into a thin line. Patrick had tensed his muscles, and was gripping the steering wheel tightly.

"What's wrong?" she asked quickly.

"We're being tailed," he answered almost too casually. "Only I don't believe the driver realizes we're on to him yet."

She resisted the urge to turn around. Instead she took her compact out of her purse, aimed it so she could see behind her, and studied the traffic for a few minutes. "The maroon Chevy?"

He nodded. "It's been with us since we left the office. I turned at the last minute back there, to see if he'd follow us, and he has."

Melanie studied their pursuer. "He's done this kind of thing before, Patrick. He's staying with you even though you're weaving through traffic. He remains just close enough not to lose you. Look how he makes sure there is always a car between us and him. How did you ever spot him at all?"

"I was checking traffic in my rearview mirror when I noticed the car. It's the same color and make as the first one I ever owned. Though, of course, this one is a more recent model."

"Can you tell anything about the driver?" She closed her compact and peered at the image behind them in the side mirror. "I can't see anything except an outline."

"Not really. He's got his visor down. I'm going to make a couple more turns and see if he sticks with us."

Patrick drove down an alleyway, then stopped at the other end. For a moment, when the other car failed to appear, they began to suspect it had all been a false alarm. Then, a few minutes after they rejoined traffic, they spotted their tail once again.

"Melanie, make sure your seat belt is fastened tight. I'm going to try to turn the tables on him. We'll see what this is all about."

"I don't think it's Clancy," Melanie commented pensively. "*He* drives a sixty-eight Ford pickup. I'm also fairly certain that it's the only vehicle he owns."

"He could have borrowed this one," Patrick ventured.

"True, but this isn't like Clancy. This guy's staying back, and he's skilled at tailing. Clancy seems more like the type to run us off the road, or pull up next to us and cut loose with a shotgun." She glanced back again. "This person has too much finesse."

"There's an old commercial section of the city directly ahead. Most of the businesses that used to be there have relocated, so it should be fairly quiet. I'll head in there, and see if he still stays with us. If he does, I'm going to whip the car around and go after him."

Chapter Eight

"Patrick, wait a minute." She studied the area they were about to enter. "These streets are narrow. You won't be able to just turn around. If he follows you in, your operating room is going to be limited."

"I know what I'm doing. Trust me." Patrick turned into the neighborhood he'd selected. "I grant you that this road is barely one lane, but the fact that it's almost deserted will help us." He glanced in his rearview mirror and smiled. "He's still behind us, hanging back a bit more because there's nobody else around. But he's there."

"There's no place to maneuver here, Patrick." Melanie glanced around.

Patrick pursed his lips, then slowly a ghost of a smile began to pull at the corners of his mouth. "So, we get a little creative and try to make a disadvantage into an advantage." He went down another block, made a left turn, then slowed down. The person following them, unaware Patrick had cut his speed, came upon them abruptly from behind. "Good. We drew the guy in. Now we have him."

"What difference . . . ?" she started to ask, but the words caught in her throat. Patrick hit the brakes hard and slid to a stop. Quickly he shifted the car into reverse, then pressed down on the accelerator.

"Patrick, what are you doing? You're going to smash into him!" her voice rose.

"Just enough to startle and slow him down," he answered quickly. "Then I'm going to force him against the curb and grab him. Hold on!"

Quickly recovering, the other driver also shifted into reverse and began to make a hasty retreat.

Praying that Patrick knew exactly what he was doing, she braced herself.

Seeing the other driver increase his speed, Patrick muttered an oath. "I'm not letting him get away." He gunned the accelerator.

Traveling at about thirty miles an hour in reverse was a new experience for Melanie. The engine sounded like it was about to explode. Her head was spinning as she kept turning from side to side, trying to see if they were about to crash into something. "He can't turn around any more than we can," she shouted above the roar of the automobile.

"There'll be a chance for him in another block, if he's sharp enough to take it. It's going to be tricky."

Melanie studied the area. "Where?"

"There!" Patrick cursed. The maroon Chevy skidded as it traveled backward around the corner of an intersecting side street. Braking, the driver changed gears and accelerated forward before they could catch him. The stretch of road was clear of traffic and he sped away quickly.

"Our turn," Patrick said, not waiting to reach the intersection. He slammed on the brakes while expertly spinning the steering wheel hard to the left. The car slid around one hundred and eighty degrees in the street, reversing its direction completely.

The vehicle bounced as the wheels spun in place when Patrick jammed the pedal to the floor. They shot off after the Chevy, careening around the corner.

Melanie had learned pursuit driving in the police department, but she never would have attempted to spin the car around in such a narrow area. She strained to focus on the car in front of them. Then, without warning, a large van backed into the street, directly across their path. Patrick stomped on the brakes, narrowly avoiding a collision.

"Get out of the way," Patrick yelled. Bluffing by grabbing his Air Force ID from his jacket pocket, he waved it in the air. "I'm pursuing a criminal suspect. Move that truck."

The driver responded, placing his ponderous vehicle into forward gear and inching out of the road.

Patrick shot forward, but there was no sign of the Chevy. Screeching to a halt at the next intersection, Patrick slammed his hand down hard against the steering wheel. "I can't believe it! We lost him! After all that, we've got absolutely nothing!"

"We have something. We know the make and approximate year of the car, and that whoever was driving is no amateur. He knew what to do to get that car to respond in any way he wanted."

"Did you get the license number?"

She stared at him incredulously. "Patrick, he was *behind* us most of the time. Then when you whipped around, I couldn't get a clear look."

"Maybe there's still a ray of hope in this mess," Patrick muttered after a moment.

"Like what?"

"If we're being tailed, we must be on the right track. Our investigation has started to make someone nervous." He paused, and mulled it over. He glanced over at her. "If he followed us today, it's because he feels the need to keep an eye on us. Now that he's managed to elude us once, he might be feeling cocky, and more inclined to try it again."

"Well, if he does, we're going to have to do more than try to match our driving skills against his. We're going to have to outsmart him."

"What do you have in mind?" Patrick asked curiously.

"Misdirection," she answered. "Remember when you placed the car in reverse and started going after him? He responded quickly, countering your move. That means he's not the sort who's going to be thrown by the unexpected— at least not easily. We'll have more luck if we try to mislead rather than surprise him."

"Mislead him? How?"

"By employing a strategy I used many years back, on a particularly tricky surveillance job. Stop by my house, and let me run in and get a few things. We'll set up a trap. Then, since we don't know when he'll follow us again, we'll just have to stay prepared. However, all that's going to entail is repeating a certain pattern until he takes the bait."

"You're being terribly cryptic, you know," Patrick said with a scowl. "I'd like details."

"You'll get them, but I'd rather show you how this will work rather than try to explain it. Be patient and do this my way."

"What's new?" he muttered acerbically.

He stopped by Melanie's house as she'd asked, but before he even switched off the ignition, she was out of the car.

"Wait here, I'll be right back," she told him, then dashed up the porch steps. She remembered how strange this technique had sounded to her the first time she'd heard it. She'd scoffed, just like Patrick would have if she'd explained, until she'd seen it work.

Going through her closet, she picked out the necessary items, then stuffed them into a large laundry bag. Then she made her way to the stairs.

Patrick met her halfway down. "Here, let me take that for you. What's in here?" he asked, hefting the bag. "It's light."

"You'll see. Now come on. We have to make one more stop before we can return to the office. Let's go to that new high-rise apartment building a couple of blocks north of the agency. They have an underground garage, just the place we need for the next phase of this."

They rode in silence. Patrick stole quick furtive looks at her from time to time, as if trying to guess what she could possibly be up to.

She wasn't worried. Her plan was very creative and had the merit of having been proved successful before.

"It looks as if we're going to have a problem," Patrick interrupted her thoughts. "This is one of those maximum security buildings. There's an attendant at the entrance to make sure no unauthorized person gets in. He'll turn us away," he warned. "You're going to have to pick another place."

"No, I'm not," she answered. "Drive up anyway. The attendant is the son of a friend of mine, there won't be any problem."

He gave her a skeptical look then, with a shrug, proceeded to follow her instructions. He stopped their car beside the attendant's booth.

"Carlos, *como andas muchacho*?" She leaned forward, angling toward Patrick's window.

"Melanie?" The attendant, a man about eighteen years old, stooped to the level of the window and smiled at her. "*Estoy bien*. It's good to see you."

"I need a small favor. How about letting me pull in here for about five minutes? A maroon Chevy's been tailing us off and on today, and I need a few moments somewhere I can guarantee he's not going to show up. Can you handle it?"

He glanced around and nodded. "If I can't trust you, then I can't trust anyone. Go ahead." He looked past them out at the street. "And don't worry. The maroon Chevy isn't getting past here."

"*Gracias*, Carlos. Say hello to your mother for me, okay?"

Patrick drove through. Giving her a quick look, he shook his head in bewilderment. "This is some 'Cubano' network you've got."

"It's a nice arrangement that works to everyone's advantage. Friends mean a lot to us."

"To me too, Melanie," he said in a gentle voice. "Remember that."

His tone unsettled her. Her skin warmed as awareness made her tingle with a different kind of excitement. Perhaps that was the most disconcerting part of it all. Patrick reminded her that despite her determination to always appear confident and collected, she was still very much a woman, and vulnerable to the right man.

She forced her thoughts away from him, though the effort it took was almost physical, and concentrated on the area ahead. "Pull into that empty parking space over there," she said.

He slowed the car to a stop and switched off the ignition. "Now what?"

"Now we do some makeshift sculpting," she replied, opening her car door and stepping out. Melanie brought out her laundry bag and extracted a jumpsuit. She sat sideways in the passenger's seat, facing outward, and dangled the suit in front of her. "Now hand me the rest of the stuff in the bag," she instructed.

Patrick came around to her side. Sliding the laundry bag toward him, he reached inside. "More clothes?"

"Mostly rags, really, but it's perfect for what we need."

"Here you go." He watched her, a puzzled expression on his face.

She began to stuff the jumpsuit, filling it with what he handed her.

"You're making a scarecrow?" he asked at last. "This isn't my day," he baited, feigning sorrow. "You ask me to take you parking, then jilt me in favor of a dummy."

She laughed. "Don't kid yourself. This bundle of rags is very special. He's going to be your stand-in."

"Melanie, if that's supposed to make it all clear for me, I've got news for you. It doesn't even come close."

"We need a way to confuse the guy who's been tailing us, and get the advantage. Well, this is going to do it for us. I'll stick the dummy in the car beside me. The seat belt and shoulder harness will hold him in place. We'll put sunglasses on him and a fedora. At a distance, no one will be able to tell it's not you." She continued. "That will give you the perfect opportunity to follow us in another car. If the person tries tailing me, you can come up from behind and trap him between us."

"It's a good idea, except for a few details," he answered skeptically.

"Like what?"

"For starters, the dummy doesn't have a head."

"It will before I'm through. I have a Styrofoam head somewhere in here that I use to put my wig on. We'll tape it around the collar with black electrical tape. Since the jumpsuit is also black, it won't show up. Then we'll slip a latex, Halloween mask over the head. The one I brought looks like Count Dracula, but between the fedora and the glasses, I think it'll pass. Also, it wouldn't hurt for you to wear the hat and sunglasses at least a few times and be seen with them."

"If this is going to work at all, you're right about that. Where are they, inside the bag?"

"Of course. The hat might be a little smashed up, though. You'll have to reshape it with your hands. I just stuffed it in there, since I didn't want to carry it out in the open."

Patrick reached into the bag and extracted the hat. He'd just finished reshaping the brim when she asked him for it.

"Before you try it on, let's see how it's going to look on my broad-shouldered partner here." She zipped up the stuffed jumpsuit and then taped the head, Dracula mask and all, onto the dummy. Last of all, she added the sunglasses and fedora. She propped him up on the passenger's seat, then stood back. "Beautiful. He'll be the perfect companion. Almost looks like you, only better. He's cuddly and he doesn't talk."

She turned around, playfully ready to face him and see his reaction. Suddenly she realized that he'd moved in behind her. She was only inches from his body.

Before she could recover, he encircled her waist and pulled her against him. "Compare me to a bunch of old rags, will you?" he murmured. "And unfavorably at that!" he added. "You need to be shown what advantages the real thing has to offer."

Splaying one hand against her back, he twined the other into the curtain of her hair, and tilted her head backward. His lips descended over hers, capturing her mouth.

His embrace was firm, preventing her from moving away. Yet she wouldn't have, even if she'd been given the opportunity. Instinctively she slipped her arms around his neck, deepening the embrace.

They parted slowly, reluctantly. The safety value that had held him in check had almost been obliterated by the pressure of his new feelings for her. "Now tell me again how you prefer that bunch of rags to my company, Melanie," he murmured.

She wanted to—just to be perverse. She tried to compose herself quickly and appear cool and unaffected, but it didn't work. Her face was still flushed, and her breathing uneven. "Actually," she started, but her voice broke.

He smiled. "Admit it. You enjoyed it as much as I did." His voice was deep, and filled with masculine pride.

She smiled back very slowly, but decided right then that the only safe course of action was to change the subject. "Are we going to stand around talking all day?"

"It wasn't my idea to go parking," he replied, taking one more playful jab.

"Help me cover up the dummy with a blanket, and place him on the floor of the car," she ordered, trying to restore their serious focus.

"Alas, he was poor competition. I'm glad you see things my way now, and are ready to put him to rest," he teased.

"Take his fedora, and start wearing it," she said, refusing again to rise to the bait. "And the sunglasses, too. I'll keep him in front of me on the floor, out of sight. We'll sneak him back to the office parking lot this way. Then, if you'll pull in next to my parking space, we'll switch the dummy to my car. Since it's just basically moving him between two open doors, we shouldn't have too much of a problem keeping him hidden." She smiled. "Can you imagine what the other tenants would think if they saw us moving the dummy?"

Patrick smiled in reply. "I can imagine trying to explain it to the cops."

She laughed. "Well, our plan's all set. Next time we go out, you can pretend to come with me to the car, but then actually duck back into the building or into your car. I'll pull the dummy onto the seat, and with the seat belt across him, no one will be the wiser.''

He slipped the fedora on, and then readjusted it, trying to keep the hat from slipping down over his eyes. ''The sunglasses fit, but where did you get this hat? It's large enough for two heads.'' He glanced in the rearview mirror.

''Don't complain. I got that hat cheap, and it fits the dummy's head.'' She paused and added, ''The other dummy I mean.''

''Don't start,'' he warned, his eyes twinkling roguishly. ''You can't win, you know.''

''As usual, I don't agree with your conclusions at all,'' she replied smoothly, smiling to take the sting out of her words.

They both kept a sharp lookout as they drove back to the office, but no one seemed to be following them. As Patrick pulled into a parking space near the side entrance, Melanie glanced over at him. ''I don't think we've been tailed. To be honest, I was rather hoping the person who'd followed us would be close by, waiting for us to return to the office. Of course, we'll still have to stay alert for him when we move the dummy to my car. He could have switched vehicles.''

''That's going to be an inconvenient certainty, I'm afraid.''

They made the transfer in a matter of seconds, moving swiftly and efficiently and walked back to the office.

Melanie spent the next twenty minutes returning calls. Prospective clients and current business demanded her attention.

Patrick returned to his paperwork, but his restlessness made it impossible for him to continue. He paced around the room, then walked to the outer office. ''I'd like to give the decoy plan a trial run,'' he said. ''What do you say we go out, and head for Donnelly's Pub? We'll consider it a dress rehearsal.''

''Fine with me,'' she answered.

''Do you know where Donnelly's is?''

''Sure. Andy and I go—used to go there for lunch quite a bit.''

His gaze softened as he noted the slip of her tongue, but he didn't comment on it. "All right then. Take the most direct route. Let's not get fancy. We won't communicate unless we absolutely have to. The mobile telephones operate on public airwaves, and those can be intercepted too easily. If you do spot someone taking the bait, then head for the north parking lot, right beside the pub. There's always room in there this time of day, and there's only one way in or out. We can trap the person there."

"Agreed, only let's make sure none of the other building tenants are hanging around when we set the dummy up. It'll make them nervous and we don't want to attract their attention," Melanie suggested. She opened her purse, and checked her revolver and extra ammunition.

"Okay, then. Let's go." Patrick locked the extra dead bolt, then accompanied her out of the building. Wearing the fedora, he stepped out into the parking lot. Melanie went to the driver's side of the car, as Patrick opened the passenger's door.

"Here we go," he told her. Patrick ducked below the level of the door, removing the fedora and placing it on the dummy. The sunglasses had already been attached to the masked figure. Reaching up carefully, he propped the dummy in his place. Patrick used the car for cover, then moved across the sidewalk where he was hidden by shrubbery. After Melanie drove away, he kept out of sight and waited for her to get a bit farther down the boulevard.

Melanie merged with the traffic, traveling slowly down the street, and staying in the right-hand lane. She was about a quarter mile away from the agency when she spotted Patrick's sedan some distance behind. She proceeded toward Donnelly's, continuing her periodic checks of the rearview mirror.

Was it a coincidence or was there another car following her? A light beige compact seemed to be staying with her, no matter where she went or turned. It was a skillful tail, if one at all. She really couldn't be certain, since the car would change lanes through traffic, then suddenly reappear several cars behind her at irregular intervals.

Had Patrick noticed it? She couldn't tell. Resisting the urge to use her car phone, she remained calm and tried not to tip her hand. In accordance to their plans, she drove to Donnelly's and headed for the large parking lot that bordered the north side of the restaurant and pub.

She thought for a few moments that she'd lost the beige compact, but as she drove toward an empty parking spot she saw it cautiously pull into the parking area. The second it entered the lot, she heard another car roar up, followed by a squeal of brakes.

Patrick pulled in immediately behind the compact and stopped, blocking the exit. Cars parked along the curb sealed the trap; the man had no way out. Melanie got a glimpse of an older man behind the wheel but she couldn't get a closer look at his face. Dark glasses and a tweed cap hid his features in the late afternoon light.

Patrick opened the door of his car, but stayed behind it as he ordered the man to come out. At last something had gone their way. Melanie ducked out the passenger's door past the dummy, drawing her weapon. She kept her car between her and the trapped driver. She didn't want to risk giving him a clear shot at her if he was armed.

Ignoring Patrick's order, their quarry jammed down his accelerator and drove straight for the wooden gate that blocked an alley leading to the residential section.

Melanie gasped, stunned by the man's actions. The gate was padlocked. There was no way out!

An instant later, the driver rammed his way through it with a crash. Boards flew everywhere as the car roared down the alley. Patrick bolted into his car and gave chase.

Suddenly Melanie heard the earsplitting screech of brakes, and the shrill sound of children's screams.

Chapter Nine

Melanie's blood turned to ice. A couple of kids stood near Patrick's car, others remained pressed against the nearby walls.

A helpless, suffocating feeling engulfed her senses and filled her with horror. Had Patrick hit one of the children with his car? She forced herself to rush to where the kids had gathered. The oldest couldn't have been more than ten years of age. Her limbs felt leaden. As if trapped in a slow motion world, she searched the ground for signs of a victim.

Her heart slowed, and relief settled over her when she failed to find anyone injured.

She saw Patrick as he walked around to the side of the car. He glanced up and gave her a hesitant smile. Unwilling to accept what was before her without confirmation, she met Patrick's eyes. "Is everyone all right? I heard screaming."

Patrick's gaze went from one child to the next. "Everyone's fine, but the way he shot through here, it's a wonder these kids were able to scatter in time. I still can't believe he did that! What an act of desperation!"

One of the boys, about seven years old, bolted down the alley, racing toward one of the houses. "Wow, my dad'll never believe this!" he shouted back at them. "It was almost like being in a real live cop show."

Another boy looked at Patrick, then at Melanie. "Are you guys cops or private eyes?"

"Something like that," Patrick admitted.

"We're glad you're all okay," Melanie joined in.

The first boy stopped halfway down the alley. "Hey, Frankie, did the bad guy get away? Dad'll want to know."

"You better not tell him, or he'll skin you alive. You know we're not supposed to be here at all," the tallest boy, who'd remained close to the wall, warned. "Let's get out of here!"

"Wait, boys!" Patrick started after them, but gave up after a moment. The children climbed a chain-link fence, scaling it easily, and scattered as soon as they hit the ground on the other side.

Melanie caught up with Patrick. "Let them go. You'll never catch them now, and besides, they've been through enough."

"Only a person willing to gamble everything would have ever smashed through that gate. He had no way of knowing what was on the other side."

"That driver's lucky to be alive." Melanie glanced around and stared at the splintered gate. Large pieces of wood had flown up in the air and lay all around the alleyway. Glass from an apparent broken headlight was scattered on the pavement.

Patrick started walking Melanie back to her car. "In all my years as an investigator, I've never seen anyone drive like that. He weaved around the kids like they were pylons on an obstacle course."

"This profile doesn't fit Clancy," she commented thoughtfully. "This person has been taught the equivalent of combat driving. What in the world are we up against?"

"A very dangerous person who's willing to take us on, but only on his own terms," he answered.

"I don't like this, Patrick," she said slowly. "I don't like this at all. When you can face an enemy head-on, there's danger, but there's also the feeling that you have a certain amount of control over the outcome. In a situation like this—" she paused "—well, all you can do is hope your instincts and training will be enough to keep you alive. We need to identify this person."

"I do have some good news." His Cheshire-cat grin took her by surprise. "I know the make and year of the car, and I memorized the license number." He took a small piece of scrap paper from his jacket pocket, and jotted down the information.

Melanie smiled. "Let's go back to the office. On my way there I'll call the department and ask them to run a make on that car for us."

"I'll follow close behind. By now the person who followed us probably realized we tricked him, and the dummy isn't likely to work anymore." He glanced at the other cars starting to pull into Donnelly's parking lot. "Let's get out of here. We can file a report with the authorities and notify the owners of the pub about what happened here later."

"I can take care of that on the way back, also," she answered, sensing his impatience.

Melanie glanced in the rearview mirror often as she led the way to their office. She realized that, for now at least, the person who'd followed them wasn't likely to reappear, yet she couldn't quite force herself to relax. She was aware of everything around her, from the shopkeepers to the stray cat who lingered around the trash bins.

As they passed the budget baker that sold day-old bread and other discounted items, she suddenly saw Shy Eddy in the shadow of the store's awning. By the time she managed to pull over, Shy Eddy had disappeared again.

She and Patrick walked around the block, searching together, but found no trace of him. Both of them questioned the shopkeepers and a few of the passersby, but no one could give them any information. Dejected, they returned to their cars.

"I have a plan," Patrick commented eagerly.

"If you're thinking what I'm thinking," she answered staunchly, her mind already racing, "we should change our clothes and hit the streets as soon as possible. If he's in the area, we might be able to find him."

"Exactly, but to be on the safe side we should stay together."

She nodded, and tried to appear very calm, even though she didn't feel that way at all. "How about posing as an unemployed couple who's been forced out of their apartment? If we run into Shy Eddy and he's with some of the others, we might have an easier time trying to talk to him. Otherwise, we'll play it by ear, okay?"

"Sounds fine. Let's get started. I'll follow you to your place and wait for you to change. Then we'll make a stop by my place . . ."

Melanie held up a hand, interrupting him. "Wait a second. I'm not going to have you baby-sitting me every second of the day. We'll both do what we have to, then I'll meet you back at the office."

"That's not a good idea," he protested. "Clancy is violent. We don't know what his connection is to the guy who tailed us, but we now have reason to suspect that there's more than one person involved in this. There's definitely more than one car."

"I'll watch my back, same as you. That's all we can do, Patrick," she countered smoothly. "We can't be together twenty-four hours a day, so let's not try to do the impossible."

"Staying together round the clock doesn't sound like such a bad idea to me," Patrick drawled. "We could give it a try. Think of all the possibilities."

"Think of all the distractions," she countered. She unlocked her car and slipped inside.

"You consider me a distraction?" he answered, turning the phrase on her.

Placing the key in the ignition, she glanced up at Patrick, who had come around to her side. She allowed her gaze to slide over him openly, taking in the contours of his masculine body slowly, and thoroughly. "You could be, under the right circumstances," she baited. Then, without giving him a chance to respond, she pulled her car door shut. As she started forward, Patrick stepped back onto the sidewalk.

Laughing, Melanie glanced back in the rearview mirror a moment later. She'd expected her boldness to shock him.

Instead she saw a wide mischievous grin on his face. He'd enjoyed every minute of her teasing as much as she had. Maybe they had more in common than she thought.

PATRICK AND MELANIE MET back at the office about thirty minutes later. Even old, patched blue jeans and a gray sweatshirt with the sleeves cut off did not detract from his virile good looks. In a way, it seemed to enhance them, giving him the comfortable, yet appreciably rumpled look of a man who'd spent, say, a week out on the streets.

By comparison, in her old overalls, she felt as attractive as Lon Chaney.

His eyes strayed over her. "Good choice of clothing. You'll still get attention," he said in a resigned voice, "but the fact I'm with you should diffuse it."

"Attention? What do you mean?" She glanced down at herself.

"You . . . well . . . stick out in some very nice places," he commented almost sheepishly, with a shrug.

She stared at him in surprise. "Where?" she glanced back down at herself. The bulky fabric made it practically impossible for anyone to discern any part of her figure. "You're crazy!"

He took a deep breath, then sighed. "Let's just go." He walked toward the door and waited for her. "Just in case, are you carrying your revolver?"

"Of course," she answered quickly. "That was why I chose these overalls. There're lots of zippered pockets in it."

He bowed his head. "Well, then I guess we're ready for whatever lies ahead."

As they left the office the deadly seriousness of their situation sobered her. She'd have to look after Patrick carefully. She'd lost one partner, something she still felt partially responsible for. She wouldn't let Patrick down, too. In a way, Andy had entrusted her with what he held most dear.

"What are you thinking about?" Patrick asked. "You were looking at me with the most peculiar expression."

"Nothing specific, really," she hedged. "I was just trying to anticipate what lay ahead tonight."

"Lots of walking, I'm afraid." He locked the door and placed a tiny piece of Scotch tape at the top and a strand of hair in the doorjamb at the bottom. "Just a precaution in case someone manages to pick the locks," he explained. Patrick walked with her outside. "Any suggestions on where to start?"

"Not really. By now, supper's been served at the refuge. The homeless will wander around for a while, then go to their favorite spots."

As they approached the corner, Patrick saw three men sitting on the curb of the sidewalk. Melanie and Patrick ambled toward them. The others, aware of their presence, grew silent.

Finally the largest of the three spoke up. "You two are new around here," he commented. "Wouldn't recommend you stick around."

"Whadda you mean?" Melanie asked.

"This used to be a quiet neighborhood, but not anymore. First there's a guy in a car that gets blowed up, then people start disappearin'. Ol' Sam's been a regular around here for three, maybe four years now. Never missed a meal at the refuge. Now he's just gone. Then a strange bald-headed woman ran Shy Eddy right out of the refuge a few days back."

Melanie stared at her shoes, fighting hard not to crack a smile.

"Haven't seen him since," the man continued. "It used to be that in the summer most of us would stay out in the streets and find our own places to sleep." He shook his head. "Not anymore."

"We don't like strangers hanging around nowadays, neither," the smallest said accusingly. "Why don't you both just move on."

"Maybe we will," Melanie replied, taking Patrick by the arm, and leading him away. "These people are never this unfriendly, Patrick," she said as soon as they were out of earshot. "The only acceptance street people ever get is from other homeless. To close themselves off from that means giving up their only source of companionship. They must be very frightened, if they're acting like this."

"Let's keep going. Maybe the next group we meet will be easier to talk to."

As they walked around the neighborhood, Melanie kept alert to danger. Her eyes darted to and fro, searching and watching the alleys and shadows. "There's usually at least one or two of the street people sleeping in doorways or under the overhangs of buildings around this area. Have you noticed that we haven't even seen one?"

"That's true." Patrick cocked his head toward an area in front of them. "Look! There's a group of four around that bench ahead."

"Within a stone's throw of the refuge," she added observantly. "Let's go see if our luck's improved. Maybe Shy Eddy will be one of them."

As they approached, the group stopped talking, and began whispering back and forth. Patrick and Melanie leaned against the building and allowed the group to study them. The minutes grew longer and longer, the silence heavier between them.

"How hard is it to get a bed at the refuge?" Patrick asked at length.

"All filled," one of the men answered. "No place for strangers. You best move on."

"Ease up, George," an elderly woman complained. "Things are hard enough as they are."

"You like strangers, Mary? You talk to them." The others walked off, leaving her behind.

"Sorry," Patrick told her candidly. "I didn't mean to make any trouble for you," he added, careful not to make her nervous by approaching closer.

Melanie sat on the little patch of grass that bordered the secondhand clothes store and leaned back against a lamppost. She kept her eyes on the street, keeping a lookout on behalf of Patrick and herself. If trouble found them, she'd be ready.

"No one wants to find themselves alone right now," Mary answered, pulling the tiny shopping cart that contained her belongings closer to her. "So, for a while, we'll stick together in groups. Eventually the trouble will pass. I've made the streets my home for a long time. Trouble comes and trouble goes, and when it's gone we'll still be here." The ragged dress she wore hung loosely over her thin body. One sleeve was held to the shoulder with four safety pins.

"It's better if you stay in groups," Patrick conceded, "but what happens to the ones like Shy Eddy? He doesn't like people. They make him nervous," Patrick commented offhandedly.

"You know about Shy Eddy?" Mary asked, instantly suspicious.

"Not really. But people talk."

Mary, seemingly satisfied, pulled a cigarette stub out of a tattered, imitation leather purse she had on top of her cart, and lit it with a worn disposable lighter. "I know he's around someplace. I saw him today, but he knows how to lay low when he needs to." She took a deep drag of the cigarette stub until the white burned away, then tossed it aside. "I expect Sam wasn't as lucky. It's not like him to disappear like that."

"Aren't you scared?" Melanie asked in a gentle voice.

"Me?" She laughed. "Hell no, I'm too old to be scared. Death's a part of living, and when it comes, there'll be nothing I can do to stop it. You haven't been on the streets long, if dying scares you," she remarked casually. "We're too busy trying to find one square meal a day, or a warm spot to sleep in during the winter, or maybe just a place out of the rain." She shrugged. "The dampness really gets to me now, more than it used to," she muttered in a resigned tone. "Out here we have to live by a different set of rules, but there are rules. Not what you should or shouldn't do, but what you *have* to do to keep going."

She reached for her cart, and started to move away. "Now I have to be leaving. It's time for me to get some sleep."

"Goodbye, Mary. It was nice talking to you," Patrick said softly.

Mary stopped and turned around. "There are no good-byes out in the streets, son, people just go."

Melanie remained seated on the grass. How could someone surrounded by hundreds of thousands of people suddenly feel so alone? She wanted to be held, to reach out to Patrick and share each other's warmth. But this wasn't the time. She had to remain alert for danger. Only she couldn't get her mind off Mary's words.

"Let's go back to the office, Melanie," Patrick offered his hand and pulled her up. "If Shy Eddy's hiding out, we'll never find him."

As they headed back, Melanie continued her thoughtful silence.

"You're so quiet all of a sudden."

"I was thinking about what Mary said, and how the street people live. I don't know how they do it, Patrick. I've always been close to my family. My relationship with them has given me a sense of security and continuity. I can't imagine being without those feelings. These people have no one. Their acquaintances provide some companionship, but they don't really share anything more than a few kind words."

"I've always felt the same way about family, Melanie. My dad and mother were always there for me, and despite what you think, Dad knew if he ever needed me, all he had to do was call or let me know. Personal differences could never get in the way of that. But now with my mother and father both gone, I do know what it's like to be without a family. Only I still have everything they taught me to fall back upon. To be alone, and without any hope of a future filled with family and love, seems like a kind of slow death."

"I wonder what gives them the strength to keep going."

Patrick didn't reply. Abruptly he quickened his pace. Melanie, instantly alert, glanced up at him. "What's wrong?"

"I'm not sure if anything is, but that's the third time I've seen that old pickup going around the corner."

Melanie noticed the vehicle just moving out of sight as it turned to the right.

"It fits the description of the one Larry Clancy owns."

Melanie's hand moved to the zippered pocket that held her revolver. "Both our cars are parked right by the office. He's undoubtedly discovered that we're not at the agency. Do you think he's out here searching for us?"

Before Patrick could answer, the truck pulled up alongside the curb to their left and slowed down. Clancy leaned forward in the seat and turned their way, making sure he held both Patrick's and her eyes for a second. Then, wordlessly, he pulled back into traffic and drove away.

"What the heck was that supposed to mean?" Melanie could feel the outline of her revolver with her hand. "Could he have tampered with our cars?" Perspiration trickled down the length of her body.

They strode quickly back toward their office building. "If he's touched either car, the alarm will have gone off, and we'll know it."

"Then what?" Melanie asked.

"I think he's just trying to rattle us, but let's check the cars carefully to be sure. If the red tamper light on the steering column is lit instead of the green that'll mean the alarm went off, and we were too far away to hear it. It only sounds for three minutes, then recycles off again. Also, we'll have to check the agency door for signs of unauthorized entry. If we find any, we're not going to go in. We'll call the police."

They arrived at their building a few minutes later and stopped by the office door. Patrick checked the tape and found it was still intact. It took Melanie a few minutes to find the hair Patrick had inserted near the bottom, but when she did, she breathed a sigh of relief. "At least he hasn't tried to get in here."

"Or he saw our markers."

She gave him an incredulous look. "Patrick, that little strand of hair is almost beside the carpet, and it's darn near the same golden color. No one would have ever spotted it. I knew the hair was there, yet still almost missed it! Let's go check the cars."

The green light was glowing on both cars. "I don't think we have anything to worry about here," he concluded. Confident no one had tempered with their automobiles, they returned to the office and let themselves in.

Melanie checked for messages, then made herself comfortable behind her desk. "Mike called, and asked me to call him at home. Maybe he's got something for us."

"Don't count on it," Patrick warned acerbically.

Melanie gave him a stern look as she proceeded to dial the number.

Mike answered on the second ring. "I've been waiting for your call," he admitted. "I've got some news, but it isn't much. We ran the plates for you, and that car turns out to have been stolen earlier this morning. We found it abandoned, and we're checking for prints, but so far we have nothing. Everything's too smudged, or belongs to the registered owner."

Melanie's spirits sagged. She avoided looking at Patrick, sensing the I-told-you-so look she'd expected to find there.

"Nothing, right?" Patrick asked in a quiet voice.

Melanie nodded. "I'm really disappointed. I was hoping for a lead." Her gaze fell on Patrick as he walked out of the office and down the hall to the soft-drink machine.

"Have you guys turned up anything new?" Mike asked, still on the line.

"No, we did have a run-in with Clancy, though." She gave him the details.

He muttered an oath. "I was afraid something like that was going to start. Be careful, Melanie. Clancy's trouble just waiting to happen. I hated like hell giving the order to have him released."

"*You* were the one who authorized his release?" It had been easier and much less personal to be able to blame the legal system for allowing Clancy to go free. Mike's failure to help her came as a harsh blow. She'd expected more from him.

"I know what you're thinking, Melanie, but stalling seemed pointless. Besides, I didn't want to give Clancy any more reasons than he had already to go after you two."

She didn't answer right away. "Mike, you knew he'd come after us anyway. You could at least have slowed down the paperwork."

There was a lengthy silence on the other end. "Melanie, all I can tell you is that I did what I had to. There was a lot of pressure on me at the time. As a cop, I have to answer to a chain of command, you know that. Certain cases have more ramifications than they seem to at first glance."

"I don't understand," she insisted. "Mike, what are you telling me?"

"Too much," he answered. "It's late, Melanie. I've got to go. Take care of yourself."

Melanie placed the receiver back, then stared at the telephone. Had Patrick been right? What if their deadliest adversary had been looking over their shoulders all along in the guise of a friend?

Chapter Ten

Patrick was already in the office by the time Melanie arrived the next morning. When she glanced through the doorway, Melanie saw him sitting there, staring at a photograph of his father on the wall. She said nothing, recognizing that the healing process for Patrick was still incomplete. Less than a month had passed since Andy's murder.

Appearing composed and quite handsome in a light blue suit, Patrick came out to meet her. "Good morning. I hope you're ready to put in some long hours today."

Melanie rested her elbows on her desk, having already rolled up the sleeves of her pale green blouse. "There's nothing much we can do about finding the driver who tailed us. We have a general physical description, but if that person was wearing a disguise, it won't do us much good. We can't even be certain if it was a man or a woman."

"What we have to figure out now, is who we could have made nervous enough that they'd want to tail us," she added. "Let's go over the list of people we interviewed. Discounting Clancy, who has neither the expertise or the finesse, who else is there?"

"One of Cartolucci's men," Patrick suggested, seating himself across from her.

"Well, that's going to be difficult if not impossible to track down. Also, it's unlikely. Cartolucci already knows what he has to hide. If anything, he'd be out covering his trail, not following ours. With the police already involved, he couldn't possibly hope to trail everyone who might be a threat to him."

"So who else does that leave us? We've closed up all of Dad's current case files. If there was anything noteworthy about any of those, we sure didn't find it."

"Well, there's one possibility we dropped, but never really investigated fully. Remember Conrad Reed, the civil engineer I spoke to? We never did take an in-depth look at him. When I found out Reed had withdrawn his job application with that defense contractor because of his father's death, I placed his file on inactive status." She pulled the folder from the cabinet and handed it to Patrick.

A flash of pain clouded Patrick's features, but he pulled himself together quickly. "I suppose we could argue that his decision to withdraw his job application might have been linked to Dad's investigation." Patrick leaned back in his chair, and studied the contents of the file she'd given him. "But I sure hate to bother that man. I sympathize with his reasons for not wanting to start on a new job immediately." Patrick met her gaze very directly.

"I know. I did check on his story, and it turns out Reed's father was killed in a gruesome car accident late one night." She shifted, tucking one leg beneath her, and adjusted the hem of her midcalf-length ivory skirt. "No matter how difficult, we're still going to have to follow this up, Patrick. We can't afford not to. The next line of investigation for us is with Andy's old files, and there are hundreds of those. I'm not really looking forward to doing that."

"Okay," he conceded. He took a deep breath, then let it out slowly. "Let's use Dad's methods for the background check. That way we'll be seeing things just as he did. It might be important since we can't be sure how far Dad really got on this. All we know is what he actually wrote down in this partial report, and there's no telling how current the stuff in here is. However, we do have the form Reed signed giving the agency permission to examine any paperwork pertaining to his personal and family history. Let's use it, and see if we can turn up anything that links Reed to our investigations. If not, we'll close the file for good.''

''We can split up the work, and that way it'll go faster. I'll concentrate on his father,'' she said. ''Since the man's deceased, I'll have to use our agency's contacts to get the information we need. They know me personally, so it would be better if I contacted them. In the meantime, see what you can find on his mother. From the file, we know that his parents were divorced when Conrad was six. Frederick, the father, raised him, and his mother remarried. It might be really interesting to get her perspective on things.''

''Yes, that might turn up something.'' He stretched and stood.

Melanie watched Patrick as he walked back inside his office. It surprised her how much a part of the agency Patrick had become. It already felt natural to have him there. She wondered if he'd stay after it was all over. The office wouldn't be the same without him. His quiet voice and warmth were a magnet to which a part of her inevitably strained.

Forcing her thoughts back to business, she picked up the telephone and made several calls, methodically conducting her background check. Slowly a curious pattern began to emerge. She hung up the phone and tried to sort it out.

A half hour later Melanie walked into Patrick's office. ''Do you have a minute? I've got an interesting development.'' She made herself comfortable on the sofa across from his desk. ''I started with Conrad Reed's father, Frederick. First, I contacted his last employer. Conrad had already notified them that we'd be doing a background check, so it was easy to get the information. It seems to match what we already had.

''But after that, things started getting really strange. I called the clerk in the rural county where Frederick Reed was supposedly born. I asked them to verify his birth records while I waited, then later have a copy of his birth certificate sent to us. The clerk couldn't find anything at all for Frederick Reed in either their computer or files. Although Conrad claimed his father lived in that area most of his early life, the bank there had no financial history for him or his family at all, and they've been in business continually since 1938. They even checked their archives. I then called the social security office where he was first issued a card. I verified that through the first three numbers of his card. Although they do have a record for him there, the application only dates back to 1945. They weren't able to find any copy of a birth certificate, though. Then I called my contact at the local credit bureau. Frederick Reed has a good credit history, but it only dates back to 1945, which is unusual for someone who was in his sixties. I asked her to verify that by checking old records, too, since it definitely seemed peculiar. She double-checked it for me, and it wasn't a clerical error."

"Something's not right." Patrick studied the information in the Reed file again. "It's true that Frederick Reed got his first teaching position in 1945. That's when he started working as an assistant professor at the University of Washington in Seattle. However, according to the information Conrad gave Dad during their first interview, Frederick worked his way through college. He must have had a social security number during that time, at least."

"I couldn't find any record of one. I checked with the office of records at the University of Washington in Seattle, and they said that Frederick Reed's file contained a letter of recommendation from the University of Pennsylvania, where he'd earned his degree. Also in there was a medical deferment from the military because of a heart murmur. Everything seemed well documented from what I could tell from my telephone conversation with them. But as far as government records, and the ordinary day-to-day official history all of us compile, it's as if Reed never existed prior to 1945."

"Interesting..." He was about to say more, when a knock sounded at their door.

Melanie answered it, and came back holding a sports coat. Her face was pale as she walked to the closet in Patrick's office to hang the jacket up.

Patrick watched her. "Where did that come from?"

"Mike brought it. Your father left his coat at Mike's house a few days before he died. Mike's wife had put it away, and he only discovered it this morning. He thought you'd want it."

Patrick said nothing, but for a moment his unguarded expression mirrored the loss and the pain that had wounded his heart. "Did he happen to mention the Clancy or Cartolucci investigation?"

"Only in passing. He couldn't stay. They're following leads, but have nothing solid yet."

Patrick watched her expression, knowing that to read her feelings he had to be alert to small nuances. He'd learned it wasn't easy for Melanie to speak her mind openly. In that way they were alike. Perhaps that was one of the reasons he had the sensation of being bonded to her on some instinctive level. "Melanie, are you having doubts about the police's handling of this investigation?"

"I've had moments of uncertainty," she admitted. She touched the fabric of Andy's coat lightly. Traces of his cologne still clung to it. She pushed the door partially closed and tried unsuccessfully to block the memories the scent evoked. "I think there's more going on there than we know, but basically I still trust the department. Their motives may not always be clear, but they're not corrupt." She stared at him defiantly, expecting opposition.

Patrick walked toward her, and for a moment they stood just inches away from each other. He touched her face in a light caress. He could almost feel the confusion and the pain Melanie carried and he wanted to help, but how could he get past her wall of reserve?

"Melanie..." He pulled her into his arms and held her tightly. "You don't have to fight me. You can trust me with anything. It's okay to tell me when you're hurting. Don't you know that?'' He tilted her head and gazed steadily into her eyes.

For a breathless second neither moved. Then slowly their mouths found each other's, seeking comfort, but still she didn't relax in his arms. The tension inside her—the apprehension that prevented her from relinquishing control—was evident even in their embrace. More than anything, he wanted to sweep away her reluctance and her resistance, to love and cherish her. But now was not the time.

Reluctantly he released her. ''One day you'll understand, Melanie. You don't have to hold back with me. Not ever.''

Patrick glanced away, needing to focus on something other than her. He walked over to the window, then to the closet where she'd just hung his father's sports coat. Something was sticking out of the inside pocket. ''What's this?''

She looked over and saw him pick out a legal-size envelope. ''I don't know. Is it anything important?''

''It's a letter from the University of Pennsylvania to Dad.'' Patrick opened the envelope and read it. ''He apparently asked for verification that Frederick Reed had received his degree there. Only their records department couldn't find his transcript.''

''That makes the elder Reed's background even more shaky. Let's ask them to look again. We'll tell them that our records indicate that he did graduate from there, and we need to rule out any possible errors due to misspelling or misfiling. By the way,'' Melanie said, ''what did you find out about Conrad Reed's mother?''

''Not much. It cost the agency a long-distance call to Grand Rapids, Michigan, but she was willing to talk to me about him. She claims that Frederick never confided in her. She remarried about a year after the divorce and became Evelyn Stamfield. Although she saw her son from time to time, when he was sent to visit in the summer, she hasn't seen Conrad since he graduated from college. Evelyn Stamfield claims she hasn't talked with Frederick in over twenty years.'' He paused, searching his memory. ''She also explained that Frederick was wonderful with their son. That was the reason she never sued for custody of Conrad."

"Well, at least that fits with what we know."

Patrick sat on the corner of her desk. "For my money, our man's still Clancy. This Reed case is nothing more than an interesting puzzle. If the police don't get anywhere with him, I'm going to tail Clancy for a few days. Maybe if I get to know the man's routine and associates, we'll be able to find out more about his whereabouts on the night Dad was killed."

"All right, but give the police a chance to do their job." She checked her watch. "I better get some of the overdue reports finished and mailed while I'm here. It's almost quitting time. What are your plans?"

He took a deep breath. "I'm going to have to rearrange the office, and get it set up for myself. There're a lot of Dad's personal belongings still in there and that makes it harder for me. Every time I come across something, I feel as if I'm uncovering another old memory."

"Do you want me to help?" she asked gently.

"No, this is something I have to do myself." His voice was taut, but steady. "If there's anything in there you want, let me know. Otherwise I'll be keeping his books and photographs, but I'm giving away the rest."

"If you change your mind and you want me to take care of that, it's all right."

"Thanks. I appreciate the thought."

Patrick walked into his office and began the task of sorting through his father's things. It was a job he'd been dreading all along. Although he'd made a space on his father's desk for himself, he'd avoided taking this final step. It seemed so conclusive, and so wrong. He'd been the one in the military, still facing dangers. His father had been semiretired. Why, then, was he still alive, while his father was not? His chest tightened. As he took a deep breath he glanced down and realized his fists were clenched. It took several minutes for him to force his body to relax again.

Hours passed by slowly. It was shortly after eight by the time Melanie peered inside. "I'm going to drive to the convenience store down the street and pick up a sandwich. Shall I bring one back for you, too?"

"No, I'm not very hungry. But if you wait another twenty minutes, I'll run the errand for you," he offered. "I'm almost through here."

"I'm just going a few blocks. I'll be back in less than ten minutes," she assured him. "And I really need something to eat."

"All right, but watch yourself."

"Always do."

Five minutes later, she pulled into the small parking lot adjacent to the all-night convenience store. She was at the cash register, paying for her purchase, when she heard a deep *thwumping* sound just outside. An instant later, the alarm in her car went off.

"Call the police," she ordered the attendant, as she dashed outside to the parking lot. Weapon in hand, she stayed next to the parked cars, using them for cover as she moved. If someone was setting her up for an ambush, they'd find her ready to fight back.

Looking around, and making sure no one was nearby, Melanie made a final dash across two empty spaces. She approached her car carefully. The center of her windshield was gone, and the vestiges that remained had shattered into a million tiny cubes. A brick lay on the seat among the glass fragments.

People came out of the restaurant and the gas station across the street and stared. She was studying the crowd when she spotted Larry Clancy. He was standing by one of the gasoline pumps, wearing gloves, apparently having just filled his pickup with gasoline. Bowing his head slightly toward her, he climbed into his truck and drove away.

The police arrived moments later. They took her statement, but without evidence, it was impossible to bring any charges against Clancy. Although the officer questioned the other people standing nearby, no one was able to help. There had been no witnesses.

Going back inside, she telephoned Patrick. He met her less than three minutes later. "Why don't you drive your car across the street to the gas station," he suggested. "The owner will probably let you keep it in one of the stalls for a small storage fee. Tomorrow we'll have the auto club come by and take it to the shop. In the meantime, I can give you a ride whenever you need it."

They were on their way to Melanie's home, when Patrick's mobile telephone rang. Patrick answered it, then handed the receiver to Melanie. "It's Mike."

Melanie recounted the events. "Clancy's the only one who could have thrown the brick, he all but announced that he did by his presence there, only I can't prove anything without witnesses," she concluded.

"I'll go have a talk with him," Mike's voice came in clearly over the receiver, "but without proof all I can do is roust him a bit, Melanie. You realize that, don't you?"

"Whatever you say, Mike," she answered curtly, and disconnected the call abruptly.

"He's not going to do anything, is he?" Patrick observed.

"Legally he can't. But I don't understand why he's giving Clancy so much latitude. Mike could have him picked up and detained, or maybe have him followed." She paused, then with a shrug added, "Of course, he may already be doing that. He wouldn't necessarily tell me," she conceded.

"Melanie, your loyalty is commendable. You're going to maintain his innocence until you prove him guilty." He smiled ruefully. "You'll have to forgive me if I'm more inclined to do the opposite at the moment."

Once they arrived at Melanie's house Patrick lingered by the door, not wanting to leave, yet hesitant to intrude.

She smiled, understanding. "Why don't you stay for a while? Try to relax. Having to constantly look over our shoulders is taking a toll on both of us."

He stepped into her living room. "It looks much better with the furniture right side up and the paintings on the walls," he teased.

"Gee, thanks!" she muttered sarcastically. She followed his gaze and realized he was staring at the painting of the Celtic warrior. "Your father gave me that last Christmas. It's supposed to be Cuchulain, one of the heroes in Irish legends. Andy knew how much I love sword-and-sorcery novels, and that this type of painting would really appeal to me."

"I recognize the painting," he commented, eyebrows furrowed. "It's like one Dad commissioned for his study at home. Only the face is different on yours. It looks familiar."

Melanie's laughter was tinged with a trace of sadness. "That's your face up there. That wily old fox, Andy, must have had plans for us." She still missed Andy, but the ache was different now. She could look back on the good times without tears. "I noticed the resemblance the first time I saw you. I didn't know he'd had it commissioned. I thought Andy had found it in a gallery, and the likeness had caught his attention."

Patrick studied the painting, a tiny smile on his face. The bare-chested hero stood, sword raised, fighting half a dozen heavily armed men who menaced him. A faint outline of a woman was etched into the misty background, which depicted a massive ivy-laden castle. He was the only protector between the men and her. Patrick's smile grew bigger as he noted the warrior's determined expression and powerful build. "It's a good likeness of me, I must admit," he teased.

She chuckled. Her eyes studied him slowly, going back and forth between him and the painting. "I'd have to see more of you to really make an accurate comparison," she goaded playfully.

Laughing, he narrowed the gap between them. "Be careful what you wish for, you just might get it."

She could feel the heat of his body as it touched her own. A primitive and elemental awareness linked them. A slight shiver ran up Melanie's spine, and she moved away. "Would you like something cold to drink?"

He laughed. "Think I might need it?"

She turned, ready to stop him with a reproving gaze. However, the moment their eyes met, she couldn't help but smile back.

Patrick followed her into the kitchen and took the cola she offered. "It was so like Dad to have a painting like that done. He always had a definite idea of what was best for those he cared about. Yet he'd invariably use the indirect approach. That way he'd take you by surprise, and you'd never know what hit you." Patrick sat on the sofa, his eyes resting on the painting.

He still grieved for his father, only now the memories came to him less often. "That was part of the problem between us, you know. We were both too strong willed to get along well. Yet I never gave up hope that someday we'd learn to be friends. I was planning to leave the Air Force in a few years and come home. I think by then we could have found the closeness we both wanted but never quite achieved." His face hardened. "His murderer robbed me of that chance."

Melanie sat beside Patrick, sharing her own memories. "I miss Andy a lot. He would drive me crazy, never quite finishing reports, and ignoring the little details that make up office business, but he was my friend.

"Even as far back as our days in the department, I always thought of him as my ally. I knew I could count on his support. Life as an officer was rough, especially on women. There were lots of unspoken rules for us. Be tough, but not macho, ambitious, but not pushy, self-reliant, but always eager for advice. It made things very difficult. The department wasn't at all what I thought it would be. I knew I'd need to find another niche for myself, a career where I could feel comfortable and useful. The agency gave me that."

"I wish you'd realize that I am also your friend, Melanie, and your ally." Patrick reached across the sofa and took her hand. "There's something very special happening between us. I know you've felt it, too."

She started to deny it, but the tenderness in his gaze stopped her.

"When you were late getting back to the office, I couldn't keep my mind on work at all. All I kept thinking about was that I should have gone with you." His words caressed her. "I was already in the car when you called." His arm, which had been draped over the back of the sofa, fell onto her shoulders. Gently he gathered her against him. "I don't want anything to happen to you, Melanie."

She allowed herself a few precious minutes in the warmth and safety of his embrace. Then, afraid her heart would betray her by enticing her to remain there, she reluctantly moved away. "I care for you, too, but it's not that simple, Patrick." She met his eyes in a plea for understanding. "I was Andy's partner, yet when he needed me the most I couldn't help him. Now you're my partner, and I intend to do everything in my power to make sure nothing happens to you. That's why I have to hold back. If I don't, my feelings for you will deepen, and then I'll become a liability to you."

She glanced away. Her heart longed to give in, but her mind refused to yield. "You need a partner who can keep her attention focused solely on this investigation. Out in the field, there's a delicate balance between covering your partner and becoming overprotective. Emotions can tip that scale. I could become so intent on looking out for you that I fail to notice danger coming from another direction entirely."

"You shared a successful partnership with my father for years. Dad was willing to work with you despite the personal friendship that existed between you. And he was a smart cop," he countered in a soft voice.

She shook her head. "You don't understand. When your dad and I were both in the police department we were business associates only. It's true, Andy became like family to me, but that only happened after we were both off the force. Working for the agency isn't usually hazardous at all. We

were more relaxed there and that's why we became so close."
She paused, and tried to choose her words carefully. "But
now, it has become dangerous work. You and I are investigating something that could cost us our lives. We can't afford to get involved."

He gathered her hand, and pressed her palm to his lips.
"It's too late, Melanie. Like it or not, the feelings between
us exist. Denying that they're there won't make them go
away."

He slipped his hand beneath the cascade of long black
hair that covered her shoulders. Wordlessly, his eyes never
leaving hers, he traced feathery patterns, teasing the sensitive skin of her shoulders through her blouse.

She knew this was not a battle she wanted to win.

Patrick held her against him. "I feel your heart against
mine," he whispered. "Don't tell me you don't want me,
Melanie, because neither of us believe that." His mouth
claimed hers. His kiss lured her into a swirling maelstrom of
desire that threatened to overcome them both.

The sudden, deafening crack of gunfire, accompanied by
shattering glass, sent them sprawling to the floor, still locked
in each other's arms.

Chapter Eleven

Patrick tried to shield her but she rolled away. "Don't hold me down. I've got to get my gun!"

Already armed, Patrick slipped the safety catch off his Beretta. "I've got mine, just stay down!" Another bullet whizzed right over their heads, imbedding itself in the plaster, and sending little chunks spraying over them. Patrick pulled the lamp cord out of the socket, throwing the room into moonlit darkness.

"I'll get to the phone," she said firmly, crawling across the carpet slowly. She pulled the telephone to her by the cord, remaining close to the floor. The call took only a few seconds, but the shooting had stopped as abruptly as it had begun. Four bullet holes, visible against the white paint, showed as telltale signs on the wall above her sofa. She peered over the lower edge of the windowsill carefully, making sure her head wasn't being silhouetted against the wall behind her. Broken glass was everywhere.

Patrick stood with his back flattened against the wall, and peered around the edge of the curtains. "Do you see him? He must have been shooting from the house across the street."

"There's someone still there, by the side door, but I can't see his face." She strained forward. "There he goes, between the buildings!" In the moonlight, she was only able to catch a glimpse of the person as he darted from shadow to shadow. "Patrick, I think he was wearing the same type of hat the person tailing us wore."

As the man disappeared over a wall, two cars came screeching up, one a police car with flashing lights, the other a shiny new Porsche.

Placing his hand gun back in the shoulder holster, Patrick left his position of cover and went to Melanie's side. "Are you okay?"

Melanie nodded, then glanced back outside. "Who's got that sports car? It can't be a cop! A Porsche like that would cost a year's salary."

"Let's go see." Patrick and Melanie met the team of officers out in the street. Mike stood by the shiny sports car, keys still dangling in his hand.

"Nice car," Patrick commented, joining him.

"Yea, she's a real beaut, isn't she?" Mike glanced at Melanie, then back at Patrick. "If you guys are okay, why don't you go back inside? I'll go upstairs in just a minute. I want to get my car out of the middle of the street."

MELANIE WATCHED the lab team carefully extract the bullets from the plaster, then place them in evidence pouches. Her mind was still spinning, and she noticed her hands were shaking. She didn't know if it was because of fear or excitement. So much had happened tonight!

"The police sure got here quickly," Melanie commented. "You did, too, Mike."

"Actually I was out taking my new car for a spin when I saw Sergeant MacKenzie. We were talking when the call came in, so I decided to follow him here."

As one of the laboratory people went past them, Mike reached out and stopped him. "Anything interesting about the bullets?"

The man shook his head. "Nine-millimeter rounds, full metal jacketed military issue. That's all I can tell you, Inspector."

Patrick made himself comfortable on one of Melanie's upholstered chairs. "Anything new on Clancy, or Cartolucci?" he asked pointedly.

Mike glared at him. "I'm leaning hard on Clancy for the stunt he pulled with Melanie's car. I think he's feeling cocky, but that's going to work to our advantage." He lowered his voice. "Off-the-record, both the captain and I believe that Cartolucci's the key. We're hoping Clancy will get overconfident and lead us to him. If we get a break on the case, I'll let you know right away." He met Patrick's stony gaze with one of his own. "Don't lose faith in us, Patrick. It's too early in the game to predict the outcome."

Two hours later the police left. The empty duplex across the street, a rental, had been scoured for evidence. So far, the only thing they knew for sure was that the sniper had broken in with a pry bar and used the second-floor window that overlooked Melanie's living room. Four nine-millimeter shell casings had been recovered. The apartment had just been repainted and the police were hoping to lift some fresh fingerprints that would be usable.

"We're busy spinning our wheels on this case, but we aren't getting anywhere with it," Patrick muttered, his hands clenched into tight fists.

He stared at the holes left by each striking round. "I'll stay here with you tonight," he offered.

"No way," she countered quickly. "The trouble's over, and you're going home. I'll just close the shutters tonight, and have the landlord worry about replacing the broken glass tomorrow. We have to at least try to get some rest," she said softly. Melanie's gaze drifted gently over Patrick as she followed him to the door. At no time had she ever felt more alive than when she'd been in his arms. She wished she could accept his offer. With effort, she banished those thoughts. They had to keep their thinking focused on survival. Everything depended on their ability to stay alert to danger.

THE FOLLOWING MORNING Melanie arrived at the office ninety minutes late. Patrick's easy smile greeted her. "I was going to call and offer you a ride," he said, "but I figured that you might try to catch some extra sleep this morning. Looks like I was right."

"I wish I had been able to," she said in a weary tone. "I got up early and went to rent a car. Then I transferred my mobile telephone over to my rental. After that, I drove to the department to pay Mike a visit. I wanted to speak to him about the Cartolucci angle. I thought I'd try to get him to talk to me off-the-record."

"Did he?"

She hesitated. "I know they're working on the case, Patrick, but they're being really cagey about the whole thing. Maybe there's an undercover operation going on. I know cops, and whenever they're involved in something sensitive, they prefer to keep things on a need-to-know basis."

Patrick gave her a long, speculative look. He had a gut feeling there was something she wasn't telling him. "Remember that the police may not necessarily be on our side in this, Melanie. The only way we can build a safety margin for ourselves is if we rely on each other more than we do on anyone else."

He still didn't realize that her loyalty to the department would never supersede her loyalty to Andy. And Andy had made Patrick her partner. She would never do anything to betray that charge. "I do rely on you as my partner, Patrick," she reassured him, "but we can't shut ourselves off from the police. It's impossible for us to handle this completely on our own. Eventually, the department will tell us what they've been doing. I guarantee it. Then we'll be able to judge them, but not before."

Meanwhile, she wasn't telling Patrick that Mike had been responsible for letting Clancy go, or that she had her doubts about him. It was bound to create more problems if he knew. Before she shared that piece of information with him, she wanted to look into a few things herself. And since Patrick was already wary of Mike, she wasn't putting him in danger by not saying anything for now.

"I'm going to have to stop by the lawyer's office this morning," Patrick said. "There are some papers he wants me to sign. Why don't you come with me?"

She shook her head. "I can't. There's too much I have to do here at the office. Go on." She smiled reassuringly. "I'll be fine."

"I shouldn't be gone long," he said, as he headed toward the door. "Keep the office door locked."

She gave him a snappy salute. "Yes, sir!"

Actually she was glad to have him away from the office. Ever since she'd seen Mike's new sports car, her mind had been in a turmoil. Could Mike have been on the take after all? She had a difficult time believing that from a man both Andy and she had known for so many years. Nevertheless she had to check it out.

An hour later, she heard footsteps in the hallway. The sound stopped just outside the door, but no knock was forthcoming. Instead she saw the knob being turned. She reached for her purse, and placed it on her lap, open to the compartment holding her revolver.

"It's me," Patrick said, inserting his key in the lock and coming inside. "I forgot about keeping the door locked. Anything happen while I was gone?"

"Not really," she answered, her voice a little shaky. "In fact I haven't even moved from my desk." She pulled a pen from her purse, although she already had one in front of her, and set the purse back down.

Patrick walked around her desk and stood behind her. Looking over her shoulder, he noticed the file she'd started on Mike. "What's that all about?"

"I'm doing a background check on Mike Cooper." She swiveled her chair around and looked directly at him as she recounted the details behind Clancy's release. "It wasn't really conclusive evidence one way or another, since there were possible explanations, but it did start me wondering. Then when I saw his new sports car, I knew it was time to take a closer look. I want to find out how he got the money to buy that Porsche.

"Patrick, cops don't make that kind of income, not legally. Of course, it's possible he's been saving for years, or maybe he's inherited some money recently. Since all the dealings we have with the department concerning this case go through him, we have to make sure he's clean."

Patrick rubbed the back of his neck with one hand. "Are you sure you're ready to face whatever you find out? What are you going to do if you discover he's on the take?"

"I'll turn him in," she answered immediately. "Did you expect anything else?" she asked, surprised. She gave him a long, pensive look. "Patrick, there's loyalty between friends, but loyalty to honor and principle supersedes that."

"I thought as much, but I needed to hear you say it," Patrick admitted. "You know, since Dad used to be a cop, it's a natural for me to think of them as the good guys. The problem is that it only takes a few bad cops in positions of authority to affect the performance of the whole department. My biggest fear is that the police will only make a halfhearted investigation into the Cartolucci allegations. Then, once that's done, they'll whitewash the entire incident."

"It's possible that there are a few crooked cops in supervisory positions, but there're going to be a lot more who aren't. They'll make sure that never happens."

He started to go back to his office, then stopped in midstride and turned around. "Melanie, I owe you an apology. I was really afraid that you were hiding facts about the Cartolucci file out of loyalty to friends in the department. I realize now that you'd never do that."

A warm feeling spread over her. She even forgot to be angry with him for doubting her integrity. A new understanding had been forged between them; the same kind of trust that had existed between Andy and her. "You know what?" she said. "Now we're really partners."

He smiled back. "Yes, and it's about time."

"Amen to that," she chuckled softly. "By the way, partner, how about going downstairs to the box and getting our mail." She waved a hand at all the paperwork scattered over the top of her desk. "I need to put some of this away, before I start an avalanche."

"You got it," he said agreeably, and returned a few minutes later. "There's an envelope in here from the University of Pennsylvania. It's so thick I think they've included a transcript, too."

Melanie handed him a letter opener, and watched him as he extracted a photocopied document. "So, Frederick Reed really did attend the university there. What does the cover letter say?" she asked.

"The university apologizes for not finding the document before," Patrick answered. "Their old records, prior to the use of microfilm or computers, are stored in boxes and kept in the basement. They've sent us a copy of the original paperwork." Patrick glanced at it, then handed it to her. "It even has a photograph of Frederick Reed."

Melanie looked through the academic records quickly. Then her attention became riveted on the photograph at the upper right-hand corner. She stared at it for quite some time. "I've seen this photograph before. It was at Conrad Reed's house the time I went over to talk to him. I recognize it from the scratch on the print that made Frederick's face look scarred. Only when I saw it, it showed Frederick with his son and daughter-in-law. This is an enlargement of Frederick's upper body with the other family members cropped out of the picture. This photo doesn't match the time sequence at all, Patrick. Frederick couldn't have had a family back then, so this transcript has to be a phony."

"But that throws suspicion on his entire background."

"Frederick is dead. Why would anyone falsify these papers?"

Patrick mulled it over for a minute. "To cover a hole in Frederick Reed's background," Patrick proposed. He straddled the chair nearest Melanie's desk, and folded his arms over the backrest. "Only that opens up a string of other questions. For instance, could any of this be connected to Dad's murder? If so, how?''

Melanie pulled Conrad Reed's file from the cabinet. ''According to the police report and the funeral home's records, Frederick Reed was cremated the day *before* Andy died so I don't see how it could be connected.''

''Let's go pay Conrad another visit,'' Patrick suggested. ''We can offer to give him a copy of the background report our agency compiled on him. Let him think we didn't follow through on checking his dad's background. We'll tell him that our client no longer has any need for the report, and we thought he might like a copy. Then, while we're there, we can check that photo you saw, and verify that it's the same one.''

''Let's not call, though, let's just drop in. If he's not there, we'll wait. I don't want to take a chance on him telling us to mail it, or make an excuse.''

Patrick locked up the office, taking his usual precautions, and accompanied Melanie to his car. They were both alert for signs of the person who'd followed them before, and for Clancy.

''We're okay,'' Patrick said, as they started off.

''I just had an idea. I'm going to try to get a new sample of Conrad's signature. We'll compare it to the registrar's on the bottom of his father's University of Pennsylvania transcript and see if they match. He might have forged this himself for some reason. I have the transcript with me.''

''It's worth a try. We can have him sign for receipt of the partial background report.''

Half an hour later, they arrived at Conrad Reed's home. A young, tired-looking brunette answered the door, introduced herself as Anna Reed, and then showed them into the living room. Conrad, clearly surprised, stood and came toward them. ''What can I do for you?'' he asked.

''I hope we're not intruding, Mr. Reed. We wanted to give you a copy of the background report our firm had started. It contains all the information we'd compiled to date. Since our client no longer has any use for it, we thought you might like to have the file."

He took the manila envelope Patrick handed him, and opened it, studying its contents. "I appreciate it, but you didn't have to go through the trouble of stopping by personally."

"We didn't feel right putting it in the mail. Information like this is strictly confidential." Melanie held out a small pad. "Would you mind signing this receipt? It's just acknowledgement for our files, that we gave you a copy."

Conrad glanced at the purse-size notebook. A few sentences had been written on the top stating that the file had been delivered to his address, then below it was the date and a place for his signature. He took it from her hand and read over her written statement very carefully. Finally he reached for her pen and signed it. "Is that all?" he asked uncertainly.

"I'm sorry if we've disturbed you, Mr. Reed," Melanie said.

"No problem, but I'd like to get back to my family now."

As soon as they were back outside, Patrick gave Melanie a puzzled look. "I never saw the photograph you were talking about."

"It wasn't there. It used to be on the mantel. I looked around the room, but I couldn't see it anywhere," she answered.

"Check out those signatures as soon as we get going," Patrick urged. "Did you notice how carefully he read over the receipt before signing? I don't think he trusts you, pretty lady."

Melanie laughed. "I seem to affect people that way sometimes."

"That's only until they get to know you." His eyes sparkled with mischief. "Then they find they're *really* in trouble."

ALBERT SMITH WATCHED from the kitchen window as his son-in-law's visitors departed. A moment later, Conrad came back into the room.

He placed the file folder they'd given him on the kitchen table. "Looks like they're finally going to let me have some peace."

"I doubt it. I don't trust people like them," Albert said slowly. "I overheard your conversation in the living room. I get the feeling they're playing a war of nerves. They're searching for something to discredit you with. Your character and life-style are above reproach. They have no right to treat you that way."

Conrad looked at the old man fondly. Albert's blond hair had lightened to white with age, but the sharp blue eyes shone with intelligence and alertness. "Well, it's finished now."

Albert shook his head. "They're too eager, too curious. Watch out for them. Any damage to your reputation can harm your ability to make a living, and the family depends on you."

"I haven't done anything wrong, Albert. They can't hurt me."

"I know people," Albert said slowly, "especially this sort. To themselves, they're the good guys. Unfortunately they usually spell trouble for everyone around them. In their zeal to do their jobs, they become a threat not only to the guilty, but to the innocent as well." His voice took on a faraway quality. "You have the right to protect yourself and your family, Conrad. Nothing supersedes your duty to those you love."

"No one's trying to harm me or mine, Albert. It's all right, really," he assured in a soft voice.

Albert poured himself a second cup of coffee. The problem with Conrad was that he was afflicted with the confidence and trust of youth. There was much life would have to teach him yet.

MELANIE SAT ON THE SOFA, which faced Patrick's desk. "My contact at the state police took a look at our two samples of Conrad's writing. In his opinion it's highly unlikely that Conrad could have signed the transcript. Conrad would have had to alter his natural style drastically and the registrar's signature showed no evidence of that. It was either an expert forgery, or the genuine thing. The letters were smooth and the writing fluid."

Patrick loosened the knot of his tie and placed his jacket on the hook behind his door. "While you were over there checking that out, I got in touch with the O.S.I. Through my contacts there, I've managed to get a hold of an agent at the CIA who has promised to check Frederick Reed's photograph against their records. I've messengered a duplicate of the photo over to him."

"Good thinking," she answered. "The evidence we've turned up on Conrad Reed's signature is inconclusive," Melanie continued thoughtfully. "But the fact that he didn't sign that transcript doesn't mean he didn't have someone else do it for him. On my way back here I came up with another idea. We know that the transcript from the University of Pennsylvania is a forgery because of the photo attached. Why don't we ask for his employment record from the University of Washington and request that a complete set of credentials for him be sent along, too. Let's see how that matches up with what we have. It'll be interesting to see what educational accreditation he presented to get his job there."

"Yes, you're right," he agreed. "We'll send for it right away using Conrad Reed's authoriziation for a background check, same as before."

Almost two hours later, Patrick came out of his office. "I'm starving. It's almost eight o'clock. How about going out to dinner with me?"

"I can't. I have to get the books ready for the accountant," Melanie explained. "I've been putting it off too much as it is." She leaned back in her chair and rubbed her eyes. "I'm hungry, too, though. After you're finished eating would you mind picking up a sandwich somewhere for me?" She paused. "On second thought maybe that's not such a good idea. Last time I tried to pick up a fast dinner, Clancy was waiting."

"Don't worry about it. Clancy's the type who's more likely to pick on you than he is on me," Patrick answered.

"I don't think so," she replied. "When he smashed my windshield, he did it while I was inside the store. He's a coward, basically. He won't confront anyone head-on, if he can help it. He much prefers the 'hit and run' approach."

"Humor me on this, then. Let's just say that if he's going to try anything, I'm hoping he'll try it with me," he answered flatly.

She chuckled. "*That* I understand. Promise me that you'll go someplace crowded?"

He smiled. "Okay. Now what do you want me to bring you?"

She mulled it over. "Get me a double-decker hamburger, fries and a large chocolate milk shake."

"Such a balanced meal!" he teased. "Anything else?"

She thought it over. "A fruit pie, or some sort of junk-food dessert."

"You know, that sounds good to me, too. Besides, eating at my desk isn't such a bad idea. I've got a lot of work piled up there." Patrick grabbed his coat, and readjusted his holster. It certainly wouldn't do for someone at the local hamburger joint to see him packing a fifteen-shot Beretta. Things like that had a tendency to make people nervous. "I'll be back in a few minutes."

With one last look at Melanie, he closed the door. He hesitated, listening for the sound of the lock latching automatically, then started down the hall. Sitting behind her desk with her legs tucked up under her, she'd looked like a kitten, curled up and comfortable. How he wanted to hold her, to lose himself in her.

His feelings for her filled him with a sense of wonder. In the midst of one of life's saddest of endings, something new and wonderful had started to blossom. His father's death had taken something precious away from both of them, yet a new beginning was springing up from the ashes.

The thought comforted him. Patrick walked to his car, glanced around quickly, then unlocked the door. Switching on his headlights in the gathering twilight, he slowly began to back out of the parking space. That's when he saw a round object tumbling toward his car as if attached to it somehow. He hit the brakes and leaned forward, trying to make out what it was. A hand grenade rolled toward him on the asphalt pavement and then disappeared beneath his car.

Chapter Twelve

Patrick scrambled out of the car, took a few running steps and dived behind the nearest concrete planter. He flattened his body against the pavement and waited for the blast, but none came.

Seconds ticked by slowly, yet nothing happened. With wary reluctance, he finally lifted his body away from the ground.

He watched his car from over the edge of the planter. Had the grenade been a dud? His stomach was as tight as a knot. He was cold, but it was that peculiar type of cold that emanated from somewhere deep inside of him.

Patrick approached his car slowly, and realized he'd left the engine running. In the glare of the headlights he could now see the grenade clearly, just between the front tires. It hadn't been a dud. It was only a child's toy made of plastic, obviously someone's sick idea of a joke. It was attached to a thin string, and taped to his right front tire.

Anger and shock mingled into something ugly that welled up inside him, and threatened to burst through the civilized exterior.

That's when he heard the honk of a car horn. He glanced around and saw Larry Clancy's laughing face.

Like a shot, Patrick ran toward Clancy's pickup. There were no thoughts in his mind, only a pulsing need for retribution.

As the pickup sped off around the corner, Patrick was forced to stop. His chest heaved as he gulped for air. What in the world was he doing? What had he expected to do with Clancy had he managed to catch him? Before today, he'd never lost control. He'd never faced that dark side of himself, and now he wasn't at all certain what to do with what he'd discovered.

Patrick slowly walked back to the office. The moment he came in, he saw the shocked look on Melanie's face.

Melanie heard his story, then called the police. It seemed like hours before their questioning was finally completed and an officer had taken away the evidence.

"It doesn't look good for prints, Patrick," Melanie told him dejectedly. "I heard one of the officers talking, and the segmented surface of that toy grenade makes fingerprinting difficult. Besides, Clancy was probably wearing gloves."

"Did you expect anything else?" he snapped. He forced himself to relax, willing the knots out of his body. "I'm sorry. Why don't you go home? It's late and it's been a long day."

"What are you going to do?"

"I'm going to take a walk. I need time to think." He met her eyes, a shadow of despair and sadness clouding the spark usually there. "Melanie, I don't know what would have happened had I caught Clancy tonight. I was so angry I actually wanted to kill him with my bare hands."

"You would have got yourself into one mean fight," she replied honestly. She picked up her eyes. "Come on. Clancy's not going to try anything else tonight. Let's go for that walk together."

"No, I can't let you do that. It might be dangerous."

"We couldn't avoid being in danger even if we wanted to," she argued logically. "Let's take that walk anyway. We both need it. Besides, if there is going to be trouble, two can meet it better than one."

They left out the back door, and mingled with the shadows of night. A veil of darkness protected them as they strolled down streets, paying no attention to which direction they chose.

"Patrick, I understand why the anger you felt scares you, but that fear is your safety valve, don't you see? You wouldn't have tried to kill Clancy." She smiled wryly. "You might have broken a few bones, and put him and yourself in the hospital for a while, but you wouldn't have killed him."

"You're wrong. All I could think of was how Dad had died, and the fact that when I thought my turn had come it was only a practical joke. I felt guilty because I was alive and Dad was dead. Then when I saw Clancy laughing, something inside me just snapped." His body shook. "It's my job to be professional, not to let emotions temper my judgments. I never thought I was capable of losing control like that."

"We all are, Patrick. We're only human. The down side of our nature is always capable of a great deal of violence, but it's the other side, the good that's in us, that keeps that in check. Whenever we come up against a situation where the balance is tested, it's always frightening. However, you always learn something about yourself from it. And remember, learning doesn't consist only of knowing what you can do, but also of knowing what you could do and should not do."

"I've just told you the worst of myself, and you don't think any less of me for it." His eyes met hers. "You amaze me sometimes, Melanie."

"All you told me tonight is that you're a human being, just like the rest of us."

They walked and though they said little, they both took comfort in the undemanding companionship they offered each other.

By the time they returned to the office parking lot, it was almost midnight. "You never did get your dinner. Let me take you out to get something to eat," he said sympathetically.

"All I want is a nice warm bed to crawl into," she replied wearily. "I think I've truly earned the title 'flatfoot' tonight," she added wriggling her toes in her shoes.

Patrick smiled at her, then brushed his palm against her face in a light caress. "I could arrange for that nice warm bed," he said slowly.

A delicious weakness seeped through Melanie and her pulse leaped to life. "It's a very tempting offer," she admitted. "But neither of us would get much rest," she added, trying to stop the images his invitation evoked.

He could see the desire in her eyes and knew that it matched his own. "Melanie..."

She shook her head and stepped back, putting more distance between them. "Don't, please. It's difficult enough."

"All right. I won't pressure you, but it will happen between us, sweetheart." His voice, filled with sensual promise, electrified her senses. "And by the way, thanks for the company tonight. it meant more to me than you know."

"That's what friends are for," she answered, walking with him to her car.

As she drove away, a peculiar restlessness gripped her. Vivid pictures of the night they might have shared came unbidden to her mind and stayed there. She rolled down the window and allowed the cool air from the bay to fill her car—but the fiery warmth that coursed through her continued unabated.

She smiled ruefully and sighed. She expected neither of them would rest easy tonight.

FOUR DAYS PASSED. Her background check on Mike Cooper was getting nowhere and, worst of all, she was starting to feel guilty for ever having doubted her friend.

"Patrick, this is a very difficult situation. If I keep looking into Mike's financial records, and his background, he's bound to find out what I've been doing. So far I haven't been able to discover anything even remotely suspicious about him, and when he hears what I've been doing, I can guarantee that all hell is going to break loose."

"What about the car?"

"It's possible that by pooling his income with his wife's he could be making payments on something like that. He really doesn't have very many debts. However, I do know he didn't purchase it by taking out a loan from his bank. Also, he hasn't made any substantial withdrawals that could account for a down payment. Of course, he could have alternate financing. Still, I'd be willing to bet he's paying quite a hefty sum each month, enough to stretch his budget to the limit."

"I say we should keep investigating and risk the consequences," Patrick replied staunchly.

She was about to answer when the mail carrier came to their door. "I have a special overnight package for Ms. Melanie Cardenas."

Melanie signed for it. "It's from the University of Washington. Let's see what we have in here." Melanie brought out an evaluation form the university had inserted along with Frederick Reed's teaching credentials. "He was an assistant professor, and very competent, according to this. Now let's take a look at the rest of what they sent." She pulled out the next set of papers. "They've included their copy of his University of Pennsylvania transcript!" she added excitedly.

"Does it match the one we already have?" Patrick asked.

Melanie extracted the other transcript from the files and placed them side by side. Her heart skipped a beat. "Except for the formats and dates, these supposedly identical transcripts aren't alike at all. One or perhaps both of these are forgeries. There's a photo attached to the one we just got, too." She handed the transcript to Patrick. "It's the same man, only younger."

"It's Frederick Reed, all right," Patrick conceded. "And the transcripts aren't the same? What in the heck have we found here?"

"My contact at the state police works primarily with forged signatures and fake ID's. But documents are out of his area of expertise. I do know someone else, however, at the FBI. Andy and I both used him on occasion."

"Let's give him a try. The CIA hasn't been able to find anything yet."

It took them almost thirty minutes to drive over, then walk from the parking garage near the Civic Center to the Federal Building. After a few minutes wait, a short but athletic-looking man in a light blue suit joined them.

Melanie introduced Patrick to Agent John McDaniels.

"I was sorry to hear about Andy," McDaniels said, shaking hands with Patrick. "He'll be missed."

Patrick nodded in acknowledgement. "Thank you."

McDaniels led them to his office. He trained his laser-sharp gaze, first on Melanie, then Patrick. "So what can I do for you?"

Melanie pulled out both transcripts. "I have two photocopied documents I'd like you to take a look at. I believe that this first transcript from the University of Pennsylvania is a forgery. The photograph on the corner is not legitimate. The time frame is wrong. I'm not sure about this other one, though, which is also supposed to be from the University of Pennsylvania, for the same person. I got this version from the University of Washington's records. Would you be willing to check out both of these for style and perhaps content, and tell me anything you can about the forgery or the forger. Also, I need to know if either is genuine."

He glanced down at the documents. "I don't understand. You want me to do this again?"

"Again?" Melanie gave him a puzzled look.

"Andy brought me the photo and a copy of the University of Washington's version of that transcript less than a month ago. We couldn't tell much from a photocopy, but I ran the photograph for him through our records. That's when we discovered that the man in the photo was Bernard Cain. He'd worked briefly at a secret atomic research facility in Oak Ridge, Tennessee, during late 1944, then just disappeared. Andy spoke to one of his police contacts in Seattle, and he managed to get me the last page of the original transcript. I was able to check out the water marks, the inks, paper and the signatures then. I thought there was something odd about them, so with Andy's permission, I sent them to an expert on old forged documents at the Imperial War Museum in England. He told me that the forgery was foreign in technique and materials.''

Melanie stared at McDaniels. ''This case is getting more peculiar by the minute.''

''Andy was really excited about the Oak Ridge and Washington connection,'' McDaniels continued. ''Not too far east of Seattle, where the University of Washington is located, is the Hanover Project Atomic Development Center in Richland.''

Patrick paced restlessly. ''That means that our man must either be or have posed as Bernard Cain while working at the Oak Ridge facility. He'd then moved to Washington state, dropped his Bernard Cain identity and emerged as Frederick Reed.''

''But what about the transcript and his credentials?''

''Andy had concluded that in order to establish credentials, Reed must have intercepted the University of Washington's original transcript request. Later he'd left his own forged transcript in their personnel department's incoming mail, making it look like it came from the University of Pennsylvania.''

Patrick ventured pensively. ''Only Frederick Reed is deceased. So what does this have to do with anything now?''

McDaniels shrugged. ''Nothing. As far as the bureau is concerned this is ancient history.''

Melanie stood and shook McDaniels's hand. ''Thanks for everything. You've really helped us out.''

''If my contact at the Imperial War Museum finds out anything more he'll let you know directly.'' He walked them to the door. ''And Melanie, once this is over, you owe me lunch. I'll be curious to know where it all leads.''

''You've got it,'' she assured him.

Patrick and Melanie walked slowly out to the car, each lost in their own thoughts. Patrick finally broke the silence between them. "I've got a theory. What if Frederick Reed was a spy sent here to learn about the development of the atomic bomb and Conrad knew about it? When he saw that Dad was going to uncover skeletons in his closet, he decided to decline the job. But that didn't stop Dad, who was already intrigued by the puzzle. Conrad then murdered my father, and tried to cover his tracks. The University of Pennsylvania's phony transcript was a recent attempt to cover for a student who never went there at all."

"Conrad's alibi for the day Andy was killed is not iron-clad," Melanie conceded. "He'd been at home alone with his daughter while his wife was at work. But by the same token, I don't think Conrad has enough of a motive to murder Andy," she countered. "Conrad is a citizen. His mother was also a citizen. Even if his father had been a spy, the worst that could happen to Conrad is that he'd be ineligible for positions requiring security clearances."

"Good point," Patrick agreed as he headed back to their office.

"You know, there's another angle we haven't considered," Melanie added after a moment. "We know there were Russian spies in the United States trying to steal atomic secrets during that era. Remember the Los Alamos spy ring that was exposed in 1949? The Rosenbergs were executed as spies then. If Frederick was a spy, perhaps his contacts are still alive and in hiding. It's possible they may be involved and could be watching his family and acting without Conrad's knowledge. That would also account for the person who's followed us, if we discount the possibility it might have been Clancy or someone linked to Cartolucci."

"The whole picture is still very unclear. I admit that during wartime if a spy was caught it meant almost certain death, a prospect he'd most assuredly want to avoid. And, during the height of the Cold War there was an anticommunist furor in this country that would have made a spy's fate uncertain. Nowadays, the most that could happen to a spy is that he'd be sent to prison or, more probably deported." He slowed the car to allow another vehicle to pass.

"Unless—" his body stiffened slightly, another possibility dawning on him "—that person was hiding other crimes as well. If that's the case it becomes a different matter entirely."

"Maybe one of Frederick Reed's accomplices murdered Andy to hide a trail of evidence that might have led back to himself. It's conceivable that one of those spies reached a position of power he's determined to hold on to." Melanie bit at the inside of her lip pensively.

Patrick exhaled loudly. "I think we're reaching, and building a house of cards out of a bunch of speculation. After that stunt Clancy pulled with the toy grenade, I tend to believe he's the one responsible. Worst of all, he's flaunting it in our faces." His fingers clenched the steering wheel so tightly, his knuckles went white. "I've been wanting to do something about that, and I think it's time I made my move. I'll drop you off at the office, then I'm going to rent a car, something that doesn't attract any attention at all, and follow him. Let's see where he takes me."

"No way you're dropping me off at the office. Clancy's threatened both of us, so we're handling him together. He's dangerous, Patrick, and if there's ever a time when we should stick together, it's when we're dealing with him."

Patrick glanced at her, noting the determination in her face. "You're not going to take no for an answer, are you?"

"That's right," she replied good-naturedly. "Accept it and let's get down to details. A few blocks north of here is a car rental agency. Let's go find what we need."

An hour later, they parked half a block up from Clancy's apartment. They could see his beat-up pickup parked on the street. "This might be a long afternoon. There's no telling when he'll come out of the building. Sit back and relax," Patrick suggested. "I'll keep the first watch, then you can take over."

Melanie leaned back in her seat. "I always hated surveillance jobs."

She glanced out the side window, staring at a bird who was hopping away, worm in its beak. "At least he gets something to show for his efforts," she mumbled.

"We just got lucky, too. Here comes Clancy now," Patrick said, sitting up and switching on the ignition. Tension made his muscles taut. He wasn't psychic, but he had a feeling that today they'd finally find some answers.

Patrick followed at a discreet distance behind Clancy's pickup. Tailing a suspect through downtown streets took a great deal of skill. The inexperienced usually tried to get too close, and thus revealed their position.

Sometimes, it seemed to Melanie that they were about to lose Clancy, but Patrick always managed to stay with him. "You're doing very well at this. I'm impressed."

"You should be," he teased. "I make one heck of a partner, in every sense of the word."

She choked. "This is no time to get sidetracked."

Patrick was about to respond when he spotted Clancy entering an underground parking area beneath a bank building. "I want to know what he's doing in there, but I'm going to follow him on foot," Patrick said. "If I drive through, he'll make us for sure. Stay with the car and keep the motor running. If he's just trying to be certain he's not being followed, I want him to think he's safe."

"Patrick, if he spots you, there could be trouble."

"I have no intention of letting him even see me," he answered flatly. "Stay here and keep the motor running. I'll be right back."

Patrick was almost at the entrance of the parking area when a Mercedes Benz whizzed past him. He stepped back instinctively. Patrick only managed to catch a glimpse of the driver's face, but the discovery took him by complete surprise. Gathering his wits, he ran back to the car. Melanie was behind the wheel.

"Clancy's driving that blue Mercedes. Get going."

"What?" She pulled out into traffic. "Patrick, get real. Clancy wouldn't have left his own car back at the garage and pulled out in a Mercedes. That doesn't make any sense!"

"That's what took me by surprise!" he snapped. "I almost blew it."

Both cars weaved through traffic, Melanie keeping hers a discreet distance behind the Mercedes. "I wish I knew what the heck we've stumbled on to."

"Stay with him, he's about to turn," Patrick warned.

"Great. Another underground parking area. What now?" Melanie pulled off to the side, and waited.

"Stay here. Same procedure. I'm going to find out what he's doing in there." He unfastened his seat belt and was about to leave the car when Melanie spotted Clancy walking out of the garage.

"What do you think's going on?" Melanie asked in confusion.

"I don't know, but he's walking fast. Stay with the car. I'll follow Clancy." He dashed off before she could reply.

"No way, partner," Melanie muttered, switching off the ignition. "I'm coming with you." She caught up to him moments later.

"I told you to stay in the car," he whispered. "Why don't you ever do what I say?"

"It sets a bad precedent," she answered, nonplussed. "Now where is Clancy?" She glanced around. "Don't tell me you lost him."

"I did *not* lose him," he shot back, annoyed. "He went through the side door of that large warehouse. He's still inside."

"Let's go take a closer look. Maybe we can peek through a window, or eavesdrop," Melanie started forward.

"No, don't." He cursed softly under his breath as she moved away. "At least wait for me, will you?"

Melanie crept up to the door and listened for a moment. "I can't hear anything. Maybe we can slip inside," she suggested.

"No, Melanie, it's too..." Before he could finish the sentence, she'd already tried the door handle.

"It's locked," she said in a whisper. "Let's try the windows." She headed for the alley.

Taking two quick strides, he grabbed Melanie by the shoulders and stopped her. "Let me do this. There's no telling what's inside that building."

"Exactly. Since I'm smaller, it's harder to spot me than it is you. Now stop trying to order me around. We're working this case as partners, remember that." Melanie led the way down the alleyway beside the warehouse. She studied the high windows, searching for a way to gain entry. "Those iron grates make getting inside almost impossible without creating lots of noise. There's something funny about the windows, too, only the way the sun's shining right now, I can't tell exactly what it is."

"They're painted over," Patrick said after a pause. "Even if you shimmied up there, you wouldn't be able to peer inside."

"We need a new plan. Fast." Frustration tore at her, but she forced herself to appear composed. "We can't just go back to the car and forget the whole thing."

"There's nothing else we can do," he answered, keeping his voice low. "All we know for sure is that Clancy parked his pickup and drove a second car here. That's it. I don't know about you, but I'm not about to go to Captain Mathers with this hot tip," he said sarcastically. "When we have something solid, then I'll turn over the information."

"We could find out if that Mercedes has been reported stolen," Melanie countered. "We could call Mike, tell him what we've found, and ask him for his help."

He grasped her arm firmly but gently and urged her back toward the car. "Wonderful idea," he replied sourly, "particularly since he's been so terrific at finding answers so far."

She jerked free and entered the car, restraining herself from slamming the door behind her. "Fine, what do *you* propose we do?"

"We stake out Clancy for a few more days. Let's see what sort of habits he has. Maybe we can get more evidence. Then we can take it to the police." The anger he'd felt earlier about his father's murder was now being replaced by a cool patience he hoped would be far more deadly.

"Even if we can tie him to something illegal, Patrick, that won't necessarily connect him to Andy's murder," she replied coldly. "We've got to get the police involved in this as soon as possible. If we get the department to look into Clancy's activities involving those cars while the trail's still warm, maybe they'll uncover crimes that provide a motive for killing your father. Since they're investigating Clancy and Cartolucci both, they might find a common thread we don't know anything about."

Patrick picked up the mobile telephone and dialed a number.

"Who are you calling?"

"Mike," he said. "You win. We'll set up a meet. I don't want to run into Mathers. I'm in a bad enough mood already."

Fifteen minutes later they met Mike Cooper at the coffee shop near their office. Melanie sat between the men. She recounted what had happened with Clancy, then looked at Patrick for confirmation. "I think that's about it. Have I missed anything?"

Patrick shook his head. "The question is," he challenged, "what have the police got on the Cartolucci connection or Clancy so far, and what do you plan to do with the information we just gave you?"

Mike stared hard at Patrick. "You've got a real attitude problem, Pat. At this stage of the game, I don't have to cooperate with you. You on the other hand, need the department's sources. So why don't you cool it a bit."

Melanie saw the shadow that fell over Patrick's face. The tension in the air was almost tangible. "Hold it." She leaned forward, forcing the men to break eye contact with each other. "This isn't getting us anywhere." She glanced at Mike. "You have to admit that the department hasn't exactly been making awe-inspiring progress on this."

"You know how we work, Melanie, so you should realize that the department doesn't go around giving updates on every move it makes. When we have something definite, we'll fill you in." Mike met her gaze with a level one of his own. "The fact that we don't have anything concrete so far, doesn't mean we're resting on our laurels."

Melanie leaned back, her gaze holding his. She understood now. The message, though carefully couched, had been clear. "All right, Mike. You know everything we know at this point. Call us as soon as you have something to share."

"What are you going to do about Clancy?" Patrick demanded.

"For now, I'll have him brought in and have a talk with him. I don't have any solid evidence to back me up at this point, so I have to be careful how I handle this. If I get him too rattled, he's likely to have harassment charges brought up against us." Mike stirred his coffee, staring pensively at the liquid.

"Things at the department are very tense right now. Captain Mathers is growing increasingly bitter about the allegations Andy was investigating. Normally we might give a suspect a hard time if the stakes are high, but with Internal Affairs looking over our shoulders, all of us are being extremely careful right now. That's just the way it is."

"It's okay, Mike," Melanie said gently. "We do understand. Between Mathers and Internal Affairs, I can see how things could be tough at the moment."

"Wait a minute," Patrick interjected.

Melanie started to slide out of the booth. "Let's go, Patrick." She could feel Patrick's rising anger and wanted him away from there before it came spilling to the surface. She knew now that Mike had his own investigation going with Clancy. That's what he'd tried to tell her indirectly. She hadn't missed his message. His evasions, she suspected strongly, were attempts to keep them from interfering. Still, explaining this to Patrick would be very difficult and this was neither the time nor the place.

"By the way," Mike added in a quiet tone as they were getting ready to leave, "there's still no word out in the street supporting the theory that Cartolucci put out a contract on

Andy. If you guys hear anything I'd appreciate you passing it along."

Patrick started to speak, but Melanie grabbed his arm. "We will, Mike, and thanks," she said, urging Patrick away.

Patrick glared at her as soon as they were outside. "You should have let me set the record straight. He expects us to turn over information to him, but he certainly isn't planning on reciprocating."

"Maybe he can't," she replied cryptically.

"That doesn't help us out much, does it? Have you found out anything from your background investigation on Mike yet?"

"His finances are average for a cop with his years on the force. There have been no large deposits to or withdrawls from his bank account. Except for the car, there's nothing unusual there, Patrick, and I *have* looked."

"You never force the issue with him, Melanie. Why not?" he challenged.

"It wouldn't do much good," she answered in a monotone. Melanie kept her body perfectly still, exhibiting that complete calm that never came without tremendous effort. "You, on the other hand, could stand a lesson or two on how not to burn your bridges behind you. We do need his help."

"So now you're siding with him? Don't you get it? He's not giving us anything in return, Melanie. I think you better start being realistic about this." When she said nothing, Patrick lapsed into silence. There were times, such as these, when he had no idea how to deal with her. He hated it when she withdrew behind the wall of reserve, shutting him out completely.

Patrick drove back to the office. "We need to find out, once and for all, whether Clancy or Reed had anything to do with Dad's murder," he said finally as he parked the car. "I've come up with a plan that will get us the evidence we need. I'm certain it'll work, but it's going to be risky."

Chapter Thirteen

Melanie didn't like the sound of it. Patrick was getting frustrated with the case, and when an investigator felt that way, it usually spelled trouble. "Let's go inside and talk about it. We're easy targets out here." She returned to the office with him.

"Have you ever placed a tap on someone's line?" He took off his coat and hung it on the wooden rack.

"Of course, but I have to admit it's been a while. Whose phone did you want to listen in on?" she asked warily.

"I want to do both Reed's and Clancy's. Before you object, let me tell you that I realize we could get into trouble if we're caught. And I'm aware that any conversations we overhear or tape can't be used as evidence. We don't exactly have a court order. However, we might get a lead this way that will put us on the right track. Then we can concentrate our efforts on getting admissible evidence." He sat in the leather chair across from her desk and leaned back, legs outstretched before him.

"The key will be tailoring our methods to fit the personality of each particular suspect. That's how we'll get the most for our efforts. For instance, with Reed my plan is to place a tap on his line, then give him something he can see to worry about. We'll park a surveillance vehicle somewhere he can't miss it and tail him for a few days. Then we'll stop. Once he thinks he's not being watched, that's when he'll be most tempted to make his move. If Reed has Soviet connections or knows of his late father's contacts, he'll probably ask them for help. We'll check out any contacts he makes very carefully."

She nodded slowly. "Okay, suppose, hypothetically, that I agree to this, what about Clancy? What kind of surveillance do you want to set up on him? We know Clancy's violent, dangerous and unstable. That's not the type of person you want to provoke."

"We couldn't ever let Clancy know he's being watched," Patrick answered. "In fact, my plan for him depends on that. I'll have to sneak into his apartment when I'm certain he's out, and place a tap on his telephone. Then I'll set up a listening post somewhere close by and monitor all his calls. Between that and visual surveillance, I should be able to turn up some good leads we can follow up on."

"Am I getting this right? You want me to take care of Conrad Reed while you handle Clancy by yourself?"

"I'll help you get set up with Reed. It's important that he believe both of us are there. It'll be safer. I was thinking we could use your dummy again."

"Conrad's not dangerous, at least we don't think so, but Clancy sure is. I can't let you go off on something like that without a backup. We're partners!"

"Melanie, both jobs need to be done right now. We can't afford to let any trails get cold by concentrating on one man at a time. If Clancy and I accidentally run into each other, there'd undoubtedly be a physical confrontation. But I'm closer to his size and can hold my own in a fight. You'd have to draw your weapon and resort to deadly force."

He was right, though she hated to admit it. Still, she felt uncomfortable with the idea. The truth was, she was afraid for him. What if the next grenade was real?

At the moment, she didn't feel at all like the cool, logical investigator she always tried hard to be. That was the problem when you started caring deeply for someone you worked with. Things changed. Andy would have expected more professionalism from her, and Patrick deserved the best she had to give. Placing her heart on the sidelines, she allowed

Patrick's logic to prevail. "All right, I see your point. We'll do it your way."

"I'm going to rent a plain white van with no rear windows, and lineman's gear," Patrick said. "Then I'll get dressed in overalls, climb the pole and place a radio relay on the telephone line that leads to Reed's home. The tap will send the calls to a voice activated recorder in the van."

"If Reed's my responsibility, I'll take care of that," she said staunchly.

"No way. A woman lineman is still unusual enough to merit a second glance. I don't want to attract anyone's attention. I'm going to disguise my appearance, and get the job done as quickly as possible."

"I'll stay in the van while you get things set up," she added, "and maintain contact with you via hand-held radios. Someone has to keep a lookout for Reed. If he recognizes you, or suspects something, he might come over and start trouble. The last thing we need is for him to report us to the police."

"All right," he conceded. "I'll also need one of those small plastic signs that attaches to the side of the van with magnets. That way it won't look suspicious. If we pull up using an all-white van with no markings, some of the neighborhood residents might get nervous."

"I know exactly who can get us what we need for that," she assured him. "You concentrate on finding the right type of van."

Patrick's plan went off without a hitch. Placing a ladder on the top of their van and wearing hard hats, they attracted no more than a cursory look from passersby and fleeting interest from a couple of neighborhood kids. Reed never knew they were there.

"Okay," Patrick said, climbing down and meeting her at the van. "Now we drive the van away from here, remove the markings and place the gear out of sight inside. Then I want to find a parking spot where Reed can see us plainly. We'll move the vehicle every once in a while so that the neighbors

don't get too nervous. However, we'll make sure Reed
knows we're around."

"I think this will work," Melanie said, driving away from
the area. "I honestly don't believe Reed is a professional
espionage agent. But if he does know anything, this war of
nerves will make him slip up."

They returned to Conrad Reed's neighborhood an hour
later. Patrick wore a blue baseball cap and sunglasses that
would eventually be placed on the dummy. Melanie parked
the van one house down from Reed's.

Ten minutes later, Patrick saw Reed's garage door open.
He leaned forward. "There he is. Let's let him know we're
here."

They didn't have to go far. At a drugstore about a mile
from his home, Reed left the car and went inside. Patrick
started to get out. "Get the dummy ready." He handed her
the sunglasses, but kept the baseball cap on. "I'll stay with
Reed and make sure he knows I'm tailing him. Then, when
he comes back out, we'll make the switch. While you're
following him, I'll go back to the office and get set up for
the Clancy surveillance. There's a cellular telephone for you
in the back, so keep in touch. Remember, if you get into any
trouble, don't try to handle it alone. Call the police and
me."

"The same goes for you," she replied, trying to mask the
concern in her tone.

Patrick followed Reed into the drugstore. About twenty
minutes later, they both emerged, one after the other. As
Reed went to his car, Melanie put the van into gear and
pulled up to where Patrick stood. With a quick goodbye,
Patrick placed the baseball cap on the dummy, and fastened the seat belt around him. At a distance it would look
like he was shielding his eyes from the sun and taking a nap.

PATRICK PARKED across the street from Clancy's apartment building, and waited. From his vantage point, he could
see Clancy's pickup in the glare of the streetlight ahead, as

well as flickering shadows moving inside Clancy's apartment.

His observation post would do for now, but he needed to find a more concealed lookout point. Seeing the For Rent sign posted at the front of the building where Clancy lived, he decided to take a look.

The corner apartment that was available had a view of the street, which suited his needs. From there he'd be able to maintain visual surveillance on Clancy should he go to his truck, as well as monitor his telephone calls.

A half hour later, having rented the apartment under an assumed name, Patrick surveyed his new working quarters. Unfortunately he couldn't duplicate the phone-tap method they'd used on Reed. Tapping Clancy's line from the complex's central control panel would be very difficult because the panel was located somewhere inside the apartment building's business office. He would have to break into that office just to search for the panel. Instead he would wait until Clancy left and then slip a listening device directly into his telephone.

The minutes ticked by slowly. Waiting was the hardest part of investigative work. Restless, he walked outside to the street. He glanced up at Clancy's second-story window while remaining as inconspicuous as possible. The shadows were still there. He returned to his rented apartment and paced. His thoughts drifted back to Melanie. Would she call him for help if she ran into trouble? He really wasn't sure. She tried so hard to appear tough, but he'd glimpsed the vulnerability beneath the image. And behind those veiled eyes lay a capacity to love and care greater than any he'd ever found. It was that softer side of her that was weaving its way into his heart.

At the same time, he resented her inscrutability. It left him with the feeling that she was holding something back.

He was in the midst of his musings, staring out the window, when he saw Clancy emerge from the building and jump into his truck. Clancy sped away as if late for an appointment. Knowing there was no time to lose, Patrick brought out several skeleton keys that had served him well in the past. They'd been his father's gift to him when he'd decided to pursue investigative work in the Air Force.

Patrick smiled, despite himself. Maybe his father had suspected all along that someday he'd return and become more involved with the agency. His intuition had always been sharp. Yet what about Melanie? Dad had been right about one thing: the sparks certainly did fly whenever they were together.

Forcing her from his mind, Patrick started down the hall toward Clancy's apartment, his nerves on edge. The hall was empty but he heard footsteps and quickly turned the corner. He waited, then realized the person had gone on down the stairs. Aware of everything around him, senses sharp and alert to danger, he continued toward Clancy's apartment.

The locks on Clancy's door were not as intimidating as he had expected. Perhaps Clancy was arrogant enough to believe that no one would ever be foolish enough to attempt to break into *his* home.

Patrick entered the apartment, and shut the door. The odor of stale cigarette smoke was oppressive. Beer cans and cigarette butts filled the plastic wastebasket beside the living-room couch. He found the telephone quickly, and immediately began to take apart the receiver. The listening device was self-adhesive, so he stuck it against the inside of the plastic cover. To a layman, the device would look like an integral part of the phone itself. He reassembled the receiver.

He was ready to leave when he heard the sound of men's voices in the hall. The louder of the two sounded like Clancy's but he couldn't be sure. Hearing them come closer, he flattened against the wall behind the door, and reached inside his holster to push the safety off his Beretta. If Clancy found him there, there'd be no talking his way out of it.

The footsteps paused, then disappeared down the hall. Patrick breathed again. A false alarm. Exiting the apartment quickly, he hurried to his own. His shirt was drenched with perspiration. He casually glanced out the window to assure himself that Clancy's truck was still gone.

In surprised confusion, Patrick stared at the street below and muttered a dark oath. Clancy and a companion were retrieving something from the truck. "We might have a long wait." Clancy's voice drifted up through the window. "This case of cold beer is the only thing that'll keep us from sweltering. I can't believe I walked off and left it in the truck."

Patrick clenched his fists, then opened his hands, flexing them. It *had* been Clancy he'd heard in the hall. Good fortune had saved him.

As he saw the men walking back to the entrance, Patrick checked his tape recorder and receiver. Ten minutes after his return, Clancy got his first call. Patrick listened in. Several more calls came in, one after another. Clancy was having a busy night. Who'd have dreamed he'd be so popular? Yet the lengthy conversations were curiously void of substance and revealed little of interest to anyone outside of Clancy himself. The only thing the man talked about was cars.

"You better be on your toes, Clancy," a man's voice crackled over the receiver. "I understand there's a lot of heat coming down on you right now."

"Just from those nickel-and-dime PIs," Clancy replied. "I can't wait to get my hands on him." He paused. "Come to think of it, I'd rather get my hands on her."

Patrick heard the derisive laughter from both ends. As his thoughts turned to Melanie his fists clenched tightly. He remembered her sitting in the office. Then he visualized the way she'd looked behind the wheel of the van, so small, yet determined to complete the job. Why couldn't he have fallen in love with a woman who'd let him protect her, or at the very least, be less eager to rush out into danger? The sudden realization stopped him short. *Fallen in love.* Is that what had happened? He felt a pleasant stirring, then a feeling of possessiveness emerging from deep within him. She was so feminine—sexy, caring—but also strong, capable and intelligent. She'd make a good partner in life.

A demanding need for her permeated his being. Patrick left the apartment, locking the door behind him. He'd use the cellular phone in his car and call her. He'd tell Melanie he was checking on her progress—one partner contacting another—but he was no longer fooling himself. It was strange how an acknowledgement of his feelings had deepened the way he felt toward her.

Patrick used the back stairs. No sense running the risk of bumping into Clancy.

Patrick decided to go through the alley and take a shortcut to his car. He was halfway through the narrow passageway when he spotted Clancy on the sidewalk directly ahead. The man turned his head casually, looking behind him, then glanced down the alley.

Their eyes met, and Patrick stopped in midstride. Clancy froze, too, his expression turning hard and vicious. Patrick braced himself, wishing now that he hadn't chosen the shortcut. From the look on Clancy's face, Patrick knew that he was in for a fight.

Slowly Clancy came toward him, his eyes never leaving Patrick's face. "Spying on me, are you?" he snarled. "Well, you're in luck. You found me." He checked the alley. "And I'm in luck, too. We're all alone." Clancy reached into his pocket and extracted a knife. With a flip of his wrist, the blade clicked into place.

Clancy crouched, slowly advancing with the knife extended. Patrick held his ground. "If you want a fight, Clancy, you'll get one." For an instant, he considered drawing his gun, but then discarded the idea. He couldn't risk fatally injuring Clancy. Then he'd never know for sure what role the man had played in his father's death. His ingrained instincts from Air Force hand-to-hand combat training was all he'd have to draw on now.

He glanced around for a weapon to use against a knife. Beside the building was an old porcelain sink and several rusted iron pipes. Picking up a four-foot-long section of pipe, he grasped it firmly, hands several inches apart. He held it diagonally across his body. "You went through basic

training, Clancy. Did you ever take a rifle butt on the chin?''
Patrick moved around to the side, keeping his opponent in
front of him, forcing Clancy back to the wall.

Clancy stopped, unsure for the first time. "A man can
loose some vital organs to a six-inch blade. Particularly one
with a serrated edge," he spat out.

"Let's make a wager. I say that a six-inch blade can't
reach nearly as far as a four-foot pipe," Patrick countered.

Clancy began to inch sideways toward the end of the alley, realizing he had lost the advantage. His eyes never left
Patrick. "There'll be another time, O'Riley. Count on it."

Patrick watched Clancy turn the corner, then emerged
cautiously from the alleyway. Seeing Clancy return to the
building, he breathed easier. He dropped the pipe and
started toward his car when out of the corner of his eye, he
noticed someone else heading toward him.

Patrick turned to face the stranger, but the man stopped
and suddenly went back in the direction he'd come. He returned to a beige sedan where another man waited inside.
Puzzled, Patrick returned to his car and started the engine.
Instinct told him there was something going on.

Patrick drove around the corner and parked by the curb.
He waited a few minutes, but no one followed him. Curious, he drove around the block and came up from the other
side. The beige car was still there, the driver and his companion watching Clancy's building. Were they after Clancy
also? Patrick's suspicions were confirmed when he saw
Clancy emerge and enter his pickup. As Clancy drove down
the street, the beige car pulled out slowly and followed the
truck.

Patrick waited a moment then drove away. Now that
Clancy had seen him, he'd have to let the tape recorder and
the receiver do their work automatically. He'd check from
time to time to see if they'd picked up anything interesting,
but he'd have to do his best to avoid Clancy. It wouldn't take
much to push that man over the edge.

Melanie picked up the telephone on the second ring. Patrick told her about meeting Clancy then asked for her report.

"Nothing as exciting as your afternoon," she answered a little dejectedly. "I think Conrad's nervous, though. I can see him parting the living-room curtains and peering out every once in a while. I move the van periodically, and I think that's making him extra edgy. I'm getting ready to lock up now and leave the machines running for the night. I'll put the dummy in the back, and cover everything with a blanket. Let Reed worry about where we are. If he gets enough courage to come close to the van and peer through the windows in the front, he still won't be able to see anything. Judging from his behavior so far, though, I doubt he will."

"So you've got nothing new?" he repeated.

"I didn't say that," she cautioned, allowing herself a brief smile.

He realized she wasn't about to enlighten him further, and cursed softly. "Lock up and sneak away. I'll pick you up by the gasoline station at the corner."

Melanie met him thirty minutes later. She slipped into the passenger's seat and gave him an apologetic look. "Sorry it took me so long. I had to make sure Conrad wouldn't see me leave."

"No problem." He waited for her to let him know how her surveillance had gone. After five minutes of silence, he gave up. "Why is it that getting information from you is like pulling teeth!" he observed impatiently.

"Is this a riddle?" she questioned with a chuckle.

"No, it is *not* a riddle," he answered brusquely. "Melanie, will you please just tell me how it went for you this afternoon?" he demanded. "Damn it, I don't like to have to worry and I don't like to play guessing games."

"Were you worried?" she questioned calmly.

His face tightened, and he remained unamused. "You are the most exasperating woman I've ever met in my life," he managed at last.

"All this flattery! It's almost embarrassing," she teased.

His glacial stare could have made icicles form inside the car, but he said absolute nothing.

"Conrad made one call," she answered at last. "He told the man at the other end that something strange was going on, and that he was being watched. The man, I didn't recognize his voice, cautioned him against communicating over the telephone, and suggested that they meet later and go for a walk at their favorite park. The conversation itself could have been innocent enough, but as per our plan, I followed Conrad there, and pulled up to the curb. I could see both of them without any problem, but the park didn't offer enough cover for me to get close enough to find out what they were talking about. I decided to stay in the van and take a few photographs using the telephoto lens. They knew I was there, but I made sure they didn't see me taking the photographs."

"Were you able to find out from the telephone number who the person was that Conrad Reed called?"

"That's what I thought was interesting. Conrad called Albert Smith, his father-in-law. I'm going to run a check on him as soon as possible. We've been concentrating so much on Frederick Reed and that side of Conrad's family, that we never made more than a cursory check into the background of Conrad's in-laws. I have a good photo of him, I think, if he's the one in the park."

"That is a new development. By the way, there's something else I forgot to mention about my afternoon stakeout of Clancy. Clancy's being watched and tailed by two men, though I don't know who they are. I didn't go close enough to get their license number, but I don't think it would be hard to do."

Melanie nodded slowly. She suspected that what Patrick had seen was part of Mike's ongoing investigation involving Clancy. The men had probably been undercover cops. "I'll call Mike."

"Why bother?"

Melanie could feel her temper starting to get the better of her. She closed her eyes for a moment, then opened them again. Giving him a look completely void of expression, she answered Patrick. "I believe he should know."

It was several minutes before Patrick trusted himself to respond civilly. "Melanie, you're one terrific woman, but you're still playing hide-and-seek with me. You never really let me in on what you're thinking, yet you want to work on this as full partners." He shook his head, then shrugged. "I can understand hiding your thoughts from strangers. But there comes a time when you have to decide who your friends are, then let go and trust them."

"Patrick, you don't understand. Why should I tell you what I'm thinking, when it's something I know we will never agree on? We'll only end up arguing and getting angry with each other. That isn't going to get us anywhere. Anger is counterproductive, and I have no intention of giving in to it. That's a sign of weakness."

"It's not a sign of weakness, Melanie." He gave her a surprised look, then focused back on the road. "If it indicates anything, it's that you're being honest and open about what you're feeling."

She said nothing for several moments. "It's all right in a personal sense, but it doesn't belong in business."

"But there's more than business between you and me. Refusing to face it isn't going to make it go away," he answered in a rich, low voice.

The startling pace of the growth of their feelings for each other left her bewildered. She'd never felt anything so strong, yet she couldn't think of a worse time to yield to those emotions. "They don't have to go away, Patrick. Just slow them down," she answered candidly.

"I'm not sure if that's possible, Melanie," he replied, "but we'll try." He pulled into the parking lot. The janitor's vehicle blocked their space near the entrance, so Patrick parked in the next row over. From there they could still see the car from inside the office.

They left the sedan and headed toward the building. They were less than five feet from the door when Melanie heard the sound of hurried footsteps coming from the far side of the janitor's truck. She strained to see over the vehicle. Three men were rushing toward them, coming from the street.

"O'Riley," one called out.

Patrick stopped by the front of the truck, his body tense. He slipped his hand inside his jacket, resting it on the hidden holster. "Yeah," he answered in a steely voice, half turning toward the men. Although he could see them clearly, his angle would make him a harder target if trouble erupted.

Melanie's fingers found her revolver's butt. As the three men came closer, she saw that none of them appeared to be armed. She relaxed her grip on the pistol, but her hand remained where it was.

Melanie and Patrick instinctively fell back, keeping the janitor's truck between them and the approaching trio. "Friends of yours?" Melanie asked in a harsh whisper.

"Hardly," Patrick answered.

"Don't run and hide, O'Riley," the man goaded. "We just want to have a little talk with you." The three split up to flank the truck.

Melanie grasped her revolver more firmly again, and took it partially out of her purse. The two who had come around to her side hesitated, looking at their leader for direction. The biggest of the three had already gone around the truck, angling toward Patrick.

Patrick, back-to-back with Melanie, flipped his jacket open, revealing his pistol. "Don't do anything you might not live to regret," he growled.

"You don't want to do that, O'Riley," the leader of the three warned in a soft, but menacing voice. His hair was greased back, a red bandanna tied to his forehead. His jeans and T-shirt were patched and grease spots covered them.

"I think you got that backward, pal," Patrick challenged smoothly, drawing his Beretta.

Melanie was taken by surprise when one of the pair facing her jumped back behind the other man, and ducked inside the building. She drew her pistol but there was no way for her to stop him without shooting through the one who'd remained. She stood her ground.

"That's why not." The leader pointed toward the door a moment later.

Melanie saw the man who'd slipped past her emerge from the building holding the elderly janitor before him. The blade of his knife had already drawn a tiny rivulet of blood from the old man's throat.

Chapter Fourteen

"Let's make this real simple, O'Riley. All we want from you are your files on Mario Cartolucci."

Patrick stood rock still. "We don't have them. Everything was turned over to the police."

"You're lying," the thug spat out.

Responding to a signal, the man holding the hostage reached up with the knife and nicked the victim's ear. More blood dripped onto the janitor's tan uniform and a cry of pain was wrenched from his lips.

Melanie's mouth went dry. Would she have to try to shoot the man wielding the knife? Their positions would make that difficult. She pulled back the hammer of her revolver with her thumb, cocking it for a more accurate single-action shot. At least the light was good.

"Reason it out," Patrick insisted. As long as his pistol never wavered from the chest of the spokesman, it would remain a standoff. "Our agency doesn't have the manpower to deal with that type of investigation...."

Melanie never took her eyes off the men before her. Her pistol was still pointed at the one holding the hostage. Her aim was steady. She held the gun with both hands, just as she had been instructed years ago. It was the first time she had ever held a gun on someone, and she was surprised that her hand wasn't shaking.

"Set your pistols down on the pavement," the leader ordered.

"No way," Patrick replied. "We'll lower them, but that's as far as we go. Keep in mind that if you kill that man, you'll leave this parking lot in the same condition."

"Be reasonable, O'Riley," the leader purred. "All we want are your records. You must have kept duplicates."

Melanie shifted sideways slightly, trying to improve her line of fire. Her new stance placed her almost shoulder to shoulder with Patrick. That's when she noticed he was slowly moving away from her and toward the leader.

She had to find a way to help him by creating a diversion that would focus everyone's attention on her. "Look, what we kept is incomplete. We read the file, so we already knew what was in it," she started speaking quickly. "That's why I only copied the page which summarized the rest. If you want to know how much the cops know, I can tell you. But please, move the knife away from that man's throat," she pleaded, exaggerating her fear. "He hasn't done anything. Give him a break."

The leader signaled his accomplice, and the knife moved away from the hostage's neck, but only a fraction of an inch. At least it was no longer pressing against the skin. She eased the hammer down on her revolver, then placed it on the hood of the car directly before her. "We know that Cartolucci bribed officers," she babbled, gesturing wildly with her hands as she spoke. As she'd hoped, their attention was riveted on her erratic movements and on her pistol sitting on the hood in front of her.

Melanie continued her rapid-fire monologue while furtively monitoring Patrick's movements. His progress was barely perceptible as he patiently edged around the truck and toward the leader. Suddenly the parking lot was bathed in an intense, harsh light. Melanie glanced toward the light and saw a patrol car aiming its spotlight directly at them.

The thug holding the hostage threw his captive forward, and the janitor fell to the pavement. As all three thugs took off running, Patrick shoved his pistol into his holster and went after them. The men, already on the move, outdistanced him easily and fled through the hedges that bordered the parking lot. A second later, Patrick heard the roar of a powerful engine as the men sped away into the night. Muttering an oath, he turned back.

Melanie was crouching by the janitor's side as Patrick approached. "It's a good thing you two came by," she told the officer.

"We were told to increase our patrols in this area. Normally we wouldn't have come around for another hour or so."

Patrick placed a handkerchief over the cut on the janitor's throat, then helped him sit up. The janitor's eyes grew wide with fear as the white compress began to soak with blood.

"It's okay," the police officer assured him. "The cut on your ear is messy, but no big deal. The other one isn't deep. You might not even need stitches," he assured.

The flashing red light of the police car drifted across them in a endless cycle. The second police officer was in the car, reporting the incident and calling for an ambulance. Melanie went to sit on the bumper of the janitor's truck.

Patrick joined her. He stood in line with the headlights, shielding her eyes partially from the glare. "You were terrific, Melanie," he said softly. "You knew I was trying to get the drop on that guy, and the way you kept talking really helped keep their attention on you." He lowered his voice to a conspiratorial whisper. "Even if the cops hadn't come along, we'd have been able to handle it."

"I don't doubt that for a moment." Melanie smiled wearily. "But I'm glad it's over."

The fire department's rescue squad, and an unmarked sedan with two men inside, pulled up beside the patrol car. Melanie glanced at Patrick. "It looks like we're going to be questioned by inspectors instead of patrolmen."

"Not just ordinary inspectors," Patrick said quietly. "That's Mathers on the left. Lucky us," he muttered sarcastically.

Melanie stood as Mathers and a plainclothes officer approached. "Good evening, Captain." Melanie offered her hand. "I'm surprised to see you here."

"I was working late on a departmental matter," he said obliquely, "and I heard the call. I thought I'd come by and see what had happened." He turned and glanced at the paramedics on the pavement examining the wounded man. "How bad is it?" he asked one of the medical team.

"Not bad at all, it's just messy. He'll need bandages for a few days and some antibiotics, but that's about it," the paramedic answered.

The janitor slowly got to his feet. "Who were those people, Ms. Cardenas? And what was all that about Mario Cartolucci?"

"We uncovered some incriminating evidence on Cartolucci while conducting a separate investigation," she answered candidly. "I'm sorry that those men involved you. If it's any comfort, I doubt they'll come back. It would probably be best if you didn't mention the details of what happened to anyone, though. In the meantime, we'll ask the building manager to increase the security patrols at night."

"I'm not talking to anyone except the police, Ms. Cardenas. You can count on that!" Wally agreed. "The last thing I need is more trouble."

Melanie accompanied Wally to the emergency medical van, then returned a moment later. Mathers glanced from her to Patrick. "Ms. Cardenas, I want to take your statement now. O'Riley, my assistant, Inspector Jaynes—" he nodded toward the man by his side "—will hear what you have to say."

As Patrick walked over to the unmarked car with Jaynes, Mathers and Melanie went inside, to the agency's office. Making himself comfortable on the chair opposite her desk, Mathers asked her to recount what had happened. When she finished, Mathers was smiling and nodding.

Melanie glared at him, annoyed. "Captain, what are you so pleased about? This isn't exactly good news. Those hoods ran off, and all we have is a description. It's going to be very difficult to find them.''

"You're looking at it from the wrong perspective. What happened here tonight confirms that all the heat the department's been bringing down on Cartolucci is paying off.'' He lowered his voice. "We've all been putting in a lot of overtime on this, and it's gratifying to see that we're getting them rattled.''

Melanie started to disagree, then thought better of it. "I'm sure the police have been working very hard," she replied noncommittally.

It was another half hour before Patrick and Melanie were alone once more. "Captain Mathers may be trying hard to pursue the Cartolucci lead but he's wrong about what happened tonight," she said.

"What's his theory?" Patrick asked, sitting on the chair Mathers had vacated.

"He believes this attack was a result of all the pressure the police investigation is supposedly putting on Cartolucci,'' she answered, leaning back. "But I disagree. I think this entire incident tonight was a ruse. The threats, muscle and hostage situation had Clancy's signature all over it. Those three men had planned on facing us when they could grab a hostage. That's why they didn't even flinch when we reached for our weapons. They were expecting it. They'd counted on using the janitor as leverage against us all along.'' Her eyes narrowed and she grew thoughtful. "I'm sure the trail that will lead us to Andy's murderer lies either with Clancy or Conrad Reed, and I can't see Reed behind anything like that.''

"Maybe," he admitted. "Both are certainly possibilities we need to keep investigating." He stood by the window, and stared at the empty parking lot outside. "However, I tend to agree with Mathers on this one." He turned around and smiled at her. "Isn't that a first?"

"You still haven't discarded the theory that the police might be involved with your father's murder, have you?'' she asked tiredly.

"If Dad had discovered Mike, Captain Mathers or any other cop on the take, Dad's life would have certainly been in danger. Ex-cops become everyone's target behind bars. It would have been a matter of choosing between their own life or Dad's."

"You're wrong to suspect Mike or Captain Mathers of killing Andy," she answered honestly. "I don't like Captain Mathers, but he's not a crooked cop. And as far as Mike goes, I really believe he cared for your father. Rather than kill Andy, either of those men would have gone underground, or skipped the country. Murder would have never come into it."

"I don't know, Melanie. For someone like Mathers, whose lifetime achievement hangs in the balance, murder might not have seemed like such a bad alternative. Remember he hated my father anyway." Patrick stared at the paperweight on Melanie's desk, lost in thought. Finally he tore his gaze away and reached into his pocket for the keys to the office. "Come on, lady. It's been a long day. The work here will keep. Let me take you home."

The next four days passed quickly. The tap Patrick had placed on Clancy's telephone proved useless. After their confrontation, Clancy had become suspicious and started using public phones for his conversations, a precaution that had stymied their efforts. Finally Patrick opted to discontinue the tap.

Melanie monitored Conrad Reed's line for a few days longer, but he, too, had become more cautious. His telephone conversations revealed nothing. Disappointed, they'd decided to conclude that angle of their operation also.

Melanie worked at her desk, studying the dossier she'd started to compile on Albert Smith. "We may not have managed to get much on Clancy, but Conrad Reed is turning out to be a very interesting subject. He's as pure as driven snow, but his male relatives sure have some peculiar backgrounds."

"You've still found nothing on Smith prior to 1945?" Patrick asked, standing in the doorway between their offices.

Melanie shook her head. "And it certainly isn't for lack of trying. I started by checking him out through our local sources. The first record I found of Albert Smith in San Francisco was in May of 1945. That's when he was first hired as a locksmith by Master Key Incorporated. The man who hired him is deceased, but his son, Jason Wainright, who handled his father's business affairs in his later years remembered Smith well. Apparently Smith never served in the military due to the fact that he's blind in one eye. From his father's old shop records Jason was able to verify that Smith worked for Master Key three years. Then he purchased the shop for a small down payment, and a long payment schedule which explains why Jason Wainright remembered him. My own investigation reveals that Smith turned around what had been a marginal operation. He then built it into such a profitable business that he had to expand and open a second shop. He paid off the elder Wainright several years early and then, last year, he sold both shops for a considerable sum. He got quite a retirement nest egg from it."

"Have you checked to see if Albert Smith has a police record?" Patrick asked.

"Yes, and he doesn't," she answered. "Of course, Albert Smith might be an alias he's using. But, if it is, he's been using it for a long time. That name can be backtracked to the very first job I can find on record for him anywhere. That brings me to one of the most interesting coincidences I discovered. It seems Albert Smith was in the state of Washington at the same time Frederick Reed was there. Only he worked as a clerk at a locksmith shop in Seattle. That job only lasted a month. Then he came down to California. I checked bank records and found out that when he first opened a savings account here in San Francisco at the Oakland Savings and Loan, he transferred money from Northwest Savings in Seattle."

"But prior to Washington, there's nothing?" Patrick queried.

"Not one single piece of information," Melanie replied flatly.

"I think we need to make a few more discreet inquiries as soon as possible," Melanie continued. "First, let's talk to his landlord. He lives in a town house in the Sunset district. While we're there, we can verify he's the man I photographed with Conrad Reed at the park."

"Good idea," Patrick replied. "Once we're certain that's a picture of Smith, I want to forward copies of the photo to the FBI, the CIA and that documents expert at the Imperial War Museum in England. The CIA wasn't much help before, but who knows, this time they might be able to find something."

"We should also question Albert ourselves." Melanie leaned forward, resting her elbows on her desk. "That way we'll be able to get a feel for the type of person we're dealing with. Only approaching Smith is going to be tricky. He has nothing to gain from talking to us, and may have something to lose."

"Let's give it a try anyway," Patrick said after a few moments. "The direct approach might be just what's needed."

That afternoon, they drove to Albert Smith's town house apartment in Sunset. First, they stopped at the manager's office. A middle-aged woman appeared at the door. She was heavily made-up in colors that were too dark for her face. She peered at them from round eyeglasses that were perched halfway down her long, beaklike nose. "May I help you?" She smiled at Patrick, and after a cursory glance at Melanie, proceeded to ignore her.

"I'd like to ask you a few questions about one of the tenants here, ma'am," Patrick said formally.

She took off her glasses and straightened her posture, thrusting out her rather ample bosom. Melanie started to smile, but then forced herself to remain stoic. Patrick had made a conquest. There was no disguising the meaning the manager's body language conveyed.

"Come in," she invited. She waited graciously for Patrick to pass, then oblivious of anything else, practically shut the door in Melanie's face. "Oh, sorry," she mumbled apologetically.

This time when Melanie looked at Patrick, she saw a mischievous twinkle in his eyes. "No harm done," she answered politely.

"You guys cops?"

Patrick shook his head, and offered her a glance at his military identification. "I work full-time for military intelligence," he answered truthfully. "Ms. Cardenas is a private investigator from your city."

"My name's Alice Hamilton," she said, shaking hands with Patrick. "I'm always pleased to help out the government." She beamed her most charming smile at Patrick, ignoring Melanie once again.

"We'd like to ask you a few questions about Albert Smith," Patrick continued.

She curled her nose. "Oh, him."

Melanie decided it was probably best to leave this interview to Patrick. The woman was much more interested in dealing with him and, therefore, would be more responsive to his questions.

"What can you tell me about Albert Smith, Alice?" Patrick focused his attention on her.

She offered Patrick a seat beside her on the couch. Melanie sat across from them, and remained a silent observer. Actually she didn't blame Alice one bit; Patrick *was* impressively handsome. Those blue eyes could melt cold steel at one glance. She watched the easy way he elicited information and used his charming smile—it could make any woman's pulse quicken. No, she didn't blame Alice at all.

"I don't really know that much about Mr. Smith," Alice admitted. "He keeps to himself. Only I think he's a little loony. His neighbor, Ms. Landower, told me that he's taken to talking to himself late at night. More like mumbling, she says. But no one's ever there except him. She works at home, so she'd know." She shrugged. "He's not a problem tenant, though. He's never rude, just unfriendly. He'll say good morning to you if you speak first, but otherwise I think he prefers to ignore everyone. I'll give you an example of what I mean. Most of us who share the building get together once a month just to socialize, but not him. I used to think he was just shy, so I dropped by a few times. He wouldn't even let me inside. Once I took a plate filled with cookies over to him, and he never even asked me in for a cup of coffee. Can you imagine that!''

"Is this the man you know as Albert Smith?" Patrick asked, holding out the photograph of the man Melanie had seen with Conrad.

"That's him, all right. Not a bad-looking man, actually. It's a shame he's so standoffish.''

Patrick stood, and offered his hand. "Thanks for all your help, Alice. It was a pleasure talking to you. I wish everyone was so cooperative.''

She smiled coyly. "Anytime—" she dropped her voice "—and I mean that, anytime.''

Melanie didn't say anything until they were out in the hall. "Hoo boy! Did you charm her! *Anytime,*" she mimicked.

Patrick glanced at her and grinned. "Jealous?''

She gave him an incredulous look. "Don't you wish!''

Patrick didn't answer right away, but considered his reply carefully. They crossed the inner courtyard, and walked to Albert Smith's door. "As a matter of fact, I do," Patrick finally replied boldly.

By the time Patrick's words registered in her mind, Albert Smith was at the door. Gathering her wits quickly, Melanie focused her attention on him. Smith wasn't at all what she'd expected.

This man whose past was shrouded in secrecy looked no more threatening than someone's favorite grandfather. One eye was faintly clouded, evidence of the blindness that afflicted him. The other was clear, but instead of hostility, all that shone there was curiosity. Even after Patrick and Melanie identified themselves, that didn't change.

"Come in. I thought sooner or later you'd stop by. Conrad explained that your father was killed—murdered," he corrected. "Apparently it happened shortly after he'd started to do a background check on Conrad for that aircraft company. I guess you want to look into my son-in-law's past a bit, just to rule him out as a suspect." He gave Patrick a look filled with sympathy. "You must want to find your father's murderer very badly," he commented quietly.

"I want to find him and turn him over to the police, unless the police get to him first," Patrick answered carefully.

Smith invited him to have a seat on the sofa. "You've undoubtedly learned that Conrad's record is spotless. He checked with the newspaper to get the date right, then determined that he was at home the day your father," he glanced at Melanie and added, "and your partner, Ms. Cardenas, was killed. I, unfortunately, can't confirm that for him. I wish I could." He paused. "Is that what you wanted to know?"

"It would have helped if you had been able to, but it's not a problem," Patrick hedged the question. "We're only trying to eliminate loose ends."

Smith nodded slowly. "Yes, I can understand that. A good investigation must be a thorough one. I wish I could be more help. Conrad, you see, was concerned you might not be satisfied with just his word, even though he had no reason to kill your father. His wife, my daughter, Anna, was at work and couldn't substantiate his alibi, either. It bothered him a great deal that you might think he had anything to do with the murder. That's when he came to me and asked if perhaps I remembered having stopped by to see him that day. That was about a month ago, and I have to admit, I didn't remember what I was doing that long ago. Who does? But I checked my calendar and discovered that I'd spent the day at the Bear Lodge's annual business meeting. All board members are required to attend and help make out the lodge's budget for the next fiscal year. It took us ten hours to come up with one everyone agreed on." He smiled ruefully. "Our new president, Mitch Sayers, is a bit tight-fisted. We ended up having to justify every expense two or three times before we managed to get it past him.''

"Did you speak to Conrad that day, perhaps on the telephone from the lodge?" Melanie asked, more to get information about Albert's alibi than out of any real concern about Conrad's.

He considered the question for several moments. "I doubt it, though I really couldn't swear that I didn't. I can't be absolutely certain, but I don't recall any time when we took a break. I think one man did leave briefly. Otherwise we were there at the office in the lodge from ten-thirty that morning until a little before eight that evening. We even had sandwiches sent in at noon, and dinner was leftovers from lunch. No one wanted to take the time to go out and eat. We just wanted to get finished."

"Would you mind if we checked with the others, sir? They might remember something, like your making a phone call to Conrad. That would support his story." Patrick asked politely, making it appear almost as if it had been an afterthought.

Albert's face tensed for a moment, then he shrugged. "No, I suppose not." He walked over to the small table in the corner of the room where the telephone was. After a brief search inside a drawer, he extracted a telephone address book. He scribbled several names and numbers down, then handed the slip of paper to Patrick. "Here are the others who were there with me. They'll verify my whereabouts, too, if you're thinking along those lines."

Patrick stood and extended his hand. "Thank you for your time, sir," he answered, deliberately avoiding any confirmation or denial.

"Those men should be able to set your mind at rest." Albert shook his hand. "You know, I hope you aren't seriously considering the possibility Conrad could have had anything to do with your father's death. That boy won't even kill spiders inside his house. He actually puts them in containers, takes them outside, then releases them."

Melanie smiled. Somehow that fit her idea of Conrad, too. "No sir, we have no reason to believe Conrad had anything to do with it," she answered, measuring her words carefully. "We're simply investigating all the possibilities. If nothing else, a process of elimination will furnish us with some answers."

He nodded thoughtfully. "Yes, I can see how it would." He walked with them to the door. "Those men will be able to account for my day. If I made any phone calls, they may remember it. And if there's anything else I can do to help, all you have to do is call," he said, glancing at one then the other. "I'm retired, you know, and my time's free."

He met Patrick's gaze with a steady one of his own. "I really am sorry about your father. I also know what it's like to lose someone you love," he added gently. "You see, my wife died several years ago. I still miss her. Relatives help, though. Do you come from a large family?" he asked.

"No, I was an only child," Patrick answered.

"Then your mother will need you more than ever," he affirmed kindly. "Is she holding up well?"

"My mother died many years back," Patrick replied, then suddenly his face grew hard. "Thank you for your time," Patrick said firmly, then walked outside.

Saying a quick goodbye to Albert Smith, Melanie went after Patrick who'd already crossed a section of the inner courtyard. "Why in the world are you so angry all of a sudden?"

"He turned it around on me, Melanie. I was there to interview him, not *be* interviewed. It was skillfully done, I'll say that for him. He was so subtle, he had me answering his questions before I realized what he was doing. I underestimated Albert Smith." He clenched his jaw. "The way I figure it, he was searching for weaknesses. I wonder how determined he'll be to find them."

"If he was hoping to learn about your family, he now knows he can't hurt you through them," she soothed. "The people you cared about are beyond his reach."

Patrick helped her into the car, then walked around to the driver's side, where his whisper-soft words trailed away, unheard in the gentle afternoon breeze. "All except one."

Chapter Fifteen

Melanie aimed the air-conditioner vent on the passenger's side of the car directly at herself. "Did you notice all the family photographs in the hall? The one nearest the entryway included Frederick Reed. He was the man wearing the 49ers cap. From the looks of it, I'd say family is very important to Albert Smith. I think he's worried we're overzealous, trying so hard to find a killer that we might attempt to pin it on his son-in-law. He practically said so. If he was probing you for weakness, he's doing it to defend his own family. You really can't blame him for that."

"Maybe," Patrick hedged. "I still want to check his alibi, Melanie, as soon as possible. We've already established that just like Frederick Reed, there's something odd about Smith's background. First, we have to figure out what he's hiding, then we'll see if it has anything to do with Dad's murder. The possibility still exists that one of them, or maybe both, are Soviet agents."

"We'll send out copies of Smith's photographs as soon as we get back to the office. We might get lucky this time," Melanie suggested. "But keep in mind that if Smith's alibi *is* valid, then the chances of this puzzle having anything to do with Andy's death go right down to zero."

"Let's contact the other board members right away." Patrick stopped at the red light and tapped his fingers impatiently against the steering wheel. "I have a strange feeling about this, Melanie. Smith seemed so sure of himself.

He's either telling the truth, or he's figured out an angle we know nothing about.''

"We'll soon find out which.''

The afternoon passed slowly. After sending off the photographs by an express service, they spent most of their time on the telephone. Melanie, sidetracked with agency business including a note from their landlord threatening eviction on the grounds that they were endangering other tenants, took only one of the men from their list. Patrick agreed to track down the other two.

It was almost six by the time Patrick walked out and made himself comfortable on the chair facing her desk. "Smith's alibi almost checks out.''

"Let me guess. You can't find Eric Higgins.'' Seeing the look of surprise on his face, she smiled. "No, I don't read minds, nor have we duplicated efforts again. Sam Mahoney, the man I just spoke to, told me that only two out of the four men there were at the office all day—Albert and Eric Higgins. Both Sam and the other board member left during the afternoon on personal errands, leaving two hours unaccounted for. Unfortunately they're at a critical time. Andy came back from lunch at two and the bomb went off at six. To clear Smith, we need to have those hours accounted for.''

"Eric Higgins is away on a trip,'' Patrick informed her. "He's put his telephone on call forwarding and it rang at his daughter's home. She told me that her father is retired. He travels frequently to Florida to look for investment property. His time's his own, so he doesn't follow any set schedule. She has no way of getting hold of him. He seldom calls, but if he does, she'll have him contact us. Until then, there's nothing else we can do.''

She could feel the frustration tear at him. "Patrick, we're doing our best.''

He stood and began to pace. "But it isn't enough.'' He stopped and faced her. "The problem is, I can't stand the idea that we've reached the end. Yet as far as I can see, we've exhausted our options.''

"All investigations have delays, time to study and consider the gains you have made. Waiting is part of our business."

He met her eyes. "I feel as if I'm failing at the most important task that's ever been given to me." He stood very still as if conserving his energy for that time when he'd need it to fight his unseen adversary. He'd be dangerous then, and lethal if need be, she had no doubt. It was at this moment that she realized how hard Patrick had struggled to keep his grief from overwhelming him—from interfering with the job.

"Your progress is being blocked at the moment, that's all. It doesn't mean you've failed," she answered gently.

He glanced around the office, then jammed his hands into his pockets. His body was tense, his back ramrod straight. "I owe my father everything—my life, who I am. Now the only thing left of the man he was, is the part of him that lives on in me. I have to find his murderer, and bring him to justice. If I can't do that, then I've failed him as well as myself."

Melanie stood and walked to where he was. His pain touched her deeply and accentuated her own. Without hesitation she wrapped her arms around him.

They held on to each other, each lost in a forest of emotions. Yet in the glorious warm haven of each other's arms, grief and loneliness slowly faded into the background. Another, infinitely more tender feeling gently guided their hearts together, beckoning them to yield.

Melanie forced herself to move out of his arms, a slight tremor shaking her body. "Patrick . . ."

He touched her face with his hand, the slight caress saying more than words could. "I know, lady, I feel it, too. It's getting more and more difficult to let you pull away."

A woman could lose herself in the intensity of that gaze. Swallowing to relieve the dryness in her throat, Melanie walked back to the desk. She sat down at her chair and stared out the window for a few moments.

She had only meant to take time to compose herself. Yet as she watched, she saw two of the street people taking the shortcut to the refuge and an idea began to form in her mind. "The apple," she said softly. "Why on earth didn't I think of that before!"

"What are you talking about?" Patrick asked, confused.

"Patrick, there *is* something we can do," she said, turning the chair around and facing him. "We've never considered the apple that Shy Eddy carries. Where does he get it? If we find that, then we'll find him."

Patrick smiled slowly, then nodded. "How about that produce market that's just down the street? Perkins Produce, I think it's called. They have their fruit stalls on the sidewalk when the weather is nice. It would be easy to steal one from there."

"Let's go talk to the proprietor."

Twenty minutes later they met with Charlie Perkins, the owner of the produce market. He smiled at their description of Shy Eddy. "I know exactly who you're talking about. He steals one apple from me every day. I pretend not to notice," he explained with a shrug. "I'm a businessman. If I can't afford to lose one apple, then I'm in more trouble than he is. He enjoys them so much that if he didn't take one, I'd hand it to him. In fact, during the winter I leave apples for him out on the window in the back. So what's the harm? You cops?"

Melanie smiled. "No, we're private investigators. But we're not out to roust Shy Eddy, all we want to do is talk to him. He might have seen something that could help us on a case."

"Talking to him is going to be tough." The man rubbed his chin in a thoughtful gesture. "The only person he gets close to is me because of my apples, and he doesn't talk to me—ever."

"Maybe you could call us when you see him," Melanie suggested.

"Wouldn't work. He doesn't stick around that long," the proprietor answered. "What do you think he saw? You're going to an awful lot of trouble just to find him."

Melanie hesitated, trying to decide how much to tell him. "The fact is, I remember seeing him hanging around the day my partner, Andy O'Riley, was murdered. It's possible he might have seen someone tampering with the car. That information could help me a great deal."

He nodded slowly. "I'll be glad to help if I can." He thought it over for a moment. Verifying that their offices were on the ground floor, he added, "I've got an idea. I'll put the stall with the apples back inside the store for the next week. Shy Eddy will never come in. In the meantime, you start leaving an apple on your windowsill for him each day. Whenever he stops by here, he comes from the north end of the street, which means he probably passes your office. If he can't get his usual apple here, he might go for yours. And just to make sure he doesn't miss it, next time he comes around, I'll tell a customer about the one you keep on your windowsill. It's my guess he'll go back up the street looking for it."

"Perfect," Melanie replied. "I really appreciate it, Charlie. A week should give me enough time to see if this plan's going to work."

"It's the least I can do for Andy," Perkins explained. "He always bought from me, and when my wife was in the hospital, he even sent her flowers. He cared about people, and that's rare nowadays."

Melanie saw the shadow of grief that crossed Patrick's features. Thanking the man, she walked with Patrick back to the office. Behind his calm exterior, she could feel the network of acutely sensitive nerves that needed to be touched and soothed. "We have each other, Patrick. And that's something I think would have pleased Andy a great deal."

"Do I have you?" he insisted in a voice that was barely audible above the sounds of the traffic.

She heard him, and the lightness of the tone felt like a feather being brushed against her naked skin. She trembled then, aware how much the gesture gave away, tried to suppress it.

He said nothing, but smiled tenderly. "Yes, that's exactly how I feel, too."

THE NEXT FEW DAYS seemed endless. Their patience was stretched to the limit.

"Listening and watching for Shy Eddy all week's been hard, but at least now we know approximately what time he shows up. I'm surprised that having you move your chair closer to the apple each day hasn't spooked him. I thought it might."

"So did I," Melanie conceded. "I guess he really wants the apple. Today's really the test, though. The second I spot or hear him, I'm moving my chair right next to the window. As usual, I'll have a file on my lap, and pretend to work. Only this time I'm going to hold the apple, too. The only thing on the windowsill will be photographs of Albert Smith, Conrad Reed and Larry Clancy."

"Do you think he'll balk?"

"I hope not, otherwise all the time that I've spent on this is going to be wasted. Keep your fingers crossed." She taped the photos onto their windowsill. "If things work out the way I hope, we'll have a breakthrough piece of evidence today." She peered out the window and glanced down the street. "Keep an eye out for Shy Eddy while I get everything else ready. Only be careful that he doesn't spot you watching for him."

Patrick moved to the window. "Get ready. Unless I miss my guess, that's him, and he's early." Patrick stepped back into the other office, ducking out of sight.

Melanie sat down and waited. As she heard the sound of muffled footsteps coming closer, she picked up the apple. She held it out, her eyes glued on the file as if reading.

Shy Eddy hesitated.

Melanie avoided looking at him. Instead she pretended to write something down. "By the way, Eddy, if you don't mind, would you glance at those photos? I'd like to know if any of these men look familiar."

After what seemed an eternity to Melanie, Shy Eddy took the apple. He studied the photographs, then nodded. "Yes, ma'am." His voice was hoarse, but cultured.

For the first time Melanie realized that Shy Eddy wasn't retarded, nor someone with a poor education. She glanced up quickly, surprised at her discovery.

Shy Eddy jumped back, and stared warily at her.

"It's all right," she assured gently. "You don't have to be frightened of me, Eddy. I would never hurt you." The truth that Shy Eddy was frightened of people touched her deeply. Of course, being out in the streets gave him plenty of reasons to distrust everyone. Unfortunately having shut people out of his life, he'd also closed off any possibility of help. "You're safe around me, you know," she added in a soft voice. "Besides, I'm in here and you're out there. If I do anything to frighten you, you can always run away. I won't go after you."

Shy Eddy nodded. "Okay."

"Did you recognize any one of these men?"

"I know why you're asking," he admitted. He studied the pictures again, then glanced up and met her eyes. "He looks like the man who placed something in that car, just before it exploded."

"Which one?" she insisted, trying not to alarm him with her excitement.

Shy Eddy was about to answer when the loud wail of a siren pierced the air. He glanced around quickly. Eyes wide, and looking like an animal about to be trapped, he took off running as fast as he could.

"Wait, Eddy, no!" Melanie leaned out the window and muttered an oath. Of all the rotten luck. If only that siren had been turned on a half minute later!

Patrick rushed into the room. "What happened?"

"The police frightened him." Melanie had started to duck back inside, when she caught sight of a tall figure wearing a tweed cap. "It's him! It wasn't the siren. That's who caused Eddy to run off!"

She scrambled out the window, jumping from a planter onto the sidewalk.

"Melanie, wait!" Patrick followed half a second later.

Melanie ran at full speed through the parking lot and toward the park. The distance between her and the person narrowed with each passing second. She dodged across the street. Chest heaving, she surged forward into the grassy park, reaching the person wearing the cap a moment later. With one last effort she grabbed the person's shoulders.

"Hey!" The young woman's cap fell off, revealing a thick mass of jet-black hair. "What are you doing, lady!" she demanded.

Melanie stared at the young woman in confusion. "I'm sorry. I thought you were someone I knew... I didn't realize..."

Patrick caught up to them a few seconds later. He picked up the girl's cap from the ground, and handed it back to her. "Here. Please accept our apologies. It was all a mistake."

The girl stared at them, eyebrows furrowed. "Do you always chase your friends like that?" She shook her head. "Just leave me alone, okay? You've got nothing to do with me, and that's just the way I'd like to keep it." Hearing her name called, she turned around and waved at a boy across the park. "That's my boyfriend, so unless you want trouble, you'll leave me alone."

Melanie gave Patrick a wry grin. "That should terrify us into good behavior." For the first time, Melanie noticed the loose grass that clung to his shirt and pants. "What happened to you?"

"I tripped over a poodle back there," he muttered.

Suddenly Melanie began to laugh. "What a day! I practically mug a teenager, and you end up being outmaneuvered by someone's pooch."

Patrick smiled sheepishly. "Let's get back to the office," he said. "We're not safe out here. This park's too open."

Melanie quickened her pace. The deadly hunt they were enmeshed in was wearing on her. Fear, however, was slowly being replaced with anger—and the need to strike back. "We did get something from Shy Eddy, Patrick." She took the mini tape recorder from her pocket and played back her conversation with him. "He definitely recognized one of the men."

"It's something, but not nearly enough. If only he could have told you which one," Patrick said wistfully. "There's also another possibility I don't believe you've considered. Maybe it was more than just the sound of the siren, or a person in a tweed hat, that made Shy Eddy run. A police car could have had a much more sinister meaning to him. There's still the Cartolucci connection to consider. What if Eddy saw police officers meeting with the murderer, or even police officers present when the bomb was planted?"

"That settles it. I'm going to find Shy Eddy again no matter what it takes."

Patrick shook his head. "We both know Shy Eddy is impossible to locate when he's frightened, which is most of the time. Charlie Perkins will be putting his apple stall back out on the street tomorrow, so leaving an apple for him isn't going to work anymore." He followed her inside the building, unlocked their office door, then walked back inside with her.

She cursed softly. "We were so close."

"Don't feel so badly, Melanie. We tried. Besides, Shy Eddy's testimony would have never stood up in court. Also, from the tape you made of your conversation, it's not really clear if he actually recognized one of the men, or was only referring to a resemblance."

"That's true," she conceded morosely.

"There is something good that has come of this, though. Do you realize that you and I are really working as a team lately? When I ran out of leads to pursue, you came up with the idea of tracking down Shy Eddy. It may not have turned out the way we'd hoped, but it was a very good plan. And we do have something to show for our efforts. Shy Eddy did respond to those photographs."

He sat on the corner of her desk and regarded her seriously. "Let's also not forget that together we were able to find a suspect neither of his had considered before, Albert Smith. Even if that turns out to have nothing to do with Dad's murder, I have a feeling there's something there that the authorities are going to be very interested in when we're through. And last but not least, don't you remember when those thugs got hold of the building janitor? You and I complemented each other's efforts then as instinctively as people who've worked together for years." He held her eyes steadily. "We fit around each other's jagged edges, Melanie. That's what teamwork's all about."

"We do work well as partners." She realized now that Patrick had finally come to accept her as a legitimate member of the firm his father had founded. Her heart swelled with pride, and another emotion she didn't want to put into words. "I'm glad you came here, Patrick," she admitted. The moment their eyes met, she realized that her heart had spoken the words out loud, and instinctively he'd sensed the truth they conveyed. "This agency needs you," she added quickly, trying to mask her slip.

"And you, Melanie, do you need me, too?" His voice was deep and smoky, reverberating with a singleness of purpose.

"Patrick, don't," she pleaded, afraid her resolve would weaken. She stood and started to move away when his hand closed over hers.

Patrick pulled her back toward him gently. "I can't keep denying what's going on, Melanie. The more I know you, the more I feel as if I've found the other half of myself. We complete each other, sweetheart, in every way there is."

He took her mouth in a searing kiss that left her weak all over. "I love you, lady, and I guess I have for some time now."

The words took her by surprise, her heart melting along with her resistance. "Patrick..." she answered, ready to tell him what he'd wanted to hear. But she never had the chance.

He brought his lips down over hers once more, smothering the words. He invaded her mouth, thrusting deeply with his tongue. When he eased his hold, she was trembling. "No protests, not now, Melanie." His gaze filled with tenderness. "I'm not asking you for anything in return, only that you accept the love I can give you."

She wanted to tell him she loved him, but as he traced a moist path down the column of her throat with his mouth all that escaped her lips was a sigh.

Patrick unbuttoned her blouse, then slipped it off her shoulders. In one easy motion he bared her breasts to his gaze and lowered his mouth over one rosy peak.

She gasped, then arched toward him. "Patrick..." She held her breath as he ran his hands over her, staking a claim, eliciting responses she'd long denied. A need, vibrant and primitive, washed over her. It was a force so powerful, conscious thought dissolved before its assault. It was enough to feel the warmth that was filling her, insisting, gathering speed and rushing her toward uncompromising surrender.

In one fluid motion, he lifted her off her feet and carried her to his office. The light from the outer room pierced the darkened interior, filling it with a soft muted glow. Tenderly he set her on the couch, and kissed her again. "I can't let you walk away from me tonight. I need you, Melanie." The rough desire in his voice excited her.

His touch made her burn and ache with the same need that pounded through his veins.

He undressed her tenderly. "No more barriers, Melanie. Tonight you're mine. I want to see you like this, naked and vulnerable, needing me as much as I do you."

Standing by the edge of the couch, he undressed before her. He watched her eyes taking him in hungrily. At last he stood naked. His hard muscular body seemed to dominate the space around him. His huge strength beckoned to her.

She opened her arms, extending them toward him. "Love me, Patrick," she asked in a hushed voice, "and let me love you in return."

He leaned over, the shadow of his body covering her, and kissed her again deeply. She pressed herself into the kiss, opening herself fully to him. Her heart soared as she heard the husky groan that came from deep within him.

He welcomed her little moans of pleasure. His weight pinned her to the soft cushions, and he entered her with one powerful movement that tore her breath away. He felt her warmth enveloping him, and the way she cried out his name, arcing toward him, made him think he'd lose himself completely in what she offered. She was wild and totally uninhibited in his arms. Fire swept through him. He wanted to bury himself inside her. His body throbbed. Then, as she cried out, his strength soared through her and, breathlessly, their spirits joined.

He gathered her against him.

Melanie buried her head against the hollow of his neck. Her fingers twined through the soft matt of golden hairs that covered his muscular chest.

She nestled beside him for a brief moment, but as he relaxed, her body began to stiffen ever so slightly in his arms. Something was wrong; he could feel it. Yet moments ago, she'd been his. "Tell me what you're thinking, sweetheart," he cajoled huskily.

"Later, perhaps," she answered, a trace of sadness in her voice.

"No," he insisted. "Talk to me. No more secrets. We're past that, Melanie," he coaxed gently.

She pushed away, a curious mixture of regret and longing etched on her features. "Our feelings could weaken us at a time we can least afford it." She ran her fingers across his shoulders in a light caress, then tore her gaze from his.

"Love could make us even stronger, if you let it, Melanie," he murmured.

"Or it could tear us apart." She sat up slowly, knowing she had to leave now or she'd never find the will. "What happened tonight is not your fault. I'm as much to blame as you for letting things go this far. But we just can't look toward the future until the past is settled.'' She gathered her clothing, and began to get dressed. ''I don't regret what we've shared, but we have a debt that must be paid first, don't you see?'' She pleaded for his understanding in a soft voice. ''We can't put our feelings ahead of the duty we have to perform. If we do, what we've found together will ultimately destroy us. We'll fail ourselves as well as each other.'' She stood and smoothed her clothing.

''I can't stop loving you, Melanie, even if the time is all wrong.'' He captured her eyes and held them. ''No more than you can stop your feelings for me.''

''We don't have a choice.'' She struggled to keep her voice steady. ''One or both of us may die before this is over, and in order to find Andy's murderer we have to be willing to accept that risk.''

He stood and dressed. ''So you're saying that love has no place in our lives.''

''We can't allow it in, Patrick. Not now.'' She had to force him away, to put some emotional distance between them. It was one of the hardest things she had ever done, but holding her head high, she started toward the door.

''It's too late for that, sweetheart, much too late,'' she heard him say.

Chapter Sixteen

Albert sat across the kitchen table, facing Conrad. "So that's the whole story," he said wearily. "Anna's my only daughter, and I love her very much. I don't ever want to see her hurt," he said softly, stirring his coffee. "That's why I have to ask you to keep this between us."

"She'll never find out the truth from me, Albert, I swear that."

"I knew you'd understand and honor my wishes. You've always had a very special place in my heart, Conrad. Your father was my best friend, and watching you and Anna grow up together was a constant source of pleasure for me. Frederick and I were both very happy when you two decided to marry. To Frederick, Anna was the daughter he never had, and to me, you've been like a son."

"I don't understand why Dad never told me about his past or yours. I would have understood and protected your secrets."

"Your father and I made new lives here in America after the war, Conrad. The past was something that we never spoke about, even to each other. We'd accepted having to live with the fear of being discovered someday, but we didn't want our families to carry that burden as well."

"If I'd known I would never have applied for a position that required security clearance."

"Don't judge your father too harshly, Conrad. Perhaps you should have been told, but remember that, by keeping the facts from you, he was trying to prevent his own past from ever harming you." Albert stared pensively at the dark liquid in his cup. "He did realize, though, that he'd made a mistake in not telling you about himself. He came to me a few days prior to the accident and admitted he'd been wrong. He never got the chance to tell you as he'd planned. Then, after his death, I postponed saying anything, although that duty had fallen to me, because I felt you needed time to adjust. I tried to help you through that difficult time as much as I could."

"And I'm grateful for that, Albert, believe me," Conrad answered in a hushed tone. He looked around to make sure his daughter had not wandered into the room, then added, "I don't think I could have faced identifying the remains, particularly the way the body had been burned."

"You've never had to face death, but your father and I have many times. It was an ever-present reality in our lives for many years." He remained quiet for several moments. "I'm glad that the life we've provided for you and Anna here in this country has sheltered you both from that."

"It still doesn't seem real, you and Dad *spies*? It's like watching a movie and getting swept up into it." Conrad sipped his coffee slowly, his voice almost in a whisper now. "I remember when you told me that it was imperative I withdraw my job application. When you explained that both you and Dad had been sent to the United States during World War II to learn the secrets of the atomic bomb, I was certain you were crazy. It still doesn't seem possible." He shook his head, bewildered.

He smiled. "You see me as an old man, a family man, Cindy's granddaddy. But there was a time during my youth when I owed no allegiance to anything or anyone, except my homeland."

Conrad leaned back in his chair and carefully studied the man before him. He didn't want to ask, but he knew he had to face the entire truth. "You were soldiers of a kind then, but those days are long past." He started to say more but Albert interrupted him.

"Not so long, and not so past," Albert snapped crossly. "That's the whole problem. Andrew O'Riley saw something was wrong with the background information you furnished him. He was a very thorough man. Even when you told him you were withdrawing your application, he didn't stop investigating. His curiosity had been aroused. I had hoped that with his death at the hands of some madman, our troubles would be over. But now his son and that woman who worked with him are snooping around. They keep coming back with more questions, and they are watching your every move. If they have discovered your father's and my own forged papers they may try to connect us to the murder."

"Albert, there's something I have to ask. I wish to God I didn't have to, but I've got to know. Were you responsible for the man's death?"

Albert glanced up quickly, surprise evident on his face. "Me? Everyone has the secrets of the atom bomb now, Conrad. There would be no reason for me to kill O'Riley."

"What if he exposed you?" Conrad insisted.

Albert shrugged. "Even if he did, nothing much would happen. The few people who knew of our mission here have been dead for years, and we stopped our espionage work when the war ended. Undoubtedly, I'd be held and questioned until they were certain I wasn't keeping anything from them," Albert continued, weighing the possibilities as he spoke. "However, after that, I'd probably be granted asylum here and the matter would be quickly dropped. You see, I'd be an embarrassment to them. Even if they threw me in prison, I'm sure the courts would take into account my age and the fact I haven't broken any of this country's laws in over forty years."

Albert took his cup to the sink and washed it out. "I wouldn't even have to worry about you and Anna. You're both United States citizens so they couldn't touch you for my crimes." He placed the cup on the drain rack and dried his hands.

They heard a car pull into the garage. "Anna's back from the grocery store. I'll go help her bring the bags in. Would you go check and see if Cindy has woken up from her nap?" Conrad stood and met his father-in-law's gaze. "I'm sorry I doubted you, Albert."

Albert gave him a quick hug. "It's not important now. We're family, and that's the only thing that really matters."

"WE'VE BEEN DRIVING around for hours, Melanie. Let's go back to the office. We're not getting anywhere with this."

"Shy Eddy could clear up several things for us. All I need is a few more minutes with him. He's got to be around someplace."

"You haven't seen him in days. He's probably hiding out," Patrick answered patiently. "What makes you think we can just spot him from the street? Be reasonable." He wiped the perspiration from his forehead. "Turn the car around, and let's go back."

Melanie said nothing. Shy Eddy was, at the moment, the only element of their case they could actually work on. Without something tangible to occupy her, Patrick would slowly become the focus of her thoughts. It was an ever-present temptation she had to struggle to resist. Andy's killer was still somewhere at large. They could be next. And if their turn came, it would happen when they'd least expect it—as it had for Andy.

When the cellular car telephone buzzed, Patrick answered it. "I was just thinking about you, Brother Paul. You must have ESP," Patrick commented. "Any news on Shy Eddy?"

"After you telephoned and told me what happened, I've been asking around." The man's voice sounded rushed. "Then this morning, he showed up at the refuge. It was obvious he was very ill, so we took him to the county hospital. Eddy's been admitted with pneumonia, and his condition isn't good."

"Could we visit with him for a few minutes?" Patrick insisted. "If nothing else, I know my partner would like to see him."

His words caught her attention. Melanie glanced at Patrick, then back to the road.

"I'll tell her. Thanks for calling, Brother Paul." Patrick placed the telephone back, and recounted what he'd just learned. "Eddy won't be allowed visitors, at least not for a few days," he added.

"I'll send him a basket filled with apples. Maybe that will cheer him up." Melanie took a deep breath, then let it out slowly. "I like Shy Eddy, you know. Not just because he's a source, either," she added with a shrug.

"I know," Patrick answered, a gentle smile playing over his lips. "You'd like to present yourself as tough and hard-hearted, a woman driven only by intellect. But you're not, lady," he said softly.

She gave him a stony glare, then turned back to her driving. "I can be, and don't you forget it."

"Yes, ma'am," he teased, undaunted.

Shortly afterward they returned to their office. "I've run out of ideas to pursue, Patrick," Melanie admitted dejectedly.

"I have one, and I think it might work." He readjusted his jacket. "We already know that Reed is the type of man who can be pressured. I think we should pay him a visit and try to rattle him. I've got a gut feeling he knows something that he's not telling us, and I want to find out what that might be."

"How?" Melanie followed Patrick back to the car.

"I'll play it by ear. In this particular case, since we lack hard evidence, we're going to have to poke and prod and see how he reacts."

"It beats sitting around and waiting to see what develops," she muttered. "I like your game plan, Patrick. If we don't start making our own breaks, we'll never solve this case."

By the time they arrived at Conrad Reed's home, Melanie was tense. They had been fighting shadows for too long.

She walked with Patrick to the front door and waited. A moment later Conrad answered. His face contorted into a scowl. "This is beginning to wear thin. What do you want now?"

"We'd like to talk to you for a few minutes," Patrick answered calmly. "I believe you'll find what we have to say very interesting."

"I've heard enough, O'Riley. Would you kindly leave me and my family alone?" He was about to close the door when Patrick lodged his foot in the way.

"Wait a second." Patrick met Conrad's gaze. "We're trying to give you a break, man. We know that you're in over your head on this. We've got an eyewitness who can place your father-in-law, Albert Smith, at the scene of my father's murder." Patrick saw the startled look on Conrad's face, and decided to continue the bluff now that he had Conrad's attention. It was all or nothing now. "You're involved with this, Reed, whether you want to be or not. You're going to take the fall with Albert Smith unless you cooperate with us."

"I don't believe you," Conrad replied, obviously shaken. "My father-in-law is not a murderer. You've been unable to find the real killer, so you're grasping at straws, looking for someone to pin it on." He collected himself quickly. "It's your way of hiding from your own incompetence and expiating your conscience," he countered boldly.

The remark struck hard. Patrick's eyes narrowed slightly.

Melanie saw the flash of pain that had crossed Patrick's face. "Mr. Reed," she interjected quickly, "my partner, Andy O'Riley, was killed when a bomb encased in a coffee can was placed inside his car. The police lab is now using a new spectrographic process that will be able to match the residue on the bomb fragments to microscopic samples of the original materials. For instance, if the bomb was made here at your house, or at Albert Smith's apartment, the lab technicians will be able to find physical evidence of it. Tiny traces of metal shavings from the bomb casing will be present, caught between rug fibers or cracks in the floor. Particles of the explosive itself could have also been absorbed into the counter surfaces where they might have been placed for a few minutes. It's impossible to clear all that out, no matter how hard you try. Armed with that evidence, the police will have enough to convict the guilty party of my partner's murder.''

''We don't believe you had anything to do with the actual murder, Reed, but we are certain you're protecting the guilty party. The police already have a search warrant in the works. Cooperate with us and we'll testify on your behalf,'' Patrick said. ''You don't want to spend the next decade in prison. You have a daughter and a wife to think about.''

''We have reason to believe that Albert Smith and your father came to the United States during World War II as spies. We're not going to stop investigating until we get to the bottom of this. You could be convicted as an accessory for withholding information. Help yourself by helping us,'' Melanie insisted.

Conrad hesitated. He chose his words carefully. ''You're both very smooth talkers, but the fact remains you're not the police, and I just don't believe you. Just because you may have uncovered a few mysteries associated with Albert's past does not make him a murderer. I'm sure both of *you* have secrets in your past, things you prefer not to even think about.'' He looked intently at Melanie then at Patrick. ''But instead of showing compassion, you're dragging my dead father's name through the mud, and accusing poor Albert of God knows what. He's not a killer.'' Conrad kicked Patrick's foot out of the way, and slammed the door shut.

Melanie was silent as they returned to the car. She remained thoughtful as Patrick drove them back to the office. The look Conrad had given her still burned in her mind. He'd been right. She did have things in her past that she wished she could forget. ''Conrad had a point, you know," she admitted sadly. "Everyone has skeletons in their closets. When he stood there staring at us, I remembered Andy. There were so many things I might have done differently if only I'd known."

"Melanie, surely by now you can accept that what happened wasn't your fault. There was no way you could have prevented Dad from being killed even if you had accompanied him to the car. If Dad didn't spot that bomb, you probably wouldn't have, either. All you could have done was get yourself killed, too."

She nodded slowly. "Intellectually I've known that all along, I guess. I just couldn't cope with the fact my partner had died so suddenly and without any warning. Nothing I could have done at the time would have prevented that, but I wanted to blame myself because that would mean I hadn't been helpless. Accepting that it was completely out of my control scared me. It meant facing that we can be separated from anyone or anything we love in an instant. It's reality at its most frightening."

He reached for her hand and gave it a squeeze. "The only thing any of us can do is face life with all the courage we can find and all the belief we can muster." He said nothing more for several minutes then continued. "I thought of Dad back there, too," he admitted, "and of all the things we might have shared someday. That's when I stopped being angry with Reed. I don't blame him, you know. He's trying to protect what he holds dear. Either one of us would do the same." He took a deep breath. "By the same token, he's wrong about me." Patrick clenched his jaw, then forced himself to relax. "I'm not trying to pin a murder on him or anyone else. I'm after the killer, and I'll do whatever it takes to find that person. But I want justice, not a scapegoat."

Melanie touched his arm lightly. "I know that. And if Reed or his father-in-law is the murderer, rest assured that we've stirred up the hornet's nest. Now we watch our backs and sit tight."

ALBERT SAT on a lawn chair in Conrad's backyard, sipping ice tea. The fringes of their patio umbrella swayed in the breeze.

"Albert, I want your word of honor that you didn't have anything to do with Andrew O'Riley's murder," Conrad demanded. He paced beneath the branches of an old maple tree, restless.

"I've already answered that question, Conrad. You shouldn't let them rattle you this way. That's their intent, you know."

"What about the bomb fragments, and the lab tests?" he countered, repeating what Melanie had said. "Albert, you use our garage on your woodworking and hobby projects all the time. What if they find something, or worse yet, plant some incriminating evidence there?"

"Conrad, first of all, it's impossible for them to find what never has been there to begin with. And I doubt very much if they'd plant anything. Also, in this country, the police need probable cause in order to obtain a search warrant. They don't have that. And even if they do manage to get a search warrant, we'd both watch them, and perhaps even get an attorney to supervise the procedure." Albert stood and walked toward his son-in-law. Placing his hands firmly on the younger man's shoulders, he gave him a confident smile. "Now get hold of yourself. I'm all for being cautious, but in this particular case, your fears are groundless."

Conrad shook free. "There's so much you kept hidden. What else are you still keeping from me?" he asked in a weary voice.

"I'm sorry that it has to come to this between us, Conrad." Albert stared hard at him. "For your information the day Andrew O'Riley was killed, I was at my lodge's annual business meeting. I arrived midmorning and didn't leave until late that evening. Patrick O'Riley hasn't been able to verify my alibi because Eric Higgins has been off on one of his jaunts to Florida. But Eric called me last night, so I know he's back in San Francisco now. All it will take to exonerate me is one phone call."

"I'm sorry that I had to press you, Albert." Shame and sorrow made his voice taut. "Once, not too long ago, I would have never said anything at all, but there've just been too many secrets between us."

HOURS LATER, Melanie leaned back in her chair, and stared at the office walls. She could sense Patrick's growing impatience with their investigation, and that knowledge just served to increase her own tension.

Patrick came out of his office. "I've got to get out of here for a while, Melanie. I'm starting to go stir-crazy again. I'm going for a drive, then home. Why don't you do the same? It's almost quitting time, anyway."

"The insurance adjuster is coming over in a little while," Melanie replied. "I have to wait until he gets here. Our landlord, thank heavens, has withdrawn his request that we move out. But our liability status is being changed and the agent wants to reclassify the business as high risk. That'll mean a hike in our premiums but it can't be helped. Since we're up for renewal anyway, I'm also going to increase our coverage all the way around, at least until we finish with the murder investigation."

"I'll stay then," he offered.

"Don't worry, I can handle it. Go ahead. As soon as I finish, I'll lock up and get out of here myself."

Patrick left the office reluctantly. Melanie would be safe enough for now. The building was still filled with people, and they were continuing to keep the door locked. Knowing she was out of danger, at least for the time being, would free him to concentrate on what to do next.

As he stepped outside he felt a late afternoon breeze ruffle his hair. He took a deep breath. This case was slowly tearing him apart, and his mood was darkening as a consequence.

He drove away from the building and merged with traffic. After a few minutes, he picked up the cellular telephone and called Mike. He'd expected resistance when he suggested a meeting. Setting up an appointment at the coffee shop, he slipped through the afternoon traffic with the skill of a professional driver. Mike's eagerness to meet with him had alerted Patrick. He sensed there had been a break on the case.

Patrick sat at one of the corner tables with Mike across from him. "I wish I had something to trade, Mike," Patrick admitted, "but we haven't really made any progress. We're doing fringe investigations at the moment that may or may not have anything to do with Dad's case. Both Melanie and I have started to run out of avenues to pursue. That's why I'm here. I wanted to find out how the department's faring on this."

"Patrick, I agreed to meet with you because there's something I want to say, man to man." Mike glanced at his coffee cup, then back up at him. "Your father and I were friends, and out of deference to him, I've tried to be patient with you. However, being a private investigator excluded you from a great deal of information that the department had. Despite what you concluded, we weren't just letting the Clancy investigation slide. The car you saw that day by Clancy's apartment complex was one of ours. My men told me you'd spotted them, but none of us were at liberty to tell you what we were doing.

"The department has been investigating a stolen-car ring for several months now. Part of the reason we released Clancy from jail so quickly was that we'd suspected he was involved with the operation. When John Hutchins showed up as his attorney, we were sure of it. Clancy's reported income couldn't have paid a third of that man's fees. We decided at that time to use Clancy to lead us to the others. We knew we needed more evidence against Clancy in order to keep him in jail for questioning. We figured he'd break down and lead us to the ring, and possibly to Cartolucci, if we confined him long enough."

Mike took a sip of his coffee, then continued. "Since the department was also conducting a full-scale investigation into the other allegations made in that file of Andy's, our manpower was stretched to the limit. Mathers couldn't spare the number of police officers needed to work our end of the case. We borrowed men from Burglary, but even then we could only stake out Clancy part of the time. Thanks to you and Melanie, and the information you gave us, we were finally able to break the ring. You two discovered their method of operation that day you tailed Clancy. This criminal organization had its members stealing cars and simply moving them to another parking area. Later, when the heat was off, they had the second team come in and drive the vehicle to their chop shop. Once you gave us the warehouse address, it was simple. We raided the place and arrested Clancy, as well as half a dozen others. Even their slick lawyer, Hutchins, was in on it. He was financing the operation."

"I'm glad we could help, Mike, but I gather you still don't have anything linking Clancy to Dad's murder." His voice held a wary edge. If Mike was hoping to divert him from that by getting Clancy on a lesser charge, it wasn't going to work. Compromise was not a word he was willing to associate with his father's murder investigation.

"It all ties in, Patrick, but you're going to be unhappy with the connection. You see, the members of the ring would dismantle the cars at the warehouse and sell the parts. The chop-shop operation was quite profitable for them. They spent a lot of time there. And as it turned out, Clancy was busy dismantling a Jaguar the day of Andy's death."

Patrick gave Mike an incredulous look. "Oh, come on! You believe him? On what basis, the corroboration of the other members of that group of car thieves?"

Mike shook his head. "A city utility crew had the street in front of the warehouse blocked off that day. They were required to remove the barriers in front of the building's only entrance anytime someone needed to enter or exit what was being passed off as an 'auto repair shop.' One of the city workers remembered Clancy going in the building's main door in a silver Jaguar just before noon, but not leaving during their shift. The reason he specifically remembers Clancy, and not just the car, was that Clancy had become angry with him when he was a bit slow removing the barrier and almost ran him down.''

Patrick's shoulders sagged. "That sounds like Clancy. Well, I guess this lets him off the hook."

"I'm afraid so," Mike agreed. "For obvious reasons, Clancy had been reluctant to clear himself of one crime by revealing another. Right now Clancy's in the hospital under guard. He resisted arrest, and ended up with a broken collarbone."

"Well, I should be grateful. At least this is one suspect we can definitely cross off our list." Patrick finished his coffee, then waited for the waitress to refill his cup. "What about Cartolucci?"

"That case has taken a very strange turn," Mike conceded. "He's just dropped out of sight. No one has seen or heard from the man in several days. There's a rumor circulating that Cartolucci has fled to South America. However, his attorneys insist that he's in seclusion at his estate."

The possibility of a police cover-up still remained. Had Cartolucci put out a contract on his father? "Have there been any suspected hit men in the area recently?"

"We're still looking into that, but remember we've been concentrating our efforts on Clancy. Until a few hours ago we thought *he'd* furnish us with the needed connection to Cartolucci. Captain Mathers, in fact, grilled him for over four hours. He wants to put an end to all the speculation concerning police corruption just as badly as you want to find your father's killer," Mike stated flatly.

"Mike, I'm not letting this case go, even if it means I've got to follow Cartolucci out of the country. If he ordered the hit, I'm going to find out. You can bank on that." Patrick accompanied Mike to the door, and together they traversed the parking lot.

"I didn't expect anything less, Patrick," Mike admitted. He stopped beside an old, beat-up four-door sedan.

"What happened to your beautiful sports car?" Patrick asked, as Mike fished the keys for the sedan out of his pocket and began to unlock the door.

Mike laughed. "*My* beautiful sports car? Don't I wish!"
He slipped behind the driver's seat. "My wife leased the car
for me as a birthday present. She could only afford one
month's lease, so I had to return it yesterday." His face grew
wistful. "It was the best birthday present I ever had."

MELANIE ESCORTED the insurance adjuster to the door. The
man had come an hour and a half early, so that left her with
part of the afternoon free. Yet she was too restless to call it
a day and just go home. There had to be something she
could do. Patrick had mistakenly taken today's mail with
him, so she sat at her desk and stared at the file she'd compiled on Andy's case. The more she studied their findings on
the Reed investigation, the more curious she became. There
was something about it that drew her back to the puzzle time
and time again. Like Andy, she, too, found it impossible to
ignore a mystery. The only real question was did it have
anything to do with Andy's death?

She decided to stake out Albert's apartment. Maybe she'd
learn something new. At any rate, it was better than going
home. Lately her place seemed even emptier than usual. The
silence there taunted her. It was as if her apartment had
suddenly grown too large for just one person. She'd begun
to feel more at home at the office than anywhere else. At
least here the scent of Patrick's after-shave clung to the air,
and his presence filled the office, warming her spirit.

Melanie stared at the telephone, trying to decide whether
to call Patrick now and tell him her plans. He'd looked so
tired and in such need of time to himself! She really didn't
want to bother him; everyone needed a break now and then.
Besides, she probably wasn't going to learn anything new.
It was mostly her way of keeping busy.

She picked up the receiver and called Patrick's home
phone. Leaving a message on the machine, she felt satisfied. He'd go for his drive, then once he came home, he'd
get the latest update on her plans.

Melanie made sure everything was locked tight, then
walked to the parking lot. She'd park near Albert Smith's

apartment and watch. She couldn't lose, even if she was spotted. In fact, if she managed to make him nervous enough, maybe he'd make a mistake and she'd finally get some answers.

PATRICK CROSSED his living room and walked into the kitchen. With a can of soda in hand, he returned to the sofa. As he tossed his jacket over the cushion beside him, his gaze fell upon the letters he'd picked up from the office mailbox on the way out to lunch today. He'd tucked the mail in his pocket, and completely forgotten about it until now.

He lifted the letters out of his jacket pocket, and began to sort through them. There was a utility bill, a letter from a corporation the agency had been doing business with, and another envelope that had become stuck to the previous one. He gently pried it loose. The return address caught his attention immediately. Since noon, he'd been carrying the response they'd been waiting for from the Imperial War Museum in London. He muttered an oath.

Patrick quickly tore open the envelope. The contents took him by surprise. The expert at the Museum had identified the early version of Frederick Reed's photograph. He'd matched it to one of Gerhard Stadt, a German intelligence officer who'd interviewed downed Allied pilots during the early part of World War II. Stadt had been a physics graduate from the University of Cologne, apparently a gifted scholar, when he'd been recruited to serve in German intelligence at the start of the war. He'd spoken perfect English. He'd dropped out of sight in Germany in 1944, and was never seen again.

An even greater bonus was the tentative identification of Albert Smith. If they were right, his real name was Emil Osterkamp. He'd been recognized from a comparison of prewar English newspaper clippings. Osterkamp had been a small-time German entertainer/magician who'd toured Europe in the mid-thirties. He'd duplicated some of Houdini's escape stunts in his act.

While in England in 1937, Osterkamp had been caught forging a check, and had been unceremoniously deported. His name later appeared in German secret service—Abwehr—documents as a training officer. He'd also disappeared during the latter part of the war.

Patrick stared at the letter for a long time. They had speculated that Reed and Smith might actually be Soviet spies, but the news that they were really *German* spies took him by complete surprise. Exactly what had his father stumbled onto? Frederick Reed had died before Andy, so that left Albert Smith responsible for the forged transcript and the substitution of photographs on the documents at least. Only it still didn't explain his father's murder, unless he'd been killed just to protect Smith's identity.

Patrick glanced at his watch. It was still early. The insurance adjuster wouldn't be at the office for another fifty minutes or so. He'd go back to the office, and give Melanie the news in person. Maybe together they could come up with some new theories, or make more sense of the old ones.

Grabbing his coat, and putting it on quickly, Patrick rushed back to his car. He slipped between two cars and emerged with a clear lane ahead. It now looked as if Reed and Smith, aka Stadt and Osterkamp, had been sent to the United States as a team to learn about the atomic bomb, and either steal the technology or sabotage its construction. That would explain Reed's connection with the Oak Ridge facility and the Hanover, Washington, site. Smith's job had probably been to support Reed's espionage efforts while remaining as unobtrusive as possible.

Patrick tried to recall what he could about that period in history. If memory served him right, the Allies had been advancing on all fronts. Hitler had been desperate, striking out with V-1 and V-2 rockets, and a few jet aircraft. When his spies had learned of the atomic bomb project in the United States, he'd probably figured Berlin would be their first target. Undoubtedly, that's how Reed and Smith had received their mission. They'd arrived in the United States in 1944. How they'd actually entered the country didn't matter.

Patrick pulled into the parking lot adjacent to the office, then switched off the ignition. Perhaps the trail leading to his father's murderer had been right before him all along. After all, the O.S.I. lab had reported that the bomb that had been placed inside his father's car had utilized World War II explosives of foreign origin. It could have been German in design.

He quickly strode down the hall. Melanie's gut feeling had been right. The case had indeed started to break open. Perhaps shadowing Albert Smith would yield some additional clues. But now the threat of danger was more pronounced than ever. How far would Smith go to keep his past a secret?

Patrick unlocked the agency door, and walked inside. So where was Melanie? The insurance representative wasn't even due to arrive for another half hour, yet Melanie's car wasn't in the parking lot. Patrick walked to her desk, and glanced around. Maybe she'd left a note. She wouldn't have left the office without letting him know where she could be reached. At one time that wouldn't have been unusual, but not anymore.

MELANIE SAT on the bus-stop bench. From her position, she could only see part of Albert's front porch, but she was within sight of the entire courtyard that faced it. She also had a clear view of his rear door. It was the perfect vantage point. If Albert left, using either exit, she'd know. The tinted plastic dome that sheltered the bus stop offered ideal cover, obscuring her from his eyes should he look out.

Her biggest problem was the heat. She wiped the perspiration from her brow. With the sun shining directly on it, the greenhouselike enclosure felt stifling.

She stood, ready to walk around for a bit, when she saw someone leaving Albert's apartment. The tweed cap immediately caught her attention. She leaned forward against the plastic, and tried to get a better look. From what she could see of his hair color, size and build, she was certain it was Albert.

She thought about following him, but then stopped. She was being given the perfect opportunity. With Albert out of the way, she could sneak into his apartment using one of her skeleton keys, and take a look around. Maybe if she could get something with his fingerprints on it, they'd be able to determine who he really was.

Melanie waited fifteen minutes, watching the apartment for signs of movement inside. Finally satisfied that she'd be safe, she approached the back door. It was several seemingly endless moments before she could find a key that would work.

Then she heard the lock yield. She slowly turned the handle and opened the door. She smiled, satisfied with herself, and slipped inside.

Chapter Seventeen

She practically collided with Albert Smith. He spun her around, and cruelly twisted her arm behind her back. "Tell me what you're doing here," he ordered. "And you better hope I like your answer."

Melanie gathered her wits quickly, her instincts working overtime. This was no time to show weakness. Maybe she could talk him into giving himself up. "I know all about you, Mr. Smith. I also know that you're working with someone else. Your partner, the man in the tweed cap I saw leaving, is the same man who fired shots into my apartment. You can't hope to hide out forever. The past always catches up to you."

"My past, Ms. Cardenas?" he asked in a soft, purring voice. "Tell me what you've learned."

Her heart lodged in her throat, hammering at a runaway pace. His voice was that of a funeral director's, soft and filled with a false sincerity that fooled no one. She began to wonder if she'd make it out of that apartment alive. "To begin with, we can link you to my partner's murder. The bomb was probably made in Conrad's garage, with or without his help, or else right here." The knowledge that she was in very serious trouble filled her with desperate bravado. Furtively she inched her free arm across the front of her body, reaching very slowly toward her purse. "There's a special spectrographic process that can match the metal filings and explosive particles found to the actual bomb fragments.''

"You tried that hustle on Conrad. You might have fooled him, but I'm a little tougher to deal with," he shot back in the same chilling tone.

"We also know that Conrad's father was a Soviet spy sent to the United States," she continued quickly. She kept her body as still as possible, hoping to mask the barely perceptible motion of her hand as she worked it toward her goal. "He'd posed as Bernard Cain while trying to steal atomic secrets at Oak Ridge, Tennessee, and used forged transcripts from the University of Pennsylvania to get that teaching job in Seattle." She paused, then in a tone as cold as his, added, "The fact that your past also seems to start in 1945, indicates that you're also a spy."

Feeling his grip tighten, Melanie held her breath. She'd struck a nerve with her last remark. He'd be far more dangerous now. "Look, in order to save your daughter and her family a lot of publicity and anguish, why don't you turn yourself in now? We may not have enough to convict you for Andy O'Riley's murder yet, but we will soon enough."

She finally reached her purse and slowly began to weave her fingertips inside. "Besides, what we know of your past is enough for the federal government to have you arrested for fraud, forgery and espionage. In fact, at this very moment, Patrick O'Riley is meeting with the authorities, showing them the trail of evidence we've uncovered. Neither Patrick nor I want to hurt your family in any way. They're innocent. Cooperate and we'll do our best to keep the reporters from getting hold of this story. All we want is to see justice served." Melanie could feel the cold steel of her gun against the tips of her fingers now.

Suddenly Albert pushed her hard. She careened across the room, off balance. Desperately she tried to break her fall with outstretched hands. Her purse, revolver still inside, flew off her shoulder. Scrambling to her feet, she dived toward it, but Smith anticipated her and kicked the handbag away.

"Admirable effort, Ms. Cardenas." He grabbed a nine-millimeter pistol from a cabinet drawer. "But not quite good enough."

Albert stood back and pointed the barrel of the Walther P-38 directly at her chest. "I tend to think that everything you've been telling me is nothing more than a skillful bluff. Not that I blame you at all," he added congenially. "I'd have probably done the same. The only problem is that your story just isn't convincing enough. You see, I don't think the authorities know as much as you claim. If they did, they would have been here by now." He laughed softly. "And by the way, Ms. Cardenas, if there's one thing I'm *not*, it's a Soviet spy. Perhaps you should have done your homework better."

Melanie slowly stood then started to edge away from him.

Albert shook his head. "Don't, Ms. Cardenas. That's a good way to get yourself killed."

She froze. "We've been working closely with the police," she warned.

He laughed. "Yes, I know how they've welcomed your help," he answered sarcastically. "I followed Patrick O'Riley to the station once, and saw the police captain throw him out." He gave her a look filled with mock sympathy.

Melanie was about to answer when she heard the soft pad of footsteps behind her. Before she could turn her head, she felt the impact of something hard as it smashed against her skull. An explosion of lights went off before her eyes and a hot wave of fire traveled through her skull. Her head began to spin, her body felt light as air and a curtain of darkness descended over her.

MELANIE AWOKE slowly. She blinked several times, annoyed that her body didn't quite seem to work. Her mouth felt swollen, and her headache was monumental. Her ears were ringing. Slowly she realized that she was bound to a chair, and a gag had been tied tightly around her mouth.

She could hear Albert's voice, like a deadly echo, in the next room. It suddenly occurred to her that she was no longer in Smith's apartment. Wherever she was now, it was in a small, simply furnished house or cottage. Trying to learn what was to happen to her next, Melanie struggled to concentrate on the words.

"That's right, Conrad. Go to Patrick O'Riley, and do as I ask, just one more time. Tell him I'm willing to turn myself over to him as a former German spy. Convince him I'm prepared to be deported or jailed, as long as our family will be protected." There was a pause. "Conrad, your father and I came to the United States with a mission for our country. To accomplish that Frederick was forced to kill an American named Cain in order to assume his identity and infiltrate the Oak Ridge facility. Whether or not you agree with what he did, your father was a loyal German officer. He did what any soldier would have done to fulfill his duties."

Melanie tried to make some sense out of what she was hearing. German soldiers? Is that what Andy had stumbled onto that had led to his murder? And what about her? Would she be killed, too? The thoughts formed and passed in a matter of seconds as she tried to work herself free.

"Until now, out of loyalty to your father, I've kept his secret. But, I'm not guilty of murder. I can prove I didn't kill Bernard Cain, or Andrew O'Riley, for that matter. If Patrick O'Riley still insists that I had something to do with his father's death, ask him to call Eric Higgins. He'll be able to clear me."

Melanie felt her body grow limp. Albert seemed so confident that Eric Higgins would be able to provide him with a perfect alibi. Was that because Higgins was involved in the conspiracy, too? All she knew about Higgins was that he traveled a lot and associated with Smith. She cursed herself for not looking into Higgins's past more carefully. Was he also an agent? He was the right age. Could he have been the man in the tweed cap? Andy had always said that it was the unknown factor that got you. Had Eric Higgins been the person who'd knocked her out?

The only thing she knew for sure right now was that it would be dangerous for Patrick to come. She had to get loose and warn him. Were they planning to use her against Patrick? Had that been the reason for her abduction?

"Conrad, all I want to do is cut a deal with Patrick O'Riley." Albert's voice filtered into the room where she was being held. "With your help, I think I've found a way to end this nightmare. The fact that I can prove I couldn't have been his father's murderer, and that I'm willing to turn myself in to him and undergo even closer scrutiny, ought to convince him. O'Riley has nothing to fear, I'm over sixty years old, and unarmed. O'Riley, of course, will be armed. Bring him here to my rental house, but only if he's alone. He has to agree to keep the police, and especially the press, away in the beginning. Once Patrick sees it's not a trap, then you can leave. I'll face this alone and keep you and the family out of it as best I can. Frederick is gone, and with me in the hands of the authorities maybe you, Anna and Cindy will be safe."

She heard the sound of a receiver being replaced on the telephone. Then Albert Smith entered the bedroom. "So, you're awake." He smiled. "Don't struggle against the ropes. You won't get loose. I guarantee it. You'll only make yourself more uncomfortable. Be patient," he said kindly. "It'll all be over soon. You have my word on that."

Something about his tone made her think of scarecrows flapping in the October winds, keeping faithful watch over their decaying fields.

CONRAD ARRIVED at O'Riley's office. He didn't relish this task. Albert had been like a father to him. Now, when times were tough, he deserved the support of his family.

Patrick was as difficult to convince as he'd expected. "Check out his alibi, O'Riley. He's a sixty-year-old man, for heaven's sake! You were the one who stirred this up. Okay, maybe he's not the murderer you hoped he'd be, but he's a human being. You started this mess when you discovered he was a spy during World War II, and dredged up events that were over forty years ago. Now finish it." He challenged Patrick with a level gaze. "Come with me. That way, we can be sure you don't bring in the reporters on this. The last thing my family needs is publicity. Then you can listen to what he has to say, and make up your mind what to do about it."

Patrick stared at him long and hard.

Conrad held his gaze. "Look, O'Riley, you'll be perfectly safe. If you're worried you can check me and my car for hidden weapons. To set your mind at ease, Albert will also be meeting you out in the open. You'll be the only one there with a gun."

Making his decision, Patrick glanced away. Where the hell was Melanie? He'd tried her car phone and apartment, and he still hadn't been able to get hold of her. He now regretted having encouraged her to take the rest of the afternoon off. "You say Higgins is back in town?"

"That's what Albert told me, and he wouldn't lie. Call Eric. He'll clear him."

Patrick opened the case file, and pulled out the telephone number. If Albert's alibi checked out, and he had a feeling it would, then they'd hit another dead end in their investigation. Catching a retired spy by coincidence would not avenge his father's murder.

The thought he might have failed utterly made his guts clench into a knot. He looked into Conrad Reed's face. Conrad had fulfilled his duty, even as they stood there. He, on the other hand, had so far managed only to complicate other lives while failing to find solutions to his own dilemma.

He dialed Eric Higgins's number. After a brief conversation with the man, Patrick hung up. Defeat left him feeling strangely void of emotions. He had nothing at all on

Cartolucci, who, by a process of elimination, seemed the only possible suspect left for his father's murder. And even that line of investigation seemed off track. He was almost back where they had started. All he had managed to do was rule out one more suspect.

Seeing Smith was almost anticlimactic now, so Melanie didn't need to be involved. He'd go and get it over with, and fill her in on the details later. Then they would join the police manhunt for Cartolucci. Maybe they'd have better luck than the cops.

"All right. Let's do it," Patrick said at last. "I'll follow you in my car." He scribbled a note for Melanie, and left it on her desk in case she came back to the office before he managed to reach her.

The ride was long. Patrick followed Conrad to a residential section south of San Francisco, near the outskirts of San Jose. At the end of one of the blocks, he spotted a house with a For Rent sign in front of it. In the last rays of light before sunset, Patrick saw Albert standing outside on the front porch.

Conrad parked in the narrow driveway while Patrick pulled up directly in front of the house. Patrick emerged from the car, and joined Albert and Conrad on the front lawn.

"I'm glad you came, O'Riley." Albert waved a hand behind him. "I've left the front door open. Go inside and check everything out. The house has only a few pieces of furniture so it should be an easy task. Once you're satisfied it's not a trap, then I'd like you to stay and hear my story. It'll be just the two of us. I don't want Conrad included from that point on. What happened back then doesn't involve him."

Albert remained outside talking to Conrad while Patrick searched the house from room to room, then glanced out at the enclosed backyard. Satisfied, he came back outside and met with the other two men. "I'm going to have to verify that you're not armed, Smith."

Conrad rolled his eyes. "Oh, for heaven's sake, O'Riley."

Albert shook his head, and held up a hand. "It's okay, Conrad. It's part of his job." Raising his hands over his head, Smith nodded. "Go right ahead. I'm not carrying a weapon."

Patrick frisked him quickly, but thoroughly. "I'm satisfied," he said at length. "What now?"

"Now we deal," Albert answered, then turned to Conrad. "Thank you for everything you've done, son, but now the time has come for you to go back to your family. Remember what we agreed."

"Are you sure that's what you want?" Conrad insisted.

"Yes, and don't worry. No matter what happens, I'll try my best to keep you and Anna safely out of this." Albert shook hands with Conrad, then embraced him. "Take care of yourself."

Conrad hesitated.

"Go now."

With reluctance, Conrad returned to the car. Albert watched him as he drove down the street, then out of his view. "Let's go inside, O'Riley. We'll have some iced tea, and try to make this as easy as possible. What I have to tell you is going to take a while."

Patrick started to close the door behind them when he heard a muffled noise coming from the kitchen. Instinctively he reached for his weapon, but he never had the chance to draw it from its holster.

A tall man wearing a tweed cap appeared at the kitchen door. He held his pistol, equipped with a long black silencer, directly in line with Patrick's chest. Behind the man was an open trap door leading into a cellar. A small rug that had concealed the hiding place had been tossed aside nearby.

Patrick stared at the smiling face in disbelief. "Frederick Reed, isn't it?" he managed at length. "Or should I call you Gerhard Stadt?" He didn't wait for an answer. "Albert's alibi for the day my father was killed is solid. And you were dead. That gave you the perfect alibi—'' he paused ''—until now.''

''Put your hands up, O'Riley,'' Frederick answered while Albert reached into Patrick's holster and claimed the Beretta. Assured that Patrick no longer posed a threat, Frederick reached behind him and shoved Melanie out into the center of the room.

With her hands tied behind her back, there was no way she could completely break her fall. Angling her body sideways, she hit the floor, absorbing the brunt of the impact with her shoulder. As she rolled, the gag pulled at her mouth harshly and a trickle of blood ran from the corner of her lips. She started to cough, choking on the fabric tangled in her mouth.

Patrick started to move toward her, when Albert stepped in his path, gun raised. ''Don't move,'' he ordered. Albert pulled Melanie to her feet, and removed the gag.

Frederick stepped farther into the room. He looked at Patrick squarely, then at Melanie. ''I'm not a common criminal, O'Riley. When your father found the discrepancies in my past, he became a very real threat to Albert's and my families. Even though they'd never known about our true backgrounds, they would have paid a severe penalty. The publicity would have destroyed their futures. We had to stop your father.''

Albert stared at Patrick his expression one of sadness and resignation. ''We thought it was all behind us. But if you know Gerhard's name, then you've probably guessed why we were sent over here. Gerhard had been a physicist in Germany, so his assignment was to infiltrate the Oak Ridge facility. Unfortunately he had to kill Bernard Cain in order to assume his identity and gain access there. I was Frederick's partner, radioman and backup. When we learned that the bomb was to be constructed and tested somewhere out west, we traveled to Washington. We'd hoped to get a look at the Hanford site there. That's when Gerhard started using his Frederick Reed identity, and obtained a job at the

University. As before, I worked at a locksmith shop nearby, and supported Frederick's work as much as I could. The war ended before we could complete our assignment. We learned too late that the bomb was being developed and tested in New Mexico."

Patrick nodded. "So when my father started to investigate Frederick Reed you decided to make a bomb and murder him. You knew he'd eventually find out all about your assumed identities. Since Gerhard Stadt's photograph was in government files under Cain's name, Dad would have been able to trace you all the way back to that time. And once he could prove Stadt had killed Cain, you two would likely spend a good deal of time in prison. It was only a matter of time before my father uncovered everything."

"Why didn't you just go back to Germany after the war?" Melanie asked. She slowly moved sideways, edging away from Patrick. Although escape at the moment seemed impossible. Maybe she could create a diversion and they could get away.

"How?" Albert countered cynically. "The government had fallen, and no one was in a position to give us the exit contacts we needed to get back. We were trapped here. We weren't about to turn ourselves in to the FBI, so we decided to stay in this country. We've spent all the years since then leading productive, happy lives. Then your father started asking the wrong questions and we knew our past was catching up to us."

"Albert wanted to drop out of sight," Frederick interjected, "but I came up with a better plan. I decided to fake my own death. My family knew I always drove a bit recklessly. That gave me the perfect cover. Since Albert and I were about the same size, I could borrow his clothes and hide out in his apartment. I went out only when we needed to tail you two. We could have used the resemblance between us to carry on the deception indefinitely."

"So you faked your own death by finding some derelict who fit your general description," Melanie added, "and killed him. You knew no one would ask questions or be overly concerned about street people being missing. Then you put his body in your car and engineered that accident.'' She glanced at Albert. ''And you were the one who identified the body?''

Albert nodded. ''Of course. I also made sure the remains were cremated in accordance to Frederick's will. I've never shirked my duty. Frederick has always known that he could count on me whenever necessary.''

''Yes, Albert, we know,'' Patrick answered. ''Or shall I call you Emil Osterkamp? You have a history of forgery, I understand. You must have manufactured all those transcripts for Frederick. Too bad you didn't have an old photograph of him when you faked the last one.'' Patrick smiled confidently. ''You made critical mistakes, that's why neither of you is going to get away with this.''

''Who's going to stop us after you two are gone? The police will blame Cartolucci for it, as we arranged. Let's face it, they already think he sent thugs after you once,'' Frederick replied easily.

''That phony file you planted in the office didn't fool us for long. The police will catch on, too,'' Melanie argued. She was now seeing the whole picture, but they had run out of time. It was too late. ''And those three thugs you hired? They'll testify against you to avoid an attempted murder rap.''

Patrick nodded his head in agreement. ''We've been on to you, Albert, for some time now. You didn't think I'd be careless enough to come here without any backup. Oh, I didn't call anyone in front of Conrad. I didn't have to. The police have been tailing me at a distance for about a week now. One of the detectives on the case is an old family friend. He insisted I carry a homing device with me.'' He grinned.

''Sure,'' Frederick chuckled softly. ''Nice try.''

''If you'll let me reach into my pocket, I'll show you.''

"Pull it out with two fingers, O'Riley," Frederick warned.

Patrick reached inside his breast pocket for a stainless-steel ballpoint pen. "I'm not lying," he assured arrogantly, tossing it onto the carpet in front of them. "Open the thing up and look for yourselves. I'll wager the cops are keeping an eye on this place right now. If you murder us, you won't be able to escape. Give yourselves up now before it's too late."

Melanie looked at Patrick's pen. It was a desperate gambit, but it looked as though it might work. They were hesitating. If they lowered their guns even a fraction, she'd take the offensive.

A car suddenly pulled into the driveway.

Albert spat out an oath. For a split second Frederick's eyes strayed to the window.

Seizing the moment, Patrick grabbed the floor lamp to his right, and smashed it against the side of Albert's head and shoulder. Simultaneously, still bound, Melanie kicked out, knocking the gun from Frederick's grasp. It discharged when it hit the floor.

"Head for the door," Patrick urged, pushing her forward. He was at her heels, shielding her with his own body.

As Frederick groped for his pistol, which had slid beneath the couch, Patrick reached around Melanie to free the lock.

The door burst open abruptly, knocking Melanie and Patrick backward onto the carpet and Conrad stumbled into the room. "What in the world is going on here?"

Frederick retrieved his gun, and pointed it toward Patrick and Melanie. "Get up. The game's over, O'Riley."

"Dad, thank God! You're alive!" Conrad started toward his father to embrace him, then stopped and stared at the gun. "Oh, no!" He stepped in front of Patrick and Melanie. "You can't do this."

Frederick moved quickly to the side, clearing his line of fire. "Son, you're caught in something you don't understand. Step aside, we have to end this once and for all."

Albert sat up slowly, the side of his head, where the lamp had struck him, covered with blood. "Why did you come back, Conrad?"

"I thought you'd need my help," he said lamely. "O'Riley, stay behind me." He glanced back quickly. "My father won't shoot me. We'll figure something out. No one has to get hurt."

Melanie felt truly sorry for Conrad. "Someone already has," she reminded him. They were trapped, their backs literally to the wall, with Conrad their only protection.

"Albert, you've been lying to me all along. You did kill this man's father," Conrad challenged, staring accusingly at his father-in-law. Receiving no answer, he turned and looked at his own father. "And you've been hiding out?"

"I killed O'Riley," Frederick said quietly.

Conrad stared at his father aghast. "You?"

"There was no choice. It had to be done." Frederick's voice grew hard. "Conrad, act like a man. Accept that there are times when you have to make a stand."

"And what would you have me do? Support you in murder? Put the gun down, Dad. There must be some other way out of this." He shook his head as if trying to take it all in. "You let me believe you were dead! How could you put me through something like that? Were you just planning to disappear out of our lives forever?"

"Of course not. After everything went back to normal, I would have returned. I was planning to tell you my car had been stolen while I was up in the mountains, and it had taken me some time to hike out. I would never have abandoned you. You're my son. Isn't your loyalty to me as strong?"

"Yes," Conrad acknowledged, and stepped aside.

Knowing that the end was inevitable, Patrick turned to Albert, who had risen to his feet. "If you stop him now, the

worst you'd be accused of is being an accessory after the fact
in each murder. It was Frederick who killed those three men,
not you."

Albert shook his head. "I made my commitment a long
time ago. I stand by my family and my friend."

"I'm truly sorry it had to end this way for both of you,"
Frederick said quietly. "I did try everything I could to mislead you. The Cartolucci file, the hoods and the shots I fired
into your home, were all meant to throw you off our trail.
Now you've left us with no other choice. We must end your
involvement once and for all." Frederick steadied his hand.
"Your deaths will give us back our lives." Frederick's fin-
ger began to tighten on the trigger.

Chapter Eighteen

Suddenly Conrad stepped back into his line of fire. Frederick smoothly shifted his pistol to his right hand. Although his angle was no longer as clear, he'd still be able to hit his mark. "Get out of the way, son. This has gone too far to stop now."

"You taught me that respect for duty and loyalty are the measure of a man," Conrad exclaimed, trying to reason with his father. "But don't you see? Those are concepts that require honor most of all. When you start doing things that are wrong, you end up corrupting the very values you're trying to defend."

"If a man doesn't protect his family, he's not much of a man," Frederick answered, moving farther to get a closer shot. "Now step away."

Conrad blocked him again. "No, Dad, there've been enough deaths. I can't support you when you're doing something that destroys the very foundation of all the beliefs you brought me up to live by." He stepped toward his father. "Give me the gun, Dad. There was honor in serving your country as a soldier. There is none in taking innocent lives."

Frederick hesitated, and Conrad started to reach for the gun. Suddenly Frederick shoved him aside hard. Conrad stumbled to his knees.

Like a released spring, Patrick leaped for cover, taking Melanie to the floor with him. Hidden behind the couch, he pulled a small, backup pistol from inside his boot. It wasn't his weapon of choice, but as an alternative in an emergency, it was worth its weight in gold.

Frederick's silenced pistol made a soft plopping sound as a bullet thumped into the wall behind them. It barely missed Patrick's head. Frederick strode toward them. "It's no use, O'Riley. You're not going anywhere."

"Don't move. I'm armed," Patrick warned.

Frederick laughed. "You're determined to go down fighting. I admire that."

The minute he stepped around the end of the sofa and into view, Patrick fired two quick shots. The impact of the bullets tore holes in Frederick's chest, and blood erupted through his shirt. He staggered back, his face a mask of confusion as he realized he was about to die.

Albert fired three unaimed shots of his own to cover his escape from the room. He positioned himself at the entryway leading to the hall. Pressed against the side wall, he was shielded from Patrick's view. He could see his lifelong friend and partner lying on the floor, his blood soaking the carpet. The bright red bubbles on his lips meant that the bullets had pierced his lungs. "Goodbye, Gerhard," he whispered.

With the thunderous roar of gunfire ended, Conrad moved to his father's side. Frederick's mouth dragged into an unnatural smile. "We'll get help," Conrad assured his father, "just hold on."

Melanie, keeping low, edged toward Patrick. Turning her back to him, she extended her bound hands. "Undo this, will you?"

He reached over blindly with one hand, feeling for the knots, his eyes still trained on the door he'd seen Albert run through. His pistol was at the ready. "Smith, you can't escape. Drop your weapon."

"No. I'll never stop fighting for my family." Smith stepped out from cover for an instant, firing two shots in rapid succession.

Patrick ducked, pulling Melanie down with him, then returned fire. The deafening reverberations of their shots in the enclosed space faded away into a silence that was as unnatural as it was deadly.

The sound of a door being slammed shut broke that vacant stillness. Patrick finished untying Melanie then, keeping low to the front, went to where Frederick lay. It didn't take a doctor to tell him the man was dead. Patrick glanced up and met Conrad's eyes.

Patrick felt a stab of sympathy as he saw the anguish mirrored there. "I know what it's like to lose a father, Conrad. I wouldn't have wished that on anyone, but he didn't give me a choice."

"I realize that, but I want you to know that my father was a good man." His voice was soft, and had a faraway quality. "Maybe he did the wrong things, but he did them out of love."

Patrick placed a hand on Conrad's arm. "I'm sorry. I wish none of this had happened." He glanced down the hallway where Albert had fled. "Is there another way out back there?"

Conrad shook his head. "There's only the two bedroom windows, and they're much too narrow for a man Albert's size to fit through." He paused. "He can't hurt anyone from there. Don't use your weapon. There's been enough bloodshed."

"He's still armed and dangerous, Conrad," Patrick countered bluntly. "I can't ignore the fact that he's shot at us twice now." He considered his options. "I give you my word, though, that I'll do everything possible to avoid violence."

Melanie traversed the room, crawling across until she reached Patrick's side. She scooped up Frederick's pistol, and checked to see that it was ready to fire. "Now what?

He's barricaded in one of the back bedrooms, and there's no way we can rush the place without risking our lives.''

"We'll call the police from my cellular phone, and let them handle it. There's no other way I can think of. Maybe they can shoot tear gas into the room, or just wait him out."

Melanie was about to answer, when they heard a voice calling from the interior of the house. "O'Riley, you still there?"

"I'm not going anywhere, Albert, and neither are you. Why don't you push your weapon into the hall, and come out with your hands up. We don't want to hurt you."

"I have a proposition for you and Ms. Cardenas," he countered.

"We're listening," Patrick answered as Melanie nodded.

"Gerhard is dead, so you have now avenged Andrew O'Riley's murder. Conrad is not to blame for any of this, and remember he tried to save your lives. For the sake of his wife and daughter, keep him out of it. He never knew what we were doing. Publicity would wreck all their futures and they've done nothing to deserve that. Let it end here with Gerhard and me. In exchange, I have one final token to offer you." His voice was steady, unnaturally so.

A single gunshot shattered the stillness again. The blood drained from Conrad's face as he looked at Patrick, then at Melanie for the answer he instinctively knew.

Melanie was overwhelmed by a feeling of helplessness. "Suicide?" she mouthed.

Patrick stood, his face had lost some color and his lips were a thin, hard line. "Stay here. I don't think there's anything any of us will be able to do, but I've got to make sure."

Melanie stood and followed him. "You shouldn't have to do this by yourself. We've come this far together, we'll face the rest the same way."

The atmosphere of brittle tension built as they made their way cautiously down the hall. Melanie prayed silently, hoping they'd find him still alive, and it wouldn't be too late to help him.

They pushed the door open and peered anxiously into the room. Melanie gasped, then choked, her breath coming in ragged gulps. What had once been a man's head was now a ruined mass of tissue and bone.

Melanie backed out of the room quickly. The bitterness at the back of her throat was threatening to come spilling out. She ran to the bathroom sink and splashed cold water on her face.

Patrick came up behind her, placing a hand gently on her shoulder. "Are you okay?"

She nodded, and took a deep breath. "I'll go talk to Conrad while you phone the police."

After using his car phone, Patrick joined Melanie in the living room. "I'd like to do as Albert asked, and let the matter end with us here. Let the past be buried with Albert and Frederick. What do you say?"

Melanie glanced at Conrad, who sat in the chair nearest his father's body, staring vacantly across the room. "Yes," she replied, "I'd like to do that, too, but how?"

"We can cut a deal with Mathers. We'll turn all the information we have on Emil Osterkamp and Gerhard Stadt over to him. He can name them as my father's killers, and expose their past as spies. We'll give him full credit for it in the press, which will increase his chances for promotion, and balance out the implications made by the Cartolucci affair.

"In exchange, he has to agree not to reveal the aliases they'd been using here, nor release photographs of either of the men. That will protect Conrad and his family."

"Conrad saved our lives. It's the least we can do," Melanie acknowledged.

Patrick and Melanie stepped outside onto the porch, needing a respite from the oppressiveness in the house. Death filled those rooms, haunting the air with traces of gunpowder and the scent of blood. Outside, as the breeze rustled through the leaves of the trees and the evening insects hummed in steady cadence, life seemed to assert its dominion. Curious neighbors began drifting out from the shelter of their homes, milling around their tiny lawns in groups.

"I always thought that once I evened the score and avenged my father's death, everything would seem better somehow."

"Justice can be satisfying but it can't erase the loss. Andy's still gone and nothing can ever change that." She glanced at Patrick, and had a sudden foreknowledge of how he would look as an old man.

Melanie and Patrick rejoined Conrad. "We'll bury the past here, Conrad," Patrick said again quietly, wondering if the man was really taking in what they were saying. "It's time to put it behind us."

Conrad stared right through them, numbness and shock forming a protective barrier around him. "Yes," he answered finally, his voice heavy with sorrow. "I think there's been enough suffering already."

"Come outside with us," Melanie said, taking Conrad's arm and leading him out onto the porch. The house felt as if it were closing in on them.

Conrad's face was white and strained, disbelief still etched on his features.

Melanie was startled as the beam of a powerful light flashed across them. Looking up quickly, she saw three police cars coming down the street.

After the officers had taken all their statements, Patrick walked Melanie to his car. "You know, there's one thing I still don't understand. I left you in the office waiting for the insurance adjuster. How in the heck did you end up here?"

Melanie smiled wearily. "I left a message on your machine at home, but I guess you didn't hear it. Actually it's a long story."

A WEEK LATER Patrick and Melanie stood inside what had once been Andy's office. Mike was leaning against the doorway, sipping at a diet cola.

"Those are the last of your father's personal effects, from the ties he kept in the bottom drawer, to his spare jacket. Are you sure you want me to give them to Brother Paul?" Melanie asked.

"Yes. He'll be able to put those things to good use." Patrick picked up the three photographs on his desk. He remembered when Melanie had used them to get Shy Eddy to identify the killer. "You might as well file these," he said, handing them back to her. "We won't be needing them anymore."

She studied the photos pensively. Mike stepped forward, looking over her shoulder. She turned sideways in her chair. "Now we know what Shy Eddy meant by confirming that one of the photos looked familiar. Conrad does bear quite a resemblance to his father, and Frederick and Albert are also very similar."

"Yes, that's true," Patrick replied.

"I never realized just how close you two were to cracking this case. The department could have been a lot more help finding Shy Eddy and catching Clancy. If only we'd known . . ." Mike paused. "By the way, did you ever get an update on how Shy Eddy's doing?"

"We sure did. Brother Paul called this morning. Eddy's out of the hospital now, and doing just fine. He said Eddy really enjoyed the apples we sent to the hospital for him."

"Sending that basket to him was a great idea, Melanie," Patrick said.

"O'Riley and Cardenas owed Shy Eddy at least that much," she ventured. "He helped us come together as a team."

When Patrick didn't comment, Melanie turned and gazed absently out the window. If only he'd put an end to her speculation. Patrick still hadn't answered the question foremost in her mind. The military was a part of him. He'd devoted the last fifteen years of his life to it. Now that his father's murder was solved, would Patrick join her at the agency or would he go back to the world he'd known? She'd been reluctant to bring up the subject, afraid of what his answer might be. The possibility of his leaving made her feel unbearably sad.

Mike broke the awkward silence.

"I think it's time you two heard the latest news on Cartolucci."

Patrick sat down and offered Mike a seat on the couch. Melanie chose the chair across from it. "I can't tell you how curious I've been about that," she confessed.

"As it turns out, Cartolucci was an undercover agent working for the Justice Department." Mike chuckled. "They'd been conducting an investigation into organized gambling. The reason Cartolucci had never been brought to trial was that his arrest had all been for show. When rumors started circulating that he'd bribed police officers, Cartolucci had gone right along with it. That type of activity suited the image he was trying to create, so he used it to enhance his cover. Captain Mathers was furious when Cartolucci, whose real name happens to be Jake Morelli, appeared at the station in disguise a few days ago. He identified himself and took over operations, directing an interagency strike force making a string of arrests."

Mike grinned widely. "It seems no one had told Mathers about the Justice Department's undercover operation, and his department ended up investing a great deal of time and effort in a fruitless investigation."

Patrick laughed loudly. "I bet he was fit to be tied!"

Melanie joined their laughter. "It couldn't have happened to a nicer guy."

Mike stood, and started toward the door. "I better get back to the station. The captain's really in a foul mood lately." He glanced at them, eyes twinkling with mischief. "Can't imagine why!"

Melanie saw Mike to the door, then returned to Patrick's office. "So now what?" she asked, unable to suppress her curiosity any longer.

"I have to go back to the base in a few days," he answered, knowing exactly what she was referring to.

Melanie's spirits plummeted. She desperately wanted to convince him to stay, but she couldn't bear to use her love to keep him from pursuing what he truly wanted in life. It wasn't right. But, oh God, the aching inside her would never stop!

"I wish you'd stay," she admitted, no longer able to hold everything back. There would be no more secrets between them. "But I understand that you have to make your own choices." Holding her tears at bay, she forced herself to smile. "When's the expiration date on that contract you have with the Air Force? You know I'll always have a job open for you here."

He grinned devilishly. "You won't be getting rid of me that easily. I've already resigned my commission. I'm only going back to pick up my things. I am, after all, the other half of this agency. How on earth could you possibly do without me?"

Anger made her cheeks burn. She glared at him, and her voice rose. "You *knew* I'd been wondering and waiting for you to say something! How can you be such an . . ."

He pulled her to him. "I love you, you know."

She sighed and let her anger fade. "And I love you," she answered.

"Just the response I'd hoped for," he said. His mouth closed over hers hungrily.

She matched his passion. This time they were in complete agreement on what they wanted—a partnership between two loving hearts.

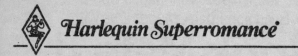
Harlequin Superromance

CALLOWAY CORNERS

Created by four outstanding Superromance authors, bonded by
lifelong friendship and a love of their home state: Sandra Canfield, Tracy Hughes, Katherine Burton and Penny Richards.

CALLOWAY CORNERS

Home of four sisters as different as the seasons, as elusive as the
elements; an undiscovered part of Louisiana where time stands
still and passion lasts forever.

CALLOWAY CORNERS

Birthplace of the unforgettable Calloway women: *Mariah*, free
as the wind, and untamed until she meets the preacher who
claims her, body and soul; *Jo*, the fiery, feisty defender of lost
causes who loses her heart to a rock and roll man; *Tess*, gentle
as a placid lake but tormented by her longing for the town's bad
boy and *Eden*, the earth mother who's been so busy giving love
she doesn't know how much she needs it until she's awakened
by a drifter's kiss...

CALLOWAY CORNERS

Coming from Superromance, in 1989:
Mariah, by Sandra Canfield, a January release
Jo, by Tracy Hughes, a February release
Tess, by Katherine Burton, a March release
Eden, by Penny Richards, an April release

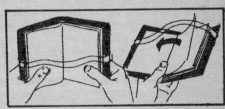

Romance the way it was *always* meant to be!

The time is 1811, when a Regent Prince rules the empire. The place is London, the glittering capital where rakish dukes and dazzling debutantes scheme and flirt in a dangerously exciting game. Where marriage is the passport to wealth and power, yet every girl hopes secretly for love....

Welcome to Harlequin Regency Romance where reading is an adventure and romance is *not* just a thing of the past! Two delightful books a month, beginning May '89.

Available wherever Harlequin Books are sold.